FLIPPING *OUT*

FLIPPING OUT

A Lomax & Biggs Mystery

MARSHALL KARP

Minotaur Books

New York

This is a work of fiction. All of the characters, organizations, and events portrayed in this novel are either products of the author's imagination or are used fictitiously.

*For Jason Wood
and the bodies to come.*

*And for my wife,
the one they call Saint Emily.*

FLIPPING OUT

CHAPTER ONE

There were five detectives at our Sunday debriefing.

That's what we call them—debriefings, because no cop is dumb enough to tell his wife or girlfriend that he'd rather spend his day off hanging out with his buddies than taking her to the mall to pick out curtain fabric.

We were on Reggie Drabyak's fishing boat, so technically this was an LAPD naval debriefing.

It started at dawn when Reggie, who works vice, and Charlie Knoll from burglary set sail to spend the day in the hot sun trying to catch the same stuff I'd rather pick up at an air-conditioned supermarket for eight bucks a pound.

They docked in the Marina at beer-thirty, and my partner, Terry Biggs and I joined them. An hour later, Tony Dominguez, who works gangs, showed up with a five-foot hero from Santoro's.

He unwrapped it, and I took in the intoxicating aroma of soppresatta, Genoa salami, provolone, and a half dozen other processed animal products that make men's hearts beat faster, burn through the night, and occasionally seize up.

Tony cut the hoagie into five pieces. "Here Biggs, you get a foot," he said, handing the first one to Terry. "Enjoy it, because when the cards are dealt, you sure as hell won't be getting a hand."

Ultimately that's what these debriefings are all about—the poker.

Terry played recklessly, raising when more cautious players would call, and calling when saner players would fold. By the end of the night he was ahead, but Tony still had a shot at a comeback. The stakes were doubled for the last deal, and no matter how much Terry raised, Tony stayed with him.

On the final raise, it was just the two of them, and Tony peeled back his hole card and took another look.

Terry picked up an empty beer bottle, held it close to his face, and talked into it, using the soft, mellow whisper of a professional golf announcer. "We're on the eighteenth green here at Augusta. Dominguez, who hasn't played well all day, is taking one more desperate look at his down card. This is the biggest pot of the night, folks—over fifty bucks—and from where I'm sitting, this one belongs to Terry Biggs."

"You're bluffing," Tony said.

"Dominguez looks rattled," Terry said into the Heineken microphone. "This game of high-low takes balls of steel, and Biggs has two that we know of. Maybe more. With an ace, three, four, five showing, he could have declared low and easily gone home with half the pot. But he went for the high *and* the low, the whole enchilada. Sadly, for Dominguez, the only enchilada he'll be getting tonight is the cold one left in the fridge by his lovely wife, Marisol."

"You know even less about women than you do about poker," Tony said. "Marisol hasn't cooked in ten years, and about the only cold thing she's got waiting for me tonight is her shoulder."

"Oooh," Terry groaned. "A big sigh of disappointment from the crowd here at Augusta, as they find out that their Latin hero is as unlucky at love as he is at cards."

"Come on, Tony, make up your mind," Charlie Knoll said. "I've got burglars to catch."

"And Lomax and I have homicides to solve," Terry said. "And Drabyak has prostitutes to frisk and pimps to shake down. If you fold, you can still go home with your last few bucks and what's left of your dignity."

Dominguez had two pair showing. Jacks and deuces. The third deuce had already popped up and was in Reggie Drabyak's discarded hand. There was only one card in the deck that would win the game for my trash-talking partner, and Tony Dominguez shoved his last remaining chips into the pot to see if Terry actually had it.

"Call."

Terry put his thumb under his hole card. "And the green jacket at this year's thrilling Masters tournament here in Augusta, Georgia, goes to . . ." He flipped over the deuce of spades. "Detective Terry Biggs, LAPD Homicide. The crowd goes wild, and his caddy, Detective Mike Lomax, is the first to run out onto the green and congratulate him."

"Your caddy?" Tony said, shoving his losing hand to the middle of the table. "Is that what you call him now that the two of you are shacking up together?"

"Let me apologize to the audience for that display of poor sportsmanship," Terry said, still broadcasting into his beer bottle. "That remark was highly inappropriate and totally inaccurate. Mike Lomax and Terry Biggs are not caddy shacking. Mike and the future Mrs. Lomax are waiting for their new house to be renovated. They're living with Terry and Marilyn Biggs on a temporary basis."

"First of all," I said, "Diana is not the future Mrs. anything. She's Miz Trantanella, and this little experiment of buying a house and cosigning a mortgage is the first of many steps we are taking before we even talk about getting married. Second of all, from what Marilyn tells me, she's also living with you on a temporary basis."

Terry shoveled the pile of chips toward him. "And when I return from the poker wars with this handsome haul, she'll stick around yet another night."

"Reg, you need help battening down the hatches?" Charlie said.

"No, I'm gonna sleep on the boat," Drabyak said. "Jo is working a wedding tonight, so she won't be home till late. She took my truck, so I'll go home in the morning and switch vehicles."

Tony and I helped clean up while Charlie counted the chips. "And the big wiener of the evening is Biggs," he said. "Sixty-two bucks."

"So then the big whiner of the night must be Touchdown," Terry said. "Nice game, T. D. Better luck next time."

Dominguez gave him a one-finger salute.

"I sense anger issues," Terry said. "You really need to see that expensive shrink of yours more often."

Tony Dominguez had grown up poor and fatherless on the predominantly Mexican streets of East LA. His mother, Luz, spent her whole life cleaning other people's houses. When Tony was ten, she started working for Ford Jameson, psychiatrist to the rich and famous. Jameson took to Tony from the get-go, and provided the positive male role model that had long been missing. The good doctor had been generous, buying Tony a used car when he needed wheels, helping him through college, and always available for therapy sessions at a hundred percent off his outrageous hourly rate.

"Hey, baby," Tony said, "if anyone needs his head examined, it's you."

"I've only got sixty-two dollars," Terry said, waving his winnings at Tony. "I don't think I could afford your guy."

"Do any of you fellas want to spend the night on the boat with me?" Reggie said. "Biggs has Lomax, and I'm feeling kind of jealous."

"If I can't have Mike, I don't want any of you," Charlie said.

"Why don't you stay here by yourself, Reg?" Terry said. "Your luck is bound to change, and you just may get the first good hand you've had all night."

That got a big laugh. We helped Reggie clean up, and by ten fifteen, Charlie, Tony, Terry, and I were on the dock, heading for our cars.

Five cops. Drinking beer, playing cards, busting balls. I'll never forget that Sunday night. It was the happiest time the five of us would ever spend together again.

CHAPTER TWO

I read Dante's *Inferno* when I was in college. From what I can remember, there are nine circles of hell. The first one is for the un-baptized, who weren't really sinners but wound up in limbo because they didn't accept Jesus. From a cop perspective, I think of it as the misdemeanor circle.

As you move your way along the ladder of sin, you go deeper and deeper into hell. The eighth circle is for those who knowingly commit evil deeds. That includes panderers, false prophets, sowers of discord, and the way I see it, building contractors who take your money, don't do the work, and never return your phone calls.

So there's a spot reserved in the eighth circle of hell for Hal Hooper.

He's the reason Diana and I are currently homeless. We'd been living together for over a year. Sometimes her place, sometimes mine. A few months ago we bought a house together. A fixer-upper. We hired Hooper to fix it up.

We were supposed to move in by the end of August, but by September first, the house was still missing half a roof, a working bathroom, and several other amenities. Hooper gave us a bunch of lame excuses and swore it would be livable in another month. He didn't say finished. Just livable.

We had each given up our rentals, our furniture was in storage, and we couldn't afford thirty nights in a hotel. In desperation, we moved in with Big Jim. I told Diana it would be a big mistake to try to live with my father, but she's a glass-half-full person. "It's only a month," she said. "How bad could it be?"

It didn't take long to find out.

I had braced Diana for the meddling. I warned her that he would pry into every corner of our personal lives and drop less-than-subtle hints about the joys of getting married and bearing children. But I never mentioned the peeing.

The first night, Diana and I went upstairs to our bedroom and Jim took the dogs out for one last pee. They stood in the yard, he yelled, "Business," and the four of them relieved themselves under our window. Three dogs and Jim.

When I called him on it the next morning, he said, "So I took a piss. For God's sake, Mike, it's dark out."

But darkness does not cover up industrial-strength farting or Big Jim's orgasmic groans of relief. You want to take the romance out of your evening? Get a three-hundred-pound teamster to empty his bladder under your bedroom window every night.

Even Jim's wife, Angel, who is usually pretty successful at reining him in, couldn't stop him from putting his nose in our business or his foot in his mouth. After five days and a variety of personal-boundary violations, the topper came when Jim, ever helpful, took our laundry from the dryer, folded it, and left it in our room. That Friday night at dinner, he suggested that Angel buy "one of those sexy black thongs like Diana wears."

Angel smacked the back of his fat head, Diana covered her eyes, and I grabbed the phone. By Saturday morning Diana and I were packed and headed to Sherman Oaks to move in with Terry, Marilyn, and the girls.

It was my first day commuting to work from the Valley, and we were creeping along the 101 at twenty miles an hour.

The ribbon of taillights in front of us went bright red, and Terry rolled the car to a stop. "So far, so good," he said.

"We're going to be late for Kilcullen's Monday morning briefing, so you can't be talking about the traffic. You must be bragging about the fact that we've managed to live under the same roof for forty-eight hours without any bloodshed."

"Hey, I know it's only been one weekend, but you've got to admit that bunking with us is more fun than living with Big Jim."

I nodded. "Bunking with the Taliban would be more fun than living with Big Jim."

We were fifteen minutes late getting to the station, but as it turned out, Kilcullen's meeting was canceled. Just as we pulled into the parking lot, about twenty cops, some in plainclothes, some in uniform, came pouring out of the station and began jumping into their cars.

We saw Wendy Burns, and Terry honked at her.

Wendy is our direct supervisor, the Detective III who assigns cases to the homicide teams. She's a total pro, smart, reasonable, and a great buffer to have between us and our less-than-reasonable boss, Lieutenant Brendan Kilcullen.

"You guys just caught a big one," she said as Terry and I got out of the car. "Follow me."

"What's going on?" I said.

"Reggie Drabyak's wife was shot."

"Jesus, is she okay?"

"She's dead."

CHAPTER THREE

Reggie Drabyak is not the most dynamic cop on the force. Average height, slightly more than average weight, slightly less than average personality. In two years, when he retires and hangs a "gone fishing" sign on his door, that's exactly what he'll be doing. Fishing. For him, police work is just a way to pay for his boat and his bait.

Jo Drabyak, on the other hand, was chatty, funny, and bubbly—a total charmer. Five years ago, after a series of colorful but unsuccessful career choices, she became an event planner. Weddings, bar mitzvahs, and because it's LA, parties of every imaginable stripe for the Weird and Famous.

Jo grew up in Summit, New Jersey, and dropped out of high school to become a modern dancer. She had the desire and the drive, but not the knees. She moved to Los Angeles to conquer Hollywood and wound up as a production assistant on *The Price Is Right*. That's where she met Petty Officer First Class Reggie Drabyak. Reggie was in the audience with a bunch of other sailors. He got the call to *come on down* and won himself a washer-dryer.

Jo's job was to ship the prizes to the winners. Reggie didn't have much use for major appliances on an aircraft carrier, so he said, "Have dinner with me, and you can ship my Maytag to your house."

A year later, Reggie quit the navy, joined LAPD, and offered Jo the chance to spend the rest of her life washing and drying his laundry with hers. From what I could tell, it was a damn good life. Until today.

"I guess you knew Jo Drabyak a lot better than I did," Terry said as we followed the caravan of cop cars west on Sunset.

"I like Reggie," I said, "but I was never a big fan of sitting in the hot sun all day hoping to catch my dinner. So, when I first met him, I didn't hang out with him much. Then my wife met his wife at a cop picnic, and they really hit it off. Joanie and Jo went to yoga classes together, they'd have lunch, go shopping—they really got close. Eventually, we wound up doing a lot of couples stuff together. When Joanie was dying, people would call or send cards, but only two cop wives were there in the flesh. Your wife was one of them. The other was Jo."

The Drabyaks lived on Alta Vista in a mission-style white stucco house with a red tiled roof. It would probably go for a million plus, which is modest by LA standards, but completely out of range for the average cop and his wife. Luckily, they bought it fifteen years ago when a two-income couple could still afford a down payment and a mortgage.

Terry pulled in behind Wendy's car. She had a street map in one hand and was already delegating detectives to spread out and canvass a six-block radius. "The lieutenant's waiting for you in the garage," she said.

Jo was lying on the floor a few feet from Reggie's pickup. Her legs were at a right angle to her torso. One arm was extended to the left, the other was pinned beneath her. Her left cheek was resting on the oil-stained concrete. Reggie had said she was working a wedding last night, and her clothes seemed to bear him out. She had on a flowery summer dress and sensible tan shoes with low heels. Her honey-blond hair fanned out across her back and shoulders, but one of the fan blades was missing.

I knelt down beside her. "I'm not sure, but it looks like a hunk of her hair has been chopped off. Can't really tell because of the blood."

"Bullet to the back of the head," Terry said. "Looks more like an execution than a random homicide."

"Don't jump to conclusions," Kilcullen said.

"I always jump to conclusions," Terry said. "It's just that you're not usually on the scene to watch me do my job wrong."

"I'm here for the same reason my boss is here. And his boss. A cop's wife was murdered in cold blood in her own home. Whatever else you're doing, shelve it. This case goes to the top of the pile."

"We both knew the victim," I said. "Is there any conflict with us handling this?"

"We all knew the victim," Kilcullen said, his voice kicking up a notch. "She's one of our own. She was killed in our jurisdiction. It's ours to solve, and you two are going to solve it."

"Right," Terry said. "And if you yell louder, maybe we'll solve it faster."

"Sorry," Kilcullen said, more to Jo than to Terry. He bent down and took a closer look. "They cut her hair. It's like a violation on top of a violation." He smacked his fist into the palm of his hand and stood up. "CSU should be here any minute. I've got half the station combing the neighborhood. You guys get the fun job. Interview Reggie."

"Rule number one," I said. "The husband is always the primary...."

"I know," Kilcullen said. "But I know Reggie, and he didn't kill her. Let's just hope he's got a solid alibi."

"He's going to want in on the investigation," Terry said.

"Well, you know the answer to that one. No fucking way. You need manpower, you let me know. Anyone but Reggie." He took one more look at the dead woman at our feet. "I don't get it," he said. "A nice girl like Jo. I can't imagine she had any enemies."

Terry shrugged. "She must've had one."

CHAPTER FOUR

Reggie was sitting on the sofa in the living room. He was dressed for work—tan pants, pale yellow short-sleeve shirt, green tie with thin blue stripes. He had showered and shaved since I saw him last night, and his face, forever tan from a life on the water, was probably a melanoma waiting to happen. But for the moment, it gave off a healthy glow. Only his eyes were a window to the shock and the grief.

He stood up when Terry and I walked in. "Oh man, am I glad to see you guys. I'm crawling the walls here. What's going on? What do you know?"

"Reg, we're all torn up about this," I said. "We're gonna solve it, but we're just getting started. First, we need to sit down and talk." I put my hand on his shoulder and tried to ease him back toward the sofa, but he didn't budge.

"Mike, I don't want to sit and talk. I want to be part of the investigation."

"Reg, you know the rules. . . ."

"Fuck the rules," he said. "I worked robbery-homicide at Central. I know what I'm doing."

"Reg, that was years ago, and you transferred out after six months."

"This is different. This is my wife."

Like a lot of cops, when Reggie made detective, he thought he could do the most good working homicide. But catching murderers doesn't bring back the victims, and Reggie has always had a passion to help people find the road to recovery. So he switched to vice, where he can help addicts kick the habit and prostitutes get off the street. Before he joined the navy he was raised as a Jehovah's Witness. While other kids were out playing ball, Reggie and his parents were knocking on doors trying to save souls. He gave up the religion years ago, but he never shook the need to point others toward the light.

"Reg," Terry said, "I can't tell you how sorry I am. We're going to catch this guy, but we're losing time here. The best way you can help right now is to let us ask you some questions."

Reggie lowered himself back onto the sofa and buried his head in his hands. "I know the drill," he said, looking back up at us. "Get to it. Ask."

"Let's start with the usual," I said. "Did Jo have any enemies?"

He shook his head. "Mike, you knew her. Everyone loved her."

"Dig deeper. What about crazy neighbors, old grudges, any of her exes, any of yours?"

"Mike, I've been digging deep for the past two hours. There's nobody. If I could've thought of somebody, I'd already be at their house."

"Did you hear anything or notice anything out of the ordinary in the past few days?" Terry said. "Anyone new hanging around the neighborhood? Weird phone calls? E-mails? Any flare-ups at work?"

"Nothing. She was happy. Busy, but happy. That was _she_ her. That was Jo."

A uniform came into the living room. "Excuse me, Detectives," she said. "Detective Burns said to tell you that the medical liaison is here."

"Thanks," I said. "Tell her Detective Drabyak will be right out."

"I don't need a doctor," Reggie said.

"It's standard procedure, Reg. Cop in trauma. Just talk to the doc. We'll have someone drive you to the station, and we'll pick up the interview there."

"I spent the night on the boat," he said.

"I know," I said. I didn't know it for sure, but I knew that's what he'd say.

"I should have come home." His eyes were starting to tear up. "I should have come home. This wouldn't have happened."

"Reggie, before you go," I said. "We need your okay to do a permissive search of the house." I handed him the paperwork and a pen.

"Do it," he said, signing the form. "Rip the place apart. I don't give a shit. Just find out who did this."

"And we'll need to secure your gun."

He grunted out a laugh. "I don't know why you need it now. I _whom_ don't know <u>who</u> to shoot yet." He reached down to his ankle, took his piece out of the holster, and handed it to me.

"Thanks. We'll talk back at the station," I said.

"The first thing we talk about is making me part of the investigation."

I looked at Terry. He had told Kilcullen that Reggie would want to help us catch Jo's killer. I also remember Kilcullen's answer. No way. Only he said it in three words.

"Did you hear me?" Reggie said. "I want in."

"We understand," Terry said. "But it's not our call. We'll ask Kilcullen. He's pretty reasonable. Let's see what he says."

CHAPTER FIVE

Kilcullen delivered the manpower we needed. At least a dozen uniformed officers plus detectives from every desk at the Hollywood Station canvassed the area and questioned everyone they could find within a six-block radius of the crime scene.

"Most people are at work," Kilcullen told them. "Which means you keep going back and knocking on doors till you speak to every single person who might have seen or heard anything last night."

Terry and I searched the house. It was neat, tasteful, and completely devoid of leads. At 11:00 A.M. we went back to the garage and were surprised to find Jessica Keating wrapping up her preliminary investigation. For my money, Jess is the best crime scene investigator in LA County. I just hadn't expected to see her till October.

"I thought you still had another month of maternity leave before you came back," I said.

"Breast-feeding and poopy diapers are highly overrated," Jess said. "Besides, Dan works at home, and we were starting to get on each other's nerves. So I bought a breast pump, left enough milk in the fridge to feed a village, and asked if I could come back to work early." She looked down at Jo Drabyak and shook her head. "I know it sounds unhealthy coming from someone who just brought a life into the world, but believe it or not, I missed this."

"Glad you did," I said. "What's the cause of death?"

"You didn't really need me to figure that out," Keating said. "She died from a good old-fashioned case of HILP: high-impact lead poisoning. A single bullet to the back of her head. Small hole, no exit wound, probably a .22, but there's no brass on the floor."

"So ballistics will be next to impossible," Terry said.

Jess shrugged. "You know the odds as well as I do. A small caliber like a .22 tends to just ping around your skull making a mess of everything in there, including itself. The slug is usually hard to trace."

"Any sign of sexual assault?" I said.

"None. It looks like the killer came to kill. He must have waited till she got out of the car, got behind her, and put a bullet in her brain."

"He?" I said.

"Sorry. That's my pronoun of choice for all assholes who commit murder. But it could easily have been a she. Women aren't traditionally shooters, but the wound indicates a small, ladylike gun."

"What about her hair?" I said.

"Bravo," Jessica said. "A man who actually can tell when a woman gets her hair cut. If I wanted Dan to notice I'd have to come home looking like Sinéad O'Connor. Someone chopped off a big hank of her hair. Unless she had a really bad hair day at the beauty salon, my guess is whoever killed her decided to take home a souvenir."

"So what do we have here?" I said. "A vendetta?"

"I'm not a profiler," she said. "I just sift through the physical evidence and try to find something that can help. But this doesn't look like a robbery, a crime of opportunity, or a random shooting."

"Time of death?"

"Around midnight—give or take."

"Give or take how much?" I said. "Her husband has an alibi for part of last night, but not for all of it."

"She probably was shot between eleven last night and one o'clock this morning. Does that help?"

"It helps us," I said. "It won't help him. You got anything else?"

"Nothing yet," she said. "The garage is covered with prints. We'll be dusting for a week. And we're going over the grounds looking for footprints, fibers, or any sign of someone who might have laid in wait outside, then followed her in when she opened the garage door."

lain

"Excuse me again, Detectives." It was the same cop who let us know when the medical liaison showed up. She was young, blond, with how-can-I-help written all over her face.

"Yes, Officer," I said.

"Julie Horner, sir. I thought you'd want to know. There's a flower delivery."

Terry rolled his eyes. "Is this your first homicide, Officer Horner?"

"Yes, sir."

"The detectives are usually too busy looking for the killer to handle flower deliveries," he said. "Maybe you can sign for them and either put them in the house or reroute them to the funeral home."

"These don't look like condolence flowers, sir," she said. "They're roses, and they're addressed to Mrs. Drabyak."

CHAPTER SIX

The guy driving the flower van was tall and blond, with a chiseled jaw, and a pair of arms that looked like they lifted more than floral arrangements.

"Soap star wannabe," Terry said, as we walked toward him.

As we got closer, I could see that the face didn't quite live up to the physique. Thin lips, eyes set close together, sharp nose. Not a problem if he could do Shakespeare or deliver posies.

"This is so cool," he said. "With the yellow crime scene tape and everything, it looks like you're shooting a movie, except there's no cameras."

"We can't afford cameras," Terry said. "We spent all our money on yellow tape. Let's see your ID."

"John G. Evans," he said, not reaching for his wallet.

"ID," Terry repeated.

"John G. Evans," he said, flashing a mouthful of expensive teeth. "I'm just delivering flowers. Is my name going to be in the police report or something?"

"If you don't show me your ID," Terry said, "your ass is going to be in a squad car or something."

He dug into his back pocket, removed his license from his wallet, and handed it to Terry.

"Well, it's got your picture, John G.," Terry said. "But the state of California seems to think your name is Evan Goldfried."

"I'm an actor. John G. Evans is my . . ."

"I'm a detective. Way ahead of you," Terry said. "Who sent the flowers?"

He shrugged. "There's probably a card in the box."

I opened it. There were two dozen long-stemmed red roses and a single white card. *Dear Jo, Thank you for last night. Everything was perfect, except me. You were right. I did have about six drinks too many. Sorry if I put a damper on an otherwise fantastic evening. Roger.*

The *O* in Roger's name had a smiley face drawn in it. I showed the card to Terry. "Who's Roger?" he asked.

"He must be the dude who sent the flowers," John G. said.

"Where do we find him? Do you have any paperwork with his name and address?"

"I'm just the delivery guy. Call Peg at the shop," he said, pointing to the phone number on the side of the van.

I dialed. The shop was Freem's Flowers. The owner, Peg Freem, was efficient, cooperative, and not the slightest bit curious about why I was trying to track down Roger.

"He came in as soon as I opened," she said. "He was about five foot eight, late fifties, curly gray hair, wearing a nice suit, no tie, gold band on the third finger of his left hand."

"I appreciate the description," I said. "But what I really need is his last name and his address."

"I never saw him before, and he paid cash."

"Not what I wanted to hear," I said, "but it makes sense. A guy with a wedding ring, sending flowers to someone else's wife—"

She interrupted. "But I told him I needed his cell in case there were any problems."

"Well, Ms. Freem, I guess you could say there's a problem."

She gave me Roger's number.

CHAPTER SEVEN

Terry and I figured if Roger shot Jo last night, he probably wouldn't have sent flowers in the morning, along with a mea culpa for getting drunk. So we sent a backup team to track him down and question him.

The two of us drove back to the station and sat down with Reggie.

"I spent the night on the boat," he said. "You guys left at ten or so. Jo called me around eleven. She was on her way home from the wedding."

"Did she say if anything happened?" I asked.

"Like what?"

"Like people at weddings get drunk. Did she have an argument? A fight over the bill? Anything out of the ordinary?"

"No. She said it was real good. The bride was happy. Her mother was happy. It was a wedding. Everybody had a good time."

"Who's Roger?" I said.

He shrugged.

"Some guy named Roger sent Jo flowers this morning. He apologized for his bad behavior last night."

"Never heard of him," Reggie said. "But I sure as hell would like to meet him as soon as I get my gun back."

"Jo didn't mention anything about it when she called?"

"No, that shit happens all the time. She's a good looking woman . . ." He stopped, put his hand over his eyes, and turned away. "Give me a minute."

I see it a lot. That excruciating moment when someone realizes that the present tense no longer applies.

Reggie took out a handkerchief and blew his nose. "I'm okay," he lied. "Jo was beautiful. She'd orchestrate these big parties, guys would get shit-faced, and sometimes make a pass. Pretty harmless. Usually she would tell them her old man was a cop, and that would be the end of it. She wouldn't tell me, because she said I'd just get all bent out of shape. I mean, who wants to hear that some guy is grab-bing his wife's ass?"

"Was that phone call the last time you spoke to her?"

"Yeah. I drove home from the boat around six thirty this morning. Jo had borrowed my pickup last night. I parked her Tercel in the driveway, took a quick look through the garage window, and I could see my truck. I walked to the front door, grabbed the paper, and went upstairs. The bed was made, so I figured she was out jog-ging. I took a shower, got dressed, but she still wasn't home, so I left her a note on the kitchen table and went to the garage to get my truck. That's when I found her. She was cold. Dead a long time. I called 911, then I called Kilcullen direct."

"Let's talk about who might have it in for you—did you bust anyone who could be that pissed?"

He shook his head. "Come on—they're low-level sex peddlers.

They get busted, they do a little time, they go back on the street again. It goes with the turf."

"What about johns?" Terry said.

"You passed the detective exam," Reggie said. "Cops don't arrest johns."

"I know. But I wonder if maybe you nailed one you shouldn't have, and caused him a problem."

"Who knows? Some of these guys are pretty twisted. Just ask the hookers. Maybe we could go over my case file. Something might jump out at me. You think I was the target?"

"We're gonna look at everything," I said.

"Maybe you're right," he said. "There was no robbery. It's not a crime of opportunity. They're laying for me, but it's dark out, Jo comes home in my truck, and they shoot her by mistake."

lying

"Reg, the lights go on in the garage when you open the door. Jo got out of the truck and the killer came up behind her. She was wearing a dress. They didn't shoot her by mistake."

"What if they came to shoot me, but I was too fat and lazy to get off the boat, so they killed her instead?"

I doubted it. The fact that the killer cut off a lock of Jo's hair made me pretty sure she was the intended victim, but that was one of the crime scene details I wasn't about to share with my primary suspect.

"You may be right, Reggie," I said. "So just in case you are the target, Kilcullen assigned someone to keep an eye on you."

"Bullshit. If I need protection, why did Kilcullen take my gun? He's not assigning someone to protect me. He knows I have other guns at home. He's just tailing me to make sure I don't go out and use them."

"So he's protecting you from yourself," Terry said. "This is your time to say good-bye to your wife, to grieve for her, not to go vigilante on us."

"Did you even bother asking Kilcullen if I could work on the case?"

"For the record, we asked," Terry said. "The three of us agree."

Reggie slumped in his chair. His tie was hanging loosely around his neck. There were dark sweat circles under the sleeves of his yellow shirt. "Who lost the coin toss?" he said.

"What do you mean?" Terry said.

"My wife was murdered. I'm an automatic suspect. Somebody's got to ask the nasty questions. I was just wondering which one of you drew the short straw. I'll tell you what—I'll spare you the embarrassment."

He stood up and looked down at the vacant chair. "So, Reggie, who were you banging?"

He sat back down and answered. "Nobody, detective. I loved my wife."

Back on his feet again. "How about Jo—all those guys hitting on her—you think she ever got involved?"

He sat down and shook his head. "No. Never."

He got up one last time. "So there were no marital problems?"

This time he didn't bother sitting down. He just stood there and stared at me and Terry. "Just the one problem," he said. "She snored, but I wouldn't say it was loud enough to shoot her. So stop wasting time and find out who the fuck did."

He walked out the door. The interview was over.

CHAPTER EIGHT

As a kid growing up in Manchester, England, Detective Chris High had two passions. Football and surfing. Manchester has two football teams but no oceans, so at seventeen Chris moved to LA, bought himself a board, and became an all-American surfer.

It was, as the Beach Boys say, fun, fun, fun. Until he broke his neck. After nine months in a halo brace and a year in therapy, he decided that becoming a cop would be a safer bet than being a surfer dude.

Chris runs the Hollywood Apprehension Team. When a detective gets a warrant, the HAT squad does the legwork and makes the arrest. Today they were called in to canvass the area where Jo Drabyak was murdered.

At six o'clock Kilcullen pulled a dozen detectives into the break room to kick around different perspectives on the case. Chris High led off with a No Progress Report.

"Nobody bloody saw anything," he said. "One bloke walking his dog heard a garage door at 23:15 hours, which is when the victim was expected home, but he didn't see anything, so he can't be sure if it was her." she

"Is that all you came up with?" Kilcullen said.

"We've only tracked down half the neighbors. We'll be sweeping the area again at 19:00 hours. But so far, nothing. Whoever did this was a bloody pro."

"What about this guy who sent the roses?" Kilcullen said.

Terry and I had sent Detectives Pat Sutula and Andy Langer to interview the guy who sent the flowers. They're known around the squad room as Penn and Teller. She does all the talking. Langer is stony silent.

"His name is Roger Levinson," Sutula said. "He's an accountant in Burbank. His daughter got married last night. Mrs. Drabyak planned the wedding. Levinson got drunk, came on to her, then tried to make nice with two dozen roses. He has an alibi for the time of death."

"Which is when?" Kilcullen asked.

"Keating gave us a two-hour spread this morning," I said. "I just spoke to her, and she's narrowed it down to somewhere between ten forty-five and eleven thirty last night. We might be able to narrow it down even more. According to Reggie, his wife called him at 11:00 P.M. She was in the car on her way home."

"Where was he when she called?" Kilcullen asked.

"His boat on the marina. It was cell to cell."

"Verify his location with cell tower records. If we can prove that he took the call on his boat at eleven that would eliminate him as a suspect."

"Isn't he already eliminated?" Tony Dominguez said. "Does anybody here actually think Reggie murdered his wife?"

"Nobody thinks he did it," Kilcullen said. "But *I was alone on the boat* is not an alibi, and the DA will crucify us if we cut him loose based on the nice-guy-we-work-with defense. I need cell records to back up his story."

"Can we talk motive?" Charlie Knoll said. "I knew this woman. I can't think of any reason why somebody would want to kill her. Does anyone think this might be a vendetta against Reggie?"

Hands went up, including mine and Terry's.

"We're working two paths," Kilcullen said. "We're digging into Jo Drabyak's life, and we're also looking at Reggie's cases." He turned to Detective Burns. "Wendy, your hand wasn't up. You don't think this is about Reggie?"

"I wouldn't rule it out. You never know who might have it in for a cop," Wendy said, "but the killer brought a pair of scissors and cut off a piece of Jo's hair. To me, that says it's about her, and it's personal."

"A boyfriend?" Kilcullen said.

Wendy smiled. "Most men don't sneak up and shoot women in the back of the head. A pissed-off boyfriend would want to confront her face to face and say, 'You see what you made me do, you bitch?'"

"Which brings us back around to her business," Kilcullen said. "We can look into every event she ever planned, but I can't imagine killing somebody over a wedding reception gone wrong."

"What about that house renovating business she's involved in?" Wendy said.

"What about it?" Tony Dominguez said.

"We should look into it," Wendy said. "Construction breeds a lot more crime than party planning."

"Are you suggesting that the women in this real estate venture are into something crooked?" Tony said.

"No," Wendy said. "I'm saying it's just another part of Jo Drab-yak's life that we should be looking into."

"Thank you for clarifying, Detective," Tony said, "because my wife is part of that group, and whatever else you might say about her, she's not involved in anything shady."

"I didn't realize Jo was one of the Flippers," Kilcullen said.

"She was," Tony said. "Charlie's wife, mine, Terry's. Us guys, we play poker and lose money to each other. Our wives get together and make a nice little profit."

"Excuse me, but I am completely flummoxed," Chris High said. "Will somebody clue me in. What's a flipper?"

"The LA Flippers," Charlie said. "It's a group of five—"

"I know," Chris said. "They play basketball."

"That's the Clippers," Charlie said. "A bunch of our wives have a business together. They call themselves the LA Flippers. You know my mother-in-law, Nora Bannister?"

High gave him a dubious look.

"For God's sakes, Chris. Nora Bannister. She's the queen of the murder mystery writers."

"I didn't realize you Yanks had a queen," High said. "I thought that's why you left England in the first place—to get away from all that monarchy rot."

"Are you telling me you never heard of Nora Bannister?" Charlie said. "She's like a cherished American writer."

"So she's more like Shakespeare than the Queen."

"You're yanking my chain, right?"

High waggled his finger. "Yes, Charles, I know who Nora Ban-nister is. I'm just not a big fan of the drivel she writes."

"To each his own, Detective High and Mighty," Charlie said.

"Anyway, five years ago, Nora helped set up my wife, Julia, and Tony's wife, Marisol, in a house-flipping business. They bought a run-down house in a good neighborhood, hired a contractor, renovated the shit out of it, then flipped it for a profit."

"Hence, the name," High said. "The LA Flippers."

"But here's the twist," Charlie said. "While the construction was going on, Nora wrote a book about a murder that takes place in that house. You might think it's drivel, but the first week *Murder at 2424 Horseshoe Canyon Road* came out, it went straight to the bestseller list. That's when the Flippers put the house on the market."

"I'm guessing it sold rather quickly," High said.

"Quickly? There was a bidding frenzy over it. Five buyers wanted to live in the house that's on the cover. It sold for a shitload more than they'd hoped to get."

"Whatever your mother-in-law lacks in literary talent, she more than makes up for in business acumen," High said. "That is bloody brilliant."

"It's so brilliant that she decided to write a bunch of them. So now she has *The House to Die For* series. A new book and a new house to flip every year. This time around Nora opened it up to a few of her friends. Terry's wife, Marilyn, and Jo Drabyak are the two newest partners."

"Actually, Marilyn and Jo are more like investors with opinions," Tony said. "My wife does most of the day-to-day work."

"And she gets a salary," Charlie said.

"She earns it. Wendy makes it sound like our wives are involved in something crooked."

"That's not what I meant," Wendy said. "We all know that

there are some real sketchy characters in the contracting business. They cut corners, they bribe inspectors, they hire illegal immigrants . . ."

"They cash your check, don't show up to do the work, so I wind up moving in with my partner," I said.

"Here's my point," Wendy said. "Some accountant hits on Jo Drabyak, she tells him to buzz off, and he sends her flowers. What if the same thing happens on the construction site with some illegal whose wife is still in Mexico? Maybe he doesn't send roses. Maybe he follows her home and kills her."

"So now you're saying some horny Mexican killed her?" Tony smiled and shook his head. "Hey, as long as you're projecting what the Mexicans would do, would you care to hear a point of view from a genuine Mexican?"

"Go ahead," Kilcullen said.

"Jo was in charge of publicity for the project," he said. "She didn't interact with the workers. Even if she had, she was a total sweetheart who got along with everyone. My wife, on the other hand, is a hot-blooded Latina with a short fuse. She's the line boss. She screams at the crew all day. She insults their mothers."

He smiled. We knew where this was headed.

"What I'm saying is, if those workers took a poll on who to shoot, Marisol would win unanimously."

Nobody argued the point. We all knew Marisol well enough to realize he was right. We spent the next half hour tossing around theories. Since we all came from different disciplines, we all had different ideas of who might want to murder a cop's wife. Gangs. Organized crime. Rappers. I'm sure if we spitballed long enough, O. J. would have come up as a suspect.

By seven thirty Terry and I were back on the 101, inching our way toward the Valley.

"Long day," I said.

"It's not over," Terry said. "We have to look into this house-flipping business. Which means when we get home, I'm gonna have to interrogate my wife."

CHAPTER NINE

Marilyn and Diana were in the living room, a bottle of wine and two glasses on the coffee table between them.

I went over and kissed Diana. Marilyn got up and hugged Terry long and hard.

"There's no dinner," she said. Her eyes were red. "I went to church, and now I'm having some wine. I'm pretty useless. Do you know who killed her?"

"Not yet," Terry said.

"She was such a wonderful person," Marilyn said. "Why? That's all I've been saying all afternoon. Why?"

It's a question Terry and I hear a lot in our line of work. We never have an answer. Usually we just say *sorry for your loss* and stand there quietly until the emotion subsides. But this was personal. Terry put his arms around her again and whispered something in her ear.

"Hey, Dad. Hey, Mike." It was Emily, Marilyn's and Terry's youngest daughter. Emily is sixteen, same red hair and green eyes as her mom, only on a smaller frame. Her older twin sisters had just started college. Sarah had decided to spend a year at LA City, so she was still living at home. But Rebecca was in St. Louis at Washington

U., which opened up a bedroom for me and Diana. As usual, Emily was being followed by Jett, the black lab my father gave her.

"Hey, honey," Terry said, not letting go of Marilyn.

"I heard about Mrs. Drabyak," Emily said. "I'm really, really sorry. But I know you and Mike are going to catch the person who did it."

"Did you finish your homework?" Marilyn said, uncoupling from her husband.

"Yes and no," Emily said.

"Pick one," her mother said.

"Madame Bouchard is making us write three hundred words describing an important event in my life, so *yes*, I have the idea for my paper, but *no*, I haven't written it yet, because I suck at French. And since you and Dad do not *parlez-vous français*, I called Carolyn Bennett, and she said she'd help me out. Can I go over there?"

"I know French," Diana said.

That was an understatement. Diana had lived in Paris for three years. So, yes, she knew French. But she didn't know the teenage mind. Emily flashed her a look that said, *Hey, lady, you're screwing up my plans to get out of the house.*

Diana recovered quickly. "Of course, it's mostly menu French. Escargot, quiche, French fries, stuff like that. And even then, I really don't know three hundred words."

"Too bad," Emily said, giving her a smile of relief. "So then, Mom, can I go over to Carolyn's house? I'll be back by ten."

"Nine thirty," Marilyn said.

"Nine forty-five."

"Nine fifteen," Marilyn countered.

"Okay, okay, nine thirty," Emily said. *"Merci beaucoup."*

"What important event are you writing about?" Terry said.

"The day Big Jim gave me Jett. Bye." She turned and headed toward the front door.

"Nine thirty," Marilyn yelled after her. "Not a minute later."

"*Oui, Mama.*" Door slam.

"There's no dinner," Marilyn said.

"I believe you mentioned that."

"You want some wine?" She reached for the bottle on the table.

"Why don't the four of us go out to Mr. Cecil's for ribs?" Terry said, removing the bottle from her hand before she could pour. "Give the wine a chance to wear off so Mike and I can ask you a few questions about Jo."

"I don't know what I can say to help, but, okay," Marilyn said. "Just promise me one thing. Promise me you'll catch the person who did this."

Terry has a voice that is magical. Soft and strong at the same time. It warms you, comforts you, reassures you. People always tell him he should be on the radio. His standard answer is, "Well, I sure got the face for it."

He put his arms around Marilyn one more time. "We'll catch him," he said. "I promise you, we'll catch him." He said it with total conviction, without a hint of the fact that we were currently clueless.

CHAPTER TEN

"You ready to answer a few questions?" Terry said, after we sat down and ordered dinner.

"Who's asking?" Marilyn said.

I "Me, Mike, does it matter?"

She sat there, hands folded on the table. "I'd be more comfortable being interrogated by somebody who's not my husband."

"*Interrogated?* Jesus, Marilyn, it's just a few simple . . ." He turned to me. "Fine, you put her through the wringer. I'll just sit here and be Bad Cop."

"How about you just be Quiet Cop," she said. "Go ahead, Mike."

"How much time did Jo spend at the flip house you're renovating?"

"Not much."

"Did she have anything to do with the contractors, any of the workers?"

Marilyn shook her head. "You think someone on the crew did it? No, they'd rather kill Marisol."

"You're the second person to say that," I said.

"Well, it's true. Marisol is on the crew's asses every day. She's a total bitch. Most of those macho construction guys hate her, but she gets the job done."

"So Marisol is there every day," I said, "and from what I understand, she gets paid extra."

"Right. Besides her partner share of the profits she gets a project management fee."

"And Jo doesn't work with the crew," I said.

"Jo and I are like the junior partners. This is our first house with them, so we're still kind of learning the ropes. We got to sit in on all the meetings with the architect, and we helped pick out the appliances and the fixtures. I worked with the landscaper, because I'm good at that, and Jo is coordinating the book launch party. It's supposed to be tomorrow night, but I spoke to Nora, and she's putting it off till after the funeral."

"What about Julia? What's her role in it?"

"Julia shows up when she wants to, which is mostly never."

"Does that piss the other partners off?"

"Just Nora. This whole thing started because Nora was looking for something for Julia to do with her life besides sit at home writing poetry. When she had the idea for *The House to Die For* series, she bought the first house and set Julia up to oversee the renovation. But Julia is a poet, a sensitive soul. If some idiot connects the water heater to the septic system, you're supposed to scream at the fucker to fix it, not agonize over the nicest way to tell him he made a mistake. So Nora went out and hired someone who can kick serious ass. Marisol."

"What about Jo? Is there anybody you can think of that's involved with the flip house that had a beef with her? Some guy who maybe had the hots for her, and she told him to screw off?"

"No. Nothing like that. A lot of these guys are illegals. There's no way they're gonna make a move on some white woman whose husband is a cop."

"They knew her husband is a cop?" I said.

"Everyone knows we're married to cops. We make a point of telling them. Plus we usually make it sound like you guys are trigger-happy psycho coppers like Dirty Harry."

Quiet Cop couldn't keep quiet any longer. "What about the partners?" Terry said. "Did they all get along with Jo?"

"No, Terry. We all got together and decided to kill her. What kind of a stupid question is that?"

"Hey," he said, "we're down to the stupid questions, because we asked all the smart ones, and we're still looking for a motive why anyone would want to kill this woman."

"Could we not talk about this anymore?" Marilyn said.

"Fine with me," Terry grumbled.

"This is going to sound dumb," Diana said, "but as long as we're down to the stupid questions, can I ask one?"

"Sure," Marilyn said. "Fire away."

"These houses that you renovate, they sell for a lot more than the market value, because Nora makes them famous. Am I right?"

"Right."

"And how does she make them famous? She makes them the scene of some fictional murder, right?"

"That's the concept."

"Okay, here's the dumb question," Diana said. "Do you think the price of the house would go up even higher if there were a real murder connected to it?"

"Wow," Marilyn said.

"That's pretty interesting," I said. "I can't wait till you come up with a smart question."

"You're saying that somebody might have wanted to drive the price of the house up, so they killed someone connected to it," Terry said.

"I don't know," Diana said. "It's just a weird thought I had."

"So maybe this has nothing to do with Jo," he said. "They just picked her at random. They could've killed any one of the . . ."

I couldn't stop him, and by the time Terry stopped himself it was too late. The idea that the victim could have been any of the partners hit Marilyn hard. She bolted from the table. "I'm going to be sick," she said, and ran toward the ladies room. Diana ran after her.

Terry put his hand to his forehead. "I must be an idiot."

"It was like watching a train wreck," I said. "I saw where you were going, but I couldn't stop you."

"She'll be okay," he said. "In the meantime, if Diana is right about the motive, that would narrow down the list of suspects. There's not too many people who would benefit if the house sold for more."

"Nora's loaded," I said. "I can't imagine she'd kill anyone for money. So that leaves Julia and Marisol."

"Don't forget about that redhead who's puking her guts out in the bathroom," Terry said. "Never did trust her."

CHAPTER ELEVEN

Traffic on the 101 is cake if you leave for work at five thirty in the morning. We had to wait till a civilized hour before we could make house calls, so we spent the first chunk of our day going over Reggie Drabyak's recent cases. At 9:00 A.M. we headed for Nora Bannister's house.

Nora is a cop groupie. She used to drop by the station under the pretense of visiting her son-in-law, Charlie Knoll, then spend the next few hours chatting it up with any homicide detective she could corner. Terry and I were her favorite targets.

Eventually, she stopped pretending and would call in advance to schedule a lunch or a drink after work, then bombard us with whatever murderous thoughts she had in her head.

If we figured out who the killer was, she'd go back and rethink the plot. Her biggest joy was getting one past us. "I've stumped the experts," she would say. "This book is going to be a bestseller."

And, of course, it always was. Nora was short, smart, tough, funny, and immensely popular in fifty countries. She was also a bit of a loon. A lot of people check their horoscopes, but Nora based every one of her life decisions on how the planets aligned with the stars. She refused to let her publisher launch a book if Mercury was in retrograde. As for her partners in the house-flipping business, any one of the wives at our station would have been thrilled to get in on the action, but Nora only invited the astrologically blessed. The sad exception was her daughter Julia, the biggest disappointment of Nora's life. Who knows if Julia would ever have been anything besides a failed poet living in her mother's shadow, but when Mom keeps telling you that you were three weeks premature, so, despite all her calculations, it's your fault that you popped out under a bad sign, your whole life is basically fucked. It doesn't matter if it was mystical or self-fulfilling, either way it was a prophecy Nostradamus would be proud to call his own.

I'd never been to her home till now. It was three stories high, pure white, and screamed art deco.

"It's like somebody broke off a piece of the Chrysler Building and dipped it in powdered sugar," Terry said.

"Does that mean you hate it?" I said.

"Are you kidding? I'd kill to own that house. Oh, wait, that's what she does."

Nora's assistant, Martin Sorensen, greeted us at the front door. We'd met him several times before at her book signings. Five years ago he had been a low-paid assistant editor at Nora's publisher. She was so impressed, she hired him to become her high-paid flunky.

Clean cut, good looking, well organized, and totally buttoned up, Martin is the perfect assistant. Even more perfect than one might imagine. At last year's book launch, after several trips to the punch bowl, Charlie let us know he was pretty sure that old Martin was banging his mother-in-law.

Of course, old Martin wasn't exactly old. He was thirty-seven.

And while Nora's Web site doesn't give her age, the consensus from the media sites put her at sixty-four.

"Julia thinks it's adorable that her mother is screwing a guy young enough to be her son," Charlie had said. "I think it's creepy. I asked around. He's got a reputation for chasing cougars, and Nora is one hell of a rich cougar."

"Terrible tragedy about Jo," Martin said as he walked us through the house to the pool. Nothing more. Just the basic pap you mumble as you shake hands with the bereaved at a funeral service and move on.

Nora and her daughter, Julia, were having coffee on the patio. Nora sprang up when we she saw us. "I'm so glad you're working this case," she said, giving each of us quick double-cheek Hollywood air kisses. "You got anything yet?"

"We're still putting it together," I said. "Good morning, Julia."

Unlike her mother, who was small and blond, Julia was big and bland. "Hi," she said.

"This is sur-freaking-real," Nora said. "Do you have any idea who might have killed her?"

"That's what we came to ask you," I said.

"The three of us have been racking our brains about it all morning," Nora said. "Nobody we know could possibly have done this. Maybe it has something to do with her past. Something none of us know about."

"Everybody loved her," Martin added helpfully.

"You all got along? No infighting? No problems?"

A chorus of three yeses.

"Would Marisol Dominguez agree with that?" I asked.

Nora laughed. She sat back in her chair and downed what was

left in her coffee cup. Without a word, Martin picked up the empty cup and refilled it from a large chrome carafe. "Well, there was no love lost between Marisol and Jo," Nora said. "They were total opposites. Sometimes Jo would bring the workers a box of pastries left over from one of her parties, and Marisol's attitude would be *we're not paying them to sit around and eat fucking donuts.* Jo was a people person. Marisol is a Marisol person. She's not there to make the workers happy. She's there to make them work. That's why she's so effective as a project manager." Nora glanced over at her daughter, the failed project manager. Julia pursed her lips but said nothing.

"So Marisol is in charge of the crew," I said. "What about the rest of the partners?"

"Well, I write the books, so I have the biggest stake," Nora said, picking up her fresh cup of coffee. "I used to own sixty percent. Julia and Marisol are twenty-percent investors, and Marisol gets a salary for overseeing all the subcontractors. On this latest house, I dropped back to fifty percent, so we could make room for Jo and Marilyn. They each have five percent. I didn't need their money as investors. It was more because it's a successful business, and I wanted to bring in a few friends, who have the talent and the karma that I thought could make it even more successful. Marilyn has an innate sense of feng shui, and she's a water sign, so she's perfect in the garden, and Jo was the quintessential Virgo, so of course I put her in charge of publicity and coming up with creative ways to showcase the house."

"The book launch was scheduled for tonight," Martin said. "Jo planned a brilliant party. We used to have the predictable champagne open house. This year, Jo has transformed it into a veritable movie set. She totally brought the murder to life."

Nora slammed her open palm down on the table. Silver, china, and Julia all jumped. "Martin, did you hear what you just said?" She turned to us. "Jo planned a stellar event. We've postponed it till after her funeral."

"Who would benefit financially with Jo gone?" I said.

"Nobody," Nora said. "She's done so much of the work already. When we sell the house, her share will go to her estate. I guess that means Reggie."

We fished for ten more minutes, but the more questions we asked, the more clear it became that no one in the group benefited from Jo Drabyak's death.

Finally, we wrapped it up. "One last question," I said. "Where were you all on Sunday night at about eleven?"

"I was in bed with a cop," Julia said. "Charlie got home from the poker game just around eleven."

"I was blogging," Nora said. "In fact, I bet you can track the fact that I posted a blog on my site around eleven thirty. It's not much of an alibi, but quite frankly, I can't imagine I actually need one."

"And I was home," Martin said.

"Alone?" I asked.

"Absolutely," he said, looking directly at Nora.

He didn't seem to care if Terry and I believed him. He was more worried about the cougar.

CHAPTER TWELVE

Martin and Julia waited on the patio, while Nora walked us to the front door. "I realize you didn't want to say anything in front of the others, but if you've got anything, feel free to share it with me. I can help."

"Nora, you've been a big help already," I said. "Thanks."

"No, Mike. I mean *help*. In case you forgot, I solve homicides for a living."

I had been in a pissy mood before I got to Nora's. I only had five hours sleep, I was tired of living out of a suitcase, and the prospect of my contractor ever calling to say my house is ready looked dim. And now this woman who invented every homicide she ever solved was telling me she could do my job. My patience was worn thin, and I tore into her. "Nora, you make this shit up," I said. "You come up with ways to kill imaginary people, and then three hundred pages later you have some other imaginary person figure out who the killer was. In case *you* forgot, this is what Terry and I do for a living. Jo Drabyak is not one of your characters. This is the real deal."

"For God's sake, Lomax, I know the difference between reality and fiction. You know what Tom Clancy said?"

"No, and quite honestly, if it's not going to help me turn this case around, I don't give a shit."

"The difference between fiction and reality is that fiction has to make sense. Killing Jo Drabyak makes no sense. I can't make heads or tails of it. I was up at four this morning. By the time you showed up I was on my third pot of coffee. I have a theory. Are you willing to listen to it?"

Terry hadn't said a word for ten minutes. He stepped in. "Yes, we'd like to hear whatever you came up with."

She smiled. "Thanks. Is it your turn to be Good Cop?"

"Yeah, but I suck at it," Terry said, "so cough up your theory fast because I can get twice as cranky as Mike."

I doubted if Nora had anything of value to offer up. The only thing on her agenda was to get involved, but she was Charlie's mother-in-law and Marilyn's partner. It was probably a good call on Terry's part to let her blather on.

"I'm sure you're looking into the Reggie connection," she said. "Cop's wife gets killed, maybe somebody's got a hard-on for the cop."

"We got it covered," Terry said.

"So I focused on Jo. Why kill her? Sure, there may be an old grudge that you dig up, but I doubt it. So I thought, what if this is not really about Jo? What if it's about someone else?"

Terry was patient. "Like who?"

"Like me," she said. "What if someone is trying to destroy my career?"

"Correct me if I'm wrong," Terry said, "but wouldn't it be easier to destroy your career by just shooting you in the head?"

"Not if the killer is a sicko who wants to toy with me. First he kills Jo, then Marisol, or Julia, or even Marilyn. Little by little he would sabotage my books, my real estate venture, everything I do. Why shoot me, if he can watch me suffer?"

I like it.

I've met a lot of self-centered people in Hollywood, but Nora was the first to suggest that someone else's murder was motivated by a desire to ruin her day.

"And who do you think might want to do that?" Terry said.

"I don't know. I haven't figured that part out yet. But even though I have millions of fans, there are always those few that don't wish me well. Maybe they're authors who are jealous, or people who were offended by something I wrote. I'm sure there are a lot more people who would rather kill me than kill Jo."

At this point I was one of them.

"It's an interesting theory," Terry said. "Maybe you can come up with a list of people who you think might have killed Jo to get at you. Meantime, Mike and I have to go. We'll be in touch."

He opened the door, and we walked down the steps into the mid-morning humidity that claws at Los Angeles every September.

"I'll fax a list to your office," she called after us. "Is there anything else I can do?"

I looked back over my shoulder. "Yeah. Switch to decaf."

CHAPTER THIRTEEN

"I was a real asshole," I said once we were back in the car. "Do I owe her an apology?"

"Hell, no," Terry said. "But you owe me one. You know I hate playing Good Cop."

"Most of the time I can deal with her," I said. "But sometimes . . . How come she never gets to you?"

"I don't have your issues."

"What issues?"

"Mike, she's smart, she's engaging, and deep down inside I'm sure she's a good person. But she's a world-class meddler. She can't keep her nose out of other people's business. Remind you of anyone?"

"Narrow it down for me," I said.

"If you moved into her house, she'd be peeing under your window every night."

"Oh, *that* world-class meddler. You think she's like my father?"

"Nora Bannister is the female version of everything that drives you crazy about Big Jim: nosy, bossy, manipulating, in your face—what did I leave out?"

"I get it," I said. "What do you think about her theory that someone killed Jo to screw up her writing career?"

"Oh yeah, I forgot egomaniac. On a scale of one to ten, I'd give her theory a zero. It pissed me off that she threw Marilyn into the mix of potential victims."

"Maybe she thinks if your wife is a target you'll work harder."

"She's playing us."

"Of course she's playing us. I don't think she shot Jo, but now that one of her partners is a homicide victim, she's going to milk it to help her sell more books. I'll bet the first thing she did when she woke up at 4:00 A.M. was call her publicist to see if she could get booked on *Good Morning America*."

We rehashed everything we had put together since we caught the case and decided that we hadn't made a hell of a lot of progress in the critical first twenty-four hours. Fifteen minutes later we were at 611 South Cherokee, the house Nora and her merry band were flipping.

There was a squad car parked outside, its lights quietly flashing. The front yard was wrapped in yellow crime scene tape. It was all part of the show.

"Murder at 611 South Cherokee," I said.

"Good title for a book," Terry said.

There was a jet black BMW 328i convertible sitting in the driveway. The vanity plates said JOAQUIN.

"Looks like Joaquin is doing pretty well for himself," Terry said.

The front door was wide open. We went inside. Marisol Dominguez was standing in the living room with a heavyset Mexican man who was dressed in paint-spattered overalls. He had a half-painted kitchen cabinet door in his hands and a puzzled look on his face.

Marisol was pissed. "No, no, no," she said, tapping on the door. *"Éste es amarillo de la mostaza. Deseo amarillo del limón."*

"Ah . . . limón," the painter said. *"Sí."*

She waved him off, and he left to fix whatever he had done wrong.

She looked up at us. "He says he's a painter, but he can't tell the difference between mustard and lemon. The book specifically says *'The kitchen cabinets were painted bright yellow. Miranda thought the color matched her sunny disposition, but Stephen said it was lemon—a perfect metaphor for their sour marriage.'* That's what I get for hiring a bunch of wetbacks."

It would be a racist comment coming from somebody else, but Marisol was Mexican, so she knew she could get away with it. I've heard her use the word before, strictly for shock value, but in this case it was just a subtle display of power. She gave us a challenging look that seemed to say, "What are you two white cops going to do? Arrest me for a bias crime?"

There were times when Terry and I wondered why Tony stayed married to her, but every time we saw her in person, we'd smack our heads and say, "Oh, yeah." Marisol might have been shortchanged in the charm department, but God had packed what little she had into a kickass body. Today, it was on display in tight jeans and a man's shirt tied in a knot at her midriff, leaving a three-inch band of smooth, dark skin.

She had a clipboard in one hand and a cigarette in the other. "I knew you two would get here sooner or later," she said.

"Good to see you too, Marisol," Terry said.

"Don't take it personally. It's just like I have a zillion things on this punch list that I still have to get done." She took an unladylike drag on the cigarette. "I feel bad about Jo's death, but if I told you I was grateful for the extra couple of days to get the house ready, would that makes me a suspect?"

"You're not a suspect," Terry lied. "We just want to know what you know about her."

"I hated her. She treated me like I was the fucking help. Well, maybe I am, but without my help, this house would never get done. She comes in as a five-percenter on the fifth house in the series, and she thinks her shit smells like strawberries. And she was always sucking up to Nora."

"Did you two argue?" Terry said. "Ever fight?"

"I fight with my husband. I fight with these dumb Mexican laborers. Her, I basically ignored. I just hated her from a distance. I'm in this for the money, not the sisterhood."

"Just for the record," Terry said, "where were you Sunday night?"

"Home. I went to sleep at ten. And just for the record, Detective Tony Dominguez can verify my alibi. I was in bed when he got back from the poker game."

She took another drag on the cigarette, then mashed the butt into an ashtray that was sitting on the mantel. "Look boys, I know you got a homicide on your hands, but I'm wasting oxygen here. Anything else before I get back to work?"

"Can we get a tour of the house?" Terry said.

"I don't see why not. Especially since your old lady has a piece of the action."

"Yeah, she's one of those annoying five-percenters."

"Marilyn's not so bad," Marisol said. "At least she doesn't think she's a princess."

← AVOID

"Right," Terry said. ("And I'd be willing to testify under oath that her shit definitely does not smell like strawberries.")

Marisol cracked half a smile. "You saw the cop car and the crime scene tape outside," she said, her tone slipping from bitch to sales-pitch mode. "Since the house is about to go on the market, it's been propped and decorated to reflect the murder house in Nora's latest book. When we actually show it, the prospective buyers will be guided around by actors wearing cop uniforms."

"And all that hoopla affects the price?" Terry said.

"People eat it up," she said. "Our open houses are so popular that vendors set up on the street to sell food to the gawkers. *The House to Die For* open houses have edged out the LaBrea Tar Pits as the fourth most popular attraction in LA."

"How about the BMW in the driveway? Is that part of the draw?"

"Hell, no. That's mine. I got it in April. You like it?"

"This house-flipping business must be pretty good. I know you can't afford it on Tony's salary," Terry said.

She grinned. "No way, José."

"Who's Joaquin?"

The grin disappeared. "My brother," she said. "He died. Tony and I don't want kids, so the car is my new baby. I gave it my brother's name. Come on, I'll show you where the previous owner of the house was murdered."

We entered the master bedroom. Just inside the door was an easel with a large card describing the room and its fictional history:

This is the 20'×30' airy master bedroom where the lifeless body of Stephen Driscoll was found sprawled on the plush Ber-

ber carpeting, the sun streaming down on the tragic scene from the three Velux electric venting skylights.

Did the killer lie in wait in the spacious walk-in closet or sneak softly across the hand-stained cedar deck through the double-paned French sliding doors?

Did he or she quickly wash away the evidence in one of the his-and-her dual Kohler sinks, or was there enough time to savor the deadly deed with a languishing soak in the fifteen-jet, multi-speed Jacuzzi tub?

Is this fiction, or could Stephen Driscoll's nightmare become the home of your dreams?

There was a chalk outline in the center of the room. Stephen's last glass of wine and his open cell phone were lying on the floor. His stamp collection book sat on the desk, open to a full page of stamps, minus one from the center. Several other clues were positioned around the room.

"So who killed him?" I said.

Marisol flashed a smile. "You'll have to buy the book. Or buy the house, and we'll throw the book in for free."

"Do you know who killed Stephen Driscoll?" Terry said.

"Damn straight I do."

"And do you know who killed Jo Drabyak?"

"No. So get off my case. Tough shit that she's dead, but I didn't have anything to do with it. I may be a bitch, but I'm not a murderous bitch."

CHAPTER FOURTEEN

We spent the rest of the day interviewing people connected to Jo, one of whom was so thrilled with her son's bar mitzvah party that she insisted on showing us pictures. We talked to a caterer, a photographer, and a DJ, all of whom worked with Jo and said they would miss her.

"Personally and financially," the DJ added. "She got me some great gigs."

"In that case, we're twice as sorry for your loss," Terry said.

Chris High tracked down a second neighbor who backed up the dog walker's story. He was sure he had heard Jo pull into the garage at around eleven fifteen Sunday night.

Almost everyone we interviewed asked the same question. Why would anyone want to kill her? It was a good question. Except that we were supposed to be asking it, and they were supposed to be coming up with answers.

By five in the afternoon we were back in the office updating Kilcullen on our most recent lack of progress.

"What about Reggie's arrests?" he said.

"We ran through the most recent busts this morning. We have

past arrests going back three years being pulled out of the archives. So far, nothing jumps out."

"Dig deeper," Kilcullen said. "It might not be obvious. It may be hiding under the surface."

"Meaning what?" Terry said.

"Okay, I'll give you a dumb scenario," Kilcullen said. "Totally hypothetical. Let's say Reggie busted a pimp. The guy wants to negotiate with Reggie, so what does he offer up as a bargaining chip?"

"I don't know," Terry said. "How horny is Reggie during the negotiation period?"

"Kiss my ass, Biggs," Kilcullen said. "I'm trying to teach you something. The pimp tells Reggie he can finger a cop who's taking bribes to look the other way when the hookers are working his beat. So now Reggie's got something on a crooked cop, and he's going to take it to IA."

"I doubt it," Terry said. "Reggie's too smart. He'd never just take some lowlife pimp's word for it."

"I told you it's hypothetical," Kilcullen said. "In this case, Reggie buys the pimp's story, but before he can report it, the rogue cop finds out, and he kills Reggie's wife."

"Why?"

"Because that would effectively put Reggie out of commission."

"Why doesn't the cop just kill Reggie?" Terry said.

"I said it was dumb, dammit. I'm just trying to get you guys to think outside of the box."

"Oh, right . . . the dumb scenario school of management,"

Terry said. He was winding up to take one more poke at the boss, when Tony and Charlie walked into Kilcullen's office. In reality, Charlie walked. Tony barreled in, steaming mad.

"What the hell are you guys doing questioning my wife?"

"What are you talking about?" Terry said. "We questioned the whole group connected to the house flipping business. Charlie's wife, his mother-in-law . . ."

"And Marilyn?" Tony said.

"Yeah, I worked her over with a rubber hose. She confessed."

"Tony, relax," Kilcullen said. "They're just doing their—"

Terry isn't the type to let the boss fight his battles. "So we interviewed Marisol," he said to Tony. "It's not like we cuffed her and carted her off. It's called police work."

"Yeah, well the next time you got police work with my family, let me know ahead of time."

"Yeah, I'll send you a registered letter," Terry said. He turned to Charlie. "How about you? You got the same beef?"

Charlie just shook his head. "Hey, man, my buddy's wife was murdered . . . whatever it takes."

"Thanks," Terry said. "And now, if it's okay with Detective Dominguez, I'm gonna take a piss."

Tony shot him the finger.

"All right, knock it off," Kilcullen said. "Get back to work."

"Yeah," Terry said. "And one more thing about your dumb scenario. I was wondering what cop would take a few hundred bucks from a pimp, and then cover up the crime by killing another cop's wife. I was thinking, how stupid can one cop be? But you're right. I gotta start thinking outside the box."

Terry stormed out and Kilcullen stood up. "Dammit,

Dominguez, the victim was in business with your wife. Of course she gets questioned."

"Marisol said he was a total wiseass," Tony said.

"It's part of his charm," Kilcullen said. "Get over it. And rein in that Latin temper. I got enough crap to deal with."

Tony threw both hands up and left the room. Charlie gave me a smile and followed.

"And Lomax," Kilcullen said. "Get your partner to start acting civil, or you're both . . . Never mind. I don't care who you piss off. Just solve it."

CHAPTER FIFTEEN

It probably would have been a good time to go home and let Terry cool down. But when I got back to my desk there was a message from the coroner's office. The autopsy was complete, and they had released Jo Drabyak's body. She was Jewish, and it's a tradition to bury the dead as soon as possible, so the funeral was scheduled for the next morning.

"You realize we're not going to get much work done tomorrow," I said. "You want to order a pizza and put in a couple of hours tonight?"

Terry, still seething from his head-to-head with Tony, grumbled something that sounded like yes. Two slices into a large pie, he was his old self again.

As promised, Nora Bannister faxed us a list of people she thought might have wanted to hurt her by murdering Jo. They included two reviewers, half a dozen authors, a Hollywood producer, a fan who she informed us "couldn't get close enough to kill me, because I have a restraining order against him," and her former publisher, who Nora informed us was the only one on the list she wanted to kill herself.

"It's hard to believe she writes murder mysteries," Terry said.

"Three of the authors live in New York, the reviewers are from Boston and Atlanta, and except for the producer and the fan, nobody else lives in LA. Most of these people probably have the same alibi—sorry, officer, but my ass wasn't even in California when the murder occurred."

"She's not stupid," I said. "The note on the cover page says, 'Don't be fooled by the geography. Just because they don't live here doesn't mean they couldn't have hired a hit man. And before you judge me, remember—even paranoids have enemies'."

"Put it on the bottom of our Help-We-Can-Do-Without pile," Terry said. "Unless she signed it, in which case we can sell it on eBay."

We recruited Muller, our superstar computer tech, to stick around and help us wade through all of Reggie's vice arrests over the past three years.

There were hundreds of files. The hookers and pimps were the usual bottom feeders you meet when you work vice, but the johns were a whole different socioeconomic demographic.

"So far I've got a high school principal, a banker, and an ad exec," Muller said.

"I'll trade you," Terry said. "I'll give you a lawyer, a neurosurgeon, a left-handed pitcher, and a first-round draft choice to be named next spring."

I didn't join in the banter. I understood all too well why some guys wind up paying for sex. My wife, Joanie, was only thirty-five when she was diagnosed with cancer. She put up a brave fight and hung on for almost three years. As the clock ticked and the chemo dripped, our sex life became as terminal as she was.

It was during one of those long dry spells that I met Coral

C. Jones. Her brother Tyrell had been accused of robbing and killing a 7-Eleven clerk. At least, that's what it looked like on the surveillance video. But Coral C. swore he was innocent, and I agreed to take one more long hard look at the evidence. She was right. Two days later I arrested the real killer.

Coral C. offered to pay me back with the oldest currency known to man. She was a hooker—big, brown, beautiful—and the very thought of losing myself in that exotic beauty for one night turned me on. But I turned her down. I didn't cheat. For better, for worse, for richer, for poorer, in sickness or in health, I was married.

Two years later, when Joanie died, I called Coral C. and took her up on her offer. With one exception. I insisted on paying for the sex.

I was drunk, but I don't blame the booze. I make no apologies, and I have no regrets. I just don't share it with anyone. Not even Terry, although he'd be the least judgmental of anyone I could ever tell.

Joanie had left me a series of letters, along with instructions to read one each month after she died. The letters were painful, heartbreaking, and one night a month for the next six months I turned to Coral C. for release. It was strictly professional. And then I met Diana, and a life I never thought I could have again began to open up to me.

Reggie Drabyak's cases had hundreds of names of men who got caught paying for sex, and the more prominent they were, the more Terry seemed to enjoy their fall from grace.

"Look at this one, Mike," he said. "A minister."

I looked at the file and didn't say a word.

Who am I to judge?

CHAPTER SIXTEEN

The funeral chapel was packed. The mayor and the chief of police sat in the front row between Reggie and Jo's parents. Behind them, friends, family, politicians, and cops. Lots of cops. Many with their wives.

Barb Brown, Jo's lifelong friend, who had flown in from New Jersey, gave a moving fifteen-minute eulogy that painted a picture of Jo from the day they met in grade school to their very last e-mail exchange.

Four other people spoke. Nora Bannister was not one of them, but her daughter, Julia, read a poem. Finally, Reggie. It was a sweet, awkward, poignant tribute. He closed by inviting everyone to the house after the funeral to eat, drink, and celebrate Jo's life. "I apologize in advance for the food," he said. "It would be a much nicer buffet if Jo were around to plan it."

And then he introduced Helen Ryan, to sing "Sail On, Little Girl, Sail On," Reggie and Jo's favorite song.

"She's blind," Marilyn whispered. It was impossible to tell. The woman walked slowly but confidently to the podium, without the help of a cane, a dog, or an escort.

Ryan was about forty, with short sandy blond hair and a totally unassuming air. She was no more than five-foot-two, but she had a powerful, bluesy voice that reminded me of Joplin. She poured her soul into the song, wrenching new meaning from lyrics that were once full of promise for Reggie and Jo. If it had been a concert instead of a funeral, the crowd probably would have leaped to its feet and yelled for more.

Killers often can't resist showing up for their victim's funeral, so despite the fact that we were there as friends, Terry and I were working. Nothing caught our radar at the chapel or the cemetery.

When we got to the house, the emotional focus shifted from Jo to Reggie. A number of women swarmed around him, bringing him food and refilling his glass. One even stood behind him and massaged his neck. I stared at Reggie as long as I could, then I closed my eyes and let the memories of Joanie's funeral flood over me.

I felt Terry's hand on my shoulder. "This isn't easy for you, is it?" he said.

"What?" I said, opening my eyes. "A funeral for a cop's wife? It's easier than the last one I went to."

"Yeah, I remember what you looked like that day. Reggie doesn't look quite as devastated."

"He's better than I am at hiding his feelings," I said.

"Plus he's got all these touchy-feely women without wedding rings to help him get through his grief."

"Once a cop, always a cop, eh, Biggs? Look, he swore to us he wasn't involved with anyone," I said. "He even offered to take a poly."

"Right. Of course, we never did take him up on his offer."

The crowd at the buffet table had thinned out, so Terry and I stepped up to grab some food. The blind woman who sang at the funeral was standing there with an empty plate in her hand.

"Need any help?" I asked.

"You're either trying to pick me up, or somebody told you I was blind," she said. "Either way, you're out of luck. I'm married, and I'm not totally blind, just legally. It's called optic atrophy. My vision is degenerating, but I can still tell the difference between a tray of lasagna and a bowl of chicken salad."

"Is that chicken salad?" I said. "I thought it was tuna."

"Trust me, it's chicken," she said, tapping her nose. "I'm Helen Ryan."

"Mike Lomax. And this is my partner, Terry Biggs."

"Nice to meet you," she said. "How long have you two been a couple?"

"He's not that kind of a partner," I said. "We work together."

"Open mouth, insert foot," she said. "Sorry, what kind of work do you do?"

"We're hairdressers," Terry said.

She giggled. "He's funny."

"We're homicide detectives," I said. "I'm the one who's not funny."

"Are you investigating Jo's death?" she asked.

"We are," I said. "How long did you know her?"

"Just about a year. I live next door to the house Nora and the girls are renovating on Cherokee. They've done such a beautiful job. I keep telling them they're doing more to drive up my property values than my husband and I have done since we bought the place."

"Is your husband here?" I said.

"He's at sea," she said. "He's a merchant marine. He left on Monday. He won't be back for a month."

We made small talk with Helen for another ten minutes. Then we stepped out into the backyard where people were still having lunch. Julia, Nora, and Marisol were sitting together at a table. My father, Big Jim Lomax, was towering over them, a beer in one hand. There were several available folding chairs, but Jim wisely didn't trust them to support a six-foot-four, three-hundred-pound teamster.

Nora waved, and we walked over. "How's it going?" she asked.

I knew what she meant by "it," but I avoided the issue. "Reggie's eulogy was touching," I said. "And Julia, I know Jo would have loved your poem."

"I think it could still use some work," Nora said, before Julia could respond. "But at least she was better than that rent-a-rabbi. It was so obvious that he didn't know Jo. All that generic crap about the fragility of life and the mysterious ways of the Lord. Plus he kept looking down at his cheat sheet every time he said her name, and even then he still pronounced Drabyak wrong."

"Well, I really enjoyed Julia's poem," I said.

"Thanks," Julia said. It was all she could get out before Nora grabbed the spotlight again.

"My book launch party is tomorrow at seven. I expect to see you boys there. You were such a huge help when I was doing research."

"I'm looking forward to it," I said, throwing in a plastic smile to go along with the phony sentiment.

"What time would you like me to pick you up tomorrow?" Big Jim said to Nora.

I winced. Jim owns a transportation business. He has over fifty cars and trucks, which he rents to film crews. He also provides a limo service for studio executives, movie stars, and just about anybody who wants to be noticed when they arrive. And if you're lucky enough to get Jim as your personal driver, don't think of yourself as a passenger. You're more like a hostage. Jim's meddling gene kicks into high gear. Put that together with Nora in the back seat, and the thought of the two of them dissecting my case annoyed the crap out of me.

Nora looked at Jim. "What are you talking about?"

"Jo arranged for me to pick you up at your house and drive you to the book party."

"In a limo?" Nora said.

Jim laughed. "I could pick you up in an eighteen-wheeler, but you'd look better getting out of a stretch Mercedes."

"Don't be silly," she said. "I can drive to my own event. Besides, I'm spending the afternoon shopping with Julia. The two of us can drive there together."

I was starting to feel a sense of relief, when Marisol jumped in.

"Absolutely not! Jo and I discussed this. We're putting on a show. We're getting press coverage. And with this . . . unfortunate incident . . . lots of press. What are you planning to do, drive up in your SUV and give it to the valet? You have to arrive looking like a rock star."

"Fine. Jim, you can pick me and Julia up at six fifteen tomorrow evening." She stared hard at me and Terry. "Maybe by then my two favorite detectives will give us something to really celebrate."

Don't split infinitives.

67

"Well, then I'll see you tomorrow," Big Jim said, slowly backing away from the table. "Nice poem, Julia. Maybe I can get a copy of it."

He turned and motioned for me and Terry to follow him. "What's going on?" he said, as soon as we were out of hearing range.

"With what?" I said.

"*Maybe my two favorite detectives will give us something to celebrate?* Why is Nora busting your chops?"

"Everyone busts our chops," I said.

"And Nora busts everyone's chops," Terry added. "It's a match made in Chop Heaven."

"She wants us to solve the murder by tomorrow night, so it can be announced at the book launch," I said.

"It would help sell a hell of a lot of books," Terry said. "Not to mention jacking up the price on the house."

"That's Nora for you. Did you notice how she was badmouthing the rabbi?" I said. "And then when I mentioned the poem . . ." I paused to give Big Jim room to jump in.

He took the bait. "Yeah, did you see the way she kept putting down her own daughter and monopolizing the conversation?"

I nodded my head.

"The woman's a pain in the ass," he added, blissfully clueless. "A bona fide, certified pain in the ass."

"You gotta feel sorry for her poor daughter," Terry said, giving Jim his best poker face.

I, on the other hand, broke into a big, broad, shit-eating grin for the first time all day. I really get off on irony.

CHAPTER SEVENTEEN

Diana and I decided to spend the night at a hotel.

"Was it something I said?" Marilyn asked.

Diana laughed. "Don't be silly."

"Then it's something Terry said."

"No, we just need a night alone," Diana said.

"Are you sure you want to spend money on a hotel, just so you can have wild sex? Our house is so noisy we'd never even hear you."

Diana smiled. "Therein lies the problem."

"Oh," Marilyn said. "You want the no-earsplitting-music, no-blaring-TV, no-barking-dog, no-screaming-kids, quiet, romantic, kind of sex?"

Diana tapped the tip of her nose. "Bingo."

"That's not possible at our house. Where you guys staying?"

"The Marriott on Ventura."

"Well, that's convenient," Marilyn said. "You can walk to the Galleria."

"We won't be walking anywhere," Diana said.

"You're making me insanely jealous," Marilyn said. "Just go."

We went. The sex turned out not to be as quiet as predicted. If you had been listening outside the door of room 313, you'd have heard the hushed rustling of clothes, tender whispers, gentle kisses, soft moans, shallow breathing, and then, suddenly, unexpectedly, a full-blown crying jag.

Much to my surprise, I was the one crying. It took me five minutes to regain my composure. Diana just stroked my face and said nothing.

"This has never happened to me before," I said.

"It's good for you to let it out," Diana said. "It's healthy."

"It's embarrassing. I don't cry. Especially in public."

"We're naked in bed. How public is that?"

"I don't understand what happened," I said.

"Yes, you do," she said. "Maybe you don't want to deal with it, but you must know why you're crying."

We were lying in each other's arms under cool sheets. I rolled over to face away from her, and she snuggled in tight behind me. I stared aimlessly at the clock radio on the night table. It jumped from 6:41 to 6:42. We had only checked in twenty minutes ago.

"She's dead almost two years," I said.

"Jo's death opened up a lot of old wounds," Diana said. "A fellow cop losing his wife. Even the names are close—Jo, Joanie."

"I get all that," I said. "Of course, I thought about Joanie at Jo's funeral. But this is too weird. Crying while I'm having sex?"

"A lot of women do it all the time."

"Oh, God," I said, "you're making it worse. Women have unpredictable hormones. Women have violent mood swings. I may not have proven it lately, but I'm a man."

She stroked the back of my neck. "I know. You're a virile, super-masculine, tough cop, macho man."

"Who just cried like a girl during sex," I said.

"Tell you what," she said, sitting up. "Let's get dressed and go out to dinner. We'll get you some steak and potatoes and beer, and we'll find a jukebox that has the theme from *Rocky*, and then we'll come back here and try it again."

She smacked me hard on my bare butt.

I rolled over, grabbed her, threw her back down on the mattress, and kissed her hard until she had to break away just to catch her breath. "I don't need no stinking steak and potatoes," I said.

And then, we made love. f- -ked.

I was glad Marilyn and Terry weren't in the next room. They'd have complained about the noise.

CHAPTER EIGHTEEN

Brendan Kilcullen has been a cop for twenty years, and he's got the scars to prove it. A bullet wound in his right thigh, a jagged gash down his left arm from a beer bottle, and three holes in his dress uniform, where service medals have been pinned.

He's been a devout Catholic for his entire forty-seven years, married for twenty-six, and sober for the past twenty-four. He's the kind of tough, smart cop I'd want backing me up in a bar fight or a shootout.

He has one failing. He doesn't do well with pressure from the top, and this was one of those cases where he was being squeezed hard, often, and from all sides.

Terry and I reported to his office at seven the next morning.

"It's Thursday," Kilcullen said.

"Yes sir," Terry said. "I caught that in today's paper."

"I'm not in the mood for comedy, Biggs. And neither is Reggie Drabyak. He called me last night. He was stinking-ass drunk."

"I think he's a candidate for AA, lieutenant. You really should think about taking him to one of your meetings." Terry said it with such a straight face that Kilcullen wasn't sure whether or not he was being played.

He let it pass. "Reggie wants to know who killed his wife, and told me if Lomax and Biggs can't solve it, he can."

Terry has his own shortcomings. Among other things, he is genetically incapable of dealing with criticism. I'm not great at it myself, but I'm better than he is. I took a half step in front of him and squared off with Kilcullen. "You and I both know that Reggie can't solve this, Loo."

"Then the question is, can *you* solve it? This is day four of the investigation. And yet, I see no progress."

"We're putting in the time, but we're running into a lot of dead ends. No ballistics, no prints, no suspects, and the biggest problem, no motive."

"You realize, of course, that Reggie is not the only one crawling up my ass," Kilcullen said.

"I know, boss. You got BUTA."

He forced out a laugh. "Oh, yeah. I got big time BUTA."

Kilcullen was not an orator. He came from humble roots and basic schooling. Somewhere along the way, he picked up the habit of turning many of the finer points of his dialogue into scatological references. He complained so often about having brass up the ass that Terry abbreviated it to BUTA. Instead of getting pissed, Kilcullen seemed to enjoy it. Like maybe we understood him better if we gave his biggest source of pain a code name.

"Everybody up the chain of command is calling me," he said. "I got so much BUTA that my shit hits the bowl with a clank."

His visual imagery is never pretty, even less so at seven in the morning.

"But that's why you get the big bucks," Terry said. "Because you always know what to say to the brass when they're screaming for justice."

"Right," Kilcullen said. "But what do I say to Reggie?"

"We're working on it, Loo," I said. "I swear we're going to solve this."

He nodded, then hit us with another of his familiar phrases. "Speed is of the essence, and failure is not an option."

He waved us out of the room. The meeting was over.

"I always feel so much more motivated after one of those locker room pep talks from Coach Kilcullen," Terry said. "Plus I feel really confident that we're going to break this case now that you officially swore we'd solve it."

"It wasn't an official swear," I said. "It was more of a contractor swear. Like that asshole Hal Hooper telling me that Diana and I would be living in the house by September first."

We spent the next eleven hours working hard and getting nowhere. We went over forensics and the statements that Chris High's team had collected. We talked to informants who had nothing to inform. We revisited the names of all the johns from Reggie's caseload who might have been damaged enough to want to commit homicide as payback. Then we spent the rest of the day on the street talking to pimps and hookers, all of whom knew Detective Drabyak, and most of whom thought he was a pretty decent cop.

By 6:00 P.M. we were back at the station documenting our failures in writing. Normally, we wouldn't get the reports out so fast, but we were killing time. We had Nora's book party to go to at seven, and having seen more than enough of her over the past few days, we had no desire to be early.

At 6:45 I suggested we wrap it up. "Let's drive over to the

party, buy a book, sneak out early, take Marilyn and Diana out for dinner, and make a decent night of it."

"Or we could bail on the party, wait for the paperback to come out next year, ply the girls with alcohol, and make a fantastic night of it."

My cell phone rang. I looked at the caller ID. "My father," I said.

Terry gave me two thumbs up. "Just when you thought your day couldn't get any better."

I flipped the phone open. "What's up, Dad?"

Big Jim was breathing heavily. "Mike, I'm at Nora's house," he said. "You better get here right away. And bring a shitload of cops."

"What's going on?"

"Somebody shot her. She's dead." *yea! I never liked her.*

CHAPTER NINETEEN

Terry bolted for the parking lot, while I ran to the watch commander's office. I was still on the phone with Big Jim.

"Dad, where are you now?"

"I'm in Nora's living room."

"Get the hell out of the house."

"But what if Julia's here too? I was supposed to pick the two of them up. What if she's lying somewhere—"

"What if she's the shooter?" I yelled. "What if she's lying somewhere with a gun waiting for some big, fat, stubborn teamster to walk in? Get out!"

Lieutenant Jack Mullen, the watch commander, picked up his Rover and was ready to key the mic. His assistant commander, Sergeant Carl Bethge, grabbed a phone and was waiting for me to give him an address. But first I had to convince Big Jim to leave the crime scene.

"C'mon, Mike, do you really think Julia would shoot her own mother?"

"If I were any closer I'd shoot my own father. Now for once in your life, follow directions, get the hell out of the house, and wait for the cops."

"Okay, okay. I'm out of here."

"And leave the front door open."

I snapped the phone shut and turned to Mullen and Bethge. "DOA at 110 South June. There could be a second victim. I need EMS, CSU, and a perimeter. Code 3."

Bethge was dialing. "I heard you tell your witness the shooter may be out there. You want an airship?"

"Yeah, thanks. Eyes in the sky might help. Guys, this is big. The dead woman is Charlie Knoll's mother-in-law, Nora Bannister. And there's a possible second vic, Charlie's wife. But for all we know, she could be the shooter. Jack, nobody enters the house till Terry and I get there."

"Good idea, Mike," he said lowering his radio, "because I was just about to call out the Evidence Contamination Squad."

Jack hates it when people tell him how to do his job, but I didn't have time to cater to his quirks. Unless the watch commander gives a specific order to wait for the detectives in charge, some cowboy cop who wants to dazzle all the girls at the bar will race into a house and corrupt the scene before CSU can get there.

Bethge swiveled in his chair. "You know South June is outside our jurisdiction."

"I don't care if it's outside the state line," I said. "Bannister was a lead in the Drabyak homicide. Notify Kilcullen and Detective Burns. If there's a turf war, it's their problem, not mine."

"How about Charlie Knoll?" Bethge said.

"He's probably waiting at the book party for Nora and Julia. Call him, but give us time to secure the premises first."

I ran out the front door and jumped into the car. Terry shot down Wilcox, then ran the lights on Santa Monica and Highland. A squad car cleared the way. We made it in five minutes, just as the EMS bus was pulling up.

Terry and I jumped out of the car and strapped on vests. I barked orders at the cops who were already cordoning off the area. Big Jim's Mercedes was parked in front of the house. There was a cluster of black and whites forty feet away, and Jim was sitting in the back of one of them.

Terry grabbed three cops and drew his gun. "Detective Lomax and I are going in first. You back us up. One woman's been shot, there may be a second victim, and the shooter may still be in there."

I pointed at one of the paramedics. "You, stay outside. Don't come in until we call for you."

The cops all drew their weapons, and the young paramedic backed up, took the stethoscope from around his neck, and pointed it at me. "Don't worry, pal, this thing is out of bullets."

Five of us ran up the white marble steps. Big Jim had left the front door open about eight inches. Terry and I stood on either side of it. He looked up at the two towering geometric stucco columns. "Rather phallic. I think they're art dicko," he said. Then he crashed the door open and bellowed, "Police. Come out with your hands up."

There were bloody footprints on the floor. I signaled for one cop to go left, and pointed the other two toward the stairs. Terry and I turned right and followed the footprints toward the living room.

And there was Nora, face down on the beige rug, wearing pink sweatpants and a white T-shirt soaked with the blood that had poured out of the back of her skull. I didn't need the paramedic to verify my father's statement. Nora Bannister was very dead.

Terry gestured for the two of us to split up. He went right. I went left.

Thirty seconds later, he yelled from down the hall, "Clear."

The living room had an arch that led to the dining room. I walked through it and did a three-sixty, gun extended. "Clear," I yelled, heading toward the next room.

The cop who had gone to the left called out from Nora's office. "Clear."

One of the cops checked in from upstairs. "Clear."

And then, from the kitchen, I heard Terry. "Shit. Get the medic in here."

"For Julia?" I yelled.

"No, goddammit. I cut myself on a chunk of broken glass. The medic is for me. Julia's gonna need the coroner."

CHAPTER TWENTY

Terry was standing in the kitchen, gun in his right hand, blood oozing out of his left. Julia was lying face up on the floor, a tiny red hole in the center of her forehead. He holstered his gun, flipped open his cell phone, and speed-dialed a number.

whom

I didn't have to ask who he was calling. Three of Marilyn's partners had been murdered.

"Shit," he said, hanging up. "My wife is the only person in LA who turns off her cell. Call Diana. The two of them are together."

The book launch party was at the flip house. Diana had read an advance copy of Nora's book and was excited to finally get to see the house in real life. I remembered the last thing she said to me this morning: "I'm looking forward to a night of murder and mayhem."

Be careful what you wish for. I dialed her number.

She picked up on the fourth ring. "Hi. Where are you?"

"Diana, are you all right?"

"I'm fine. I'm drinking champagne, and I finally heard from my long-lost boyfriend. I love this house. Would you buy it for me?"

"Are you with Marilyn?"

"Yes, but I'd rather be with you." The champagne was working.

I gave Terry a quick thumbs up, and he exhaled loud and hard.

"Listen carefully," I said. "I need you to be calm, and I need you to do exactly what I say."

Diana is a nurse in a pediatric oncology ward. She knows the sound of an emergency, and she knows how to respond. The giddiness was gone in an instant. "What's the matter?"

"I have bad news. Someone shot Nora and Julia. They're dead."

"Oh my God."

"Don't say anything else. I don't want people at the party to know what's going on. I need to get you, Marilyn, and Marisol out of there now."

"Are they after us too?"

"No. It's just a precaution. Is Tony Dominguez there?"

"Yes. I saw him a few minutes ago."

"Give the phone to Marilyn. Then find Tony for me."

I handed the phone to Terry, who repeated the bad news to Marilyn.

He spoke calmly in that soothing, reassuring, practically hypnotic voice of his. I'm sure he used it all four times he proposed marriage and a thousand times in between. He was using it now to keep Marilyn calm.

"You'll be fine. Tony is gonna bring you here. No, I don't think the girls are in any danger, but just to be on the safe side, why don't you call Sarah and Emily and tell them to go to a friend's house till they hear from me. Honey, I don't think you have to call Rebecca in St. Louis, but whatever makes you feel better. I know, baby. It's gonna be okay. Put Tony on. I promise. I love you too."

As soon as she handed the phone to Tony, Terry's voice went from comforting husband to cop in charge.

"Nora and Julia are dead. Shot. Same as Jo Drabyak. Three partners in this house-flipping business have been murdered, and I don't want my wife and yours to be numbers four and five. Get the two of them and Diana out of the building."

There was a short pause while Tony did the talking, then Terry jumped back in. "What I would do," he said, "is pull the plug on the party and lock up the house. Just tell everyone that Nora took sick, and shut it down without going public with the truth. Good. We're on the same page. Mike and I are at Nora's house. We'll send a couple of units to back you up. You're welcome, bro. See you soon."

He hung up. There was a roll of paper towels on the counter. He pointed to it. I tore some off and began to wrap it around his bloody left hand, while he called for Tony's backup. When he finished, he gave me my cell back.

"Sorry," he said. "I got blood all over your phone."

"What happened?" I said.

"I'm no Sherlock Holmes," he said, looking down at Julia, "but I'm gonna go out on a limb and guess that someone put a bullet through her head."

"What happened to *you*, asshole?"

"Oh, that. I sliced my hand on this Pellegrino bottle."

There was a shattered green bottle on the floor. It must have been full when it broke, because the pool of red around Julia was a lot more liquid than could possibly have come from the single dot in the middle of her skull.

"It looks like Julia tried to fend off her killer with a liter of imported sparkling water," Terry said. "Never the best choice against a gun. All she managed to do was get the floor sopping wet, so the first cop on the scene would slip on it, cut open his hand and wet his pants."

"There's a medic out there," I said.

"What I really need is a dry cleaner. These are my good pants."

One of the cops walked in. "Nothing upstairs, Detectives," he said. "And no sign of forced entry."

"Keep everyone out till CSU gets here." I said.

"No problem," he said. "Detective Lomax, I know you're busy in here, but you know that big guy out there—the one who found the bodies?"

"What about him?"

"He's a major pain in the ass. Says he wants to talk to you. I told him to wait till you're good and ready."

"What'd he say to that?" I asked.

The cop laughed. "He says he's your father."

I laughed along with him. "He's full of shit," I said. "Tell him to wait."

CHAPTER TWENTY-ONE

Terry and I took stock of the kitchen. There was a phone cradle on the counter, but no handset. I pressed the locator button and heard it beep back from another room.

"Well, even if Julia heard Nora get shot, that solves the mystery of why she didn't dial 911," Terry said.

He knelt down at the edge of the puddle of blood and Pellegrino. Julia was dressed for the evening. Black skirt, a silky blue blouse, heels. The hair near her left temple had been cut, and some of the little clippings were floating in the bloody soup.

"She's having a really bad hair day," he said.

We walked back through the living room and took another look at Nora. Her hair too had been chopped.

"She's wearing sweats," I said. "I know the two of them were supposed to go shopping this afternoon. They must have come back here together, and Nora probably put on something comfortable and was planning on changing her clothes at the last minute. What time do you think she would have gotten dressed for the party if she was expecting Big Jim to pick her up at six fifteen?"

Terry gave me a blank stare. "Mike, I'm the last guy you should be asking for fashion tips. I would have figured she was just gonna wear her gym clothes to the book signing."

I looked at his hand. The blood had already soaked through the paper towels. "You really should have EMS bandage that."

He stood up. "I'd rather try to solve this shit first before this maniac shoots my wife next."

We went outside and found Big Jim. He had talked his way out of the backseat of the squad car and was standing in the road, cell phone to his ear. He saw us coming and snapped it shut. "It's about time," he said. "One of your cops said something about bodies. As in more than one."

"Julia's dead," I said. "Tell us what you heard, saw, and did from the time you got here."

"I got here at six ten, five minutes early. I waited twenty minutes and called Nora from my cell. All I got was her machine. I said something like, 'Pick up if you're there,' but she didn't. So I got out of the car, walked up the steps, and rang the bell. No answer, so I tried the door, and it was open."

"Open, like wide open, or open like not locked?"

"Open like an inch, so that it looks closed, but it's not latched, so when you push it, it opens."

"Then what?"

"I knew something was wrong. I go in and call Nora's name. No answer, so I walk to the living room, and I see her on the floor. Dead. Then I called you."

"On the phone you said she was shot. Did you hear anything?"

"No. But I could see the gunshot wound and there's blood on the floor by her head. I'm sorry, but I stepped in it."

"Yeah, we saw your tracks. The crime lab will need your shoes, and since you touched the door, your prints. Then I want you to write out a statement."

"Anything you need."

"Terry and I have to get back to work. I'm going to have one of the officers stay with you."

"Okay. But I knew you were wrong about Julia."

"Meaning what?"

"Did you really think she could kill her own mother?"

"No," I said. "Most people don't kill their parents. They just fantasize about it." *yes!*

He gave me the finger.

I gave him a quick hug and went back to the house.

CHAPTER TWENTY-TWO

Jessica Keating was waiting for us at the front door.

"Nice going, Biggs," she said. "It's not every day that my lead detective bleeds all over the evidence."

"Your job's been too easy lately," Terry said. "I decided to make it a little more challenging. And I didn't bleed *all* over. Just the kitchen. My partner's father helped out by slogging through the blood in the living room."

"Darn," she said. "My guys followed those bloody footprints right out to the squad car. I figured the killer must have turned himself in. Give me your hand. I need a swab of your blood for my Dumb Cop file."

"Only if you promise to bandage me up."

Jessica took a blood sample from Terry, sprayed the cut with an antiseptic, and began wrapping it.

"I walked the scene," she said. "First impression—same MO on Mrs. Bannister as on Jo Drabyak. Small-caliber bullet to the back of the head. The killer took a lock of hair. With Mrs. Knoll it looks like she saw him coming and tried to defend herself with the Pellegrino bottle. He shot her head on. Then he cut the hair."

"There's no sign of a forced entry," I said. "It looks like the shooter rang the bell, Nora knew him, and invited him in."

"Him or her," Jessica said.

"Right. Nora leads the way, she gets to the living room, the killer pops her from behind."

"But he doesn't cut her hair yet," Terry said.

"Why?" I already knew the answer, but Terry and I work best when we try to reconstruct the crime out loud.

"Because he knows that Julia is in the kitchen," Terry said, "and he's got to do her right away."

"How does he know she's in the kitchen?"

"Okay, so maybe he doesn't know what room she's in, but he knows she's here somewhere. Otherwise, he'd have shot Nora and took off."

"So Julia is in the kitchen," I said. "She hears a gun go off. Bang."

"Or he used a silencer. But even if she did hear it, she's afraid to come running out. She's unarmed. She goes for the phone. It's not there. She hears him coming, so she grabs the bottle, but that's useless. He walks in, shoots her, she falls down, bottle breaks, end of story."

"Not quite," Jessica said. "There are bits of green glass on the edge of the counter in the kitchen. I think she smashed it in the hopes of using it as a weapon."

"Julia is so mousy," Terry said. "Hard to think of her breaking a bottle to fight someone off."

"I work in a lab. You'd be amazed at what some mice will do when they're threatened. It's easy enough to check. The glass would break differently if it hit the ground when she fell. Not to mention that you wouldn't have glass chips on the edge of the counter."

My cell phone rang. It was Sergeant Bethge, the assistant watch commander.

"Mike, Lieutenant Kilcullen should be there any minute. Same with Detective Burns. I held off calling Charlie Knoll to give you time to get squared away. I just got off the phone with him. He should be there in ten. What's the story on his wife?"

"Dead. We got a double homicide."

"Oh, Jeez." I heard him repeat the news to Jack Mullen. "Mike, I have the medical liaison on the way. Charlie's gonna need him. Let me know if you need anything else."

"Thanks, Carl."

"One more thing," Bethge said. "You said Charlie was waiting for his wife and mother-in-law at the book party. It sounded to me like he started partying before they got there."

"Drunk?"

Carl hesitated. "Let's just say impaired."

I hung up and turned to Terry. "Brace yourself. Charlie Knoll is on his way."

"And we get to break the bad news to him about his wife?"

"Unless you know someone else who'd be willing to do it."

Jessica finished bandaging Terry's hand. "Don't look at me, boys," she said. "I only work with the dead."

"Thanks," Terry said. "In that case, I'm not scheduling another appointment."

CHAPTER TWENTY-THREE

The second-biggest pain in the ass at a crime scene is having to put up with the vultures who want to capture it all on film. Since Nora was a semi-celebrity, there were more media trucks and paparazzi than usual. When word got out that one of victims was the second cop wife to be shot, all hell broke loose.

"If I ever meet the guy who taught civilians how to use police scanners," Terry said, "I will personally shove a five-thousand-channel Bearcat up his ass."

Fortunately Wendy Burns showed up. Wendy is one of those bosses who says "How can I help?" more than she says "What have you done for me lately?" She immediately offered to take over the job of keeping the gawkers and stalkers at bay.

"They must have taken twenty thousand pictures by now," Terry said. "How many more can they possibly need?"

"Maybe if you smile for one they'd go away," she said.

"One more favor, Wendy," I said. "Big Jim found the body."

"Got it. Don't let the press get near him," she said.

"It's more like don't let him get near the press. Thanks."

Kilcullen arrived just in time to help us deal with the first-biggest pain in the ass at a crime scene. The brass. Everyone from the chief on down was either there or on the way. And they'd have plenty of questions.

"You know the first thing they're going to ask," Kilcullen said. "Is somebody targeting cops' families?"

"We can't say for sure," I said, "but these three victims were all in business together. Business means money. And money is a motive for murder. I think it's about these women and not about the fact that their husband or their son-in-law is a cop."

"You're probably right," Kilcullen said. "But we should still let the wife of every cop on the force know that her life may be in danger."

"None of my business, Loo," Terry said, "but I wouldn't do that if I were you."

Whatever friction there was between the two of them, Kilcullen still respected Terry's instincts. "Why not?" he said.

"Because if the morning paper reads like it's just some business deal gone sour, the average cop will turn to the sports section. But if a cop thinks someone is targeting his old lady, the first thing he's going to do is give her a gun. And what do you think will happen then?"

Kilcullen has good instincts himself. He laughed. "A lot of cops are going to come home drunk and wind up getting shot by their wives."

"Give that man a kewpie doll," Terry said.

"Thanks, Biggs," Kilcullen said. "I'll go talk to the . . . oh, shit. It's Charlie."

Charlie Knoll was running through the maze of parked cars. "Lomax. Biggs. Where's my wife?"

Kilcullen still had time to walk off and deal with the brass. To his credit, he didn't.

Charlie raced up to the three of us. He was sweating, disheveled, and smelling of booze. Kilcullen stepped up to the plate. He put a hand on each of Charlie's shoulders.

Charlie already knew what was coming, but he went through the motions anyway. "Julia," he whimpered.

Kilcullen shook his head. "I'm so sorry, Charlie. Both Nora and Julia were shot. They're dead. I promise we'll get whoever did this."

Charlie's face contorted, and then the grief, the anger, and the alcohol took over. He shoved Kilcullen out of the way and ran toward the house.

It took the three of us and two patrol officers to stop him.

"It's a crime scene," Kilcullen said. "You know you can't go in there."

"I want to see her. I want to see both of them."

"Not till we're done," Kilcullen said. "You'll contaminate the scene."

That was true. Of course, with Big Jim's bloody footprints, Terry taking a nosedive on the kitchen floor and commingling his blood with Julia's, plus a platoon of cops tromping from room to room, the crime scene was now about as immaculate as a three-dollar hooker. But there was another reason we couldn't let Charlie go in. The husband is Suspect One. If he answers one of our questions with something that only the killer could know, we don't want him to explain it away by saying he saw it when we gave him a tour of the house.

"It might be a good idea if you gave us your gun," Kilcullen said.

"Is that the rule now?" Charlie screamed. "The killer gets to keep his gun and the victim's husband has to turn his in? This is insanity. Who would kill a cop's family? First Reggie. Now me. You guys should get home and protect Marilyn and Diana. Terry, what about your kids? How do we know who's next? I'm not turning in my—"

He grabbed his chest and started gasping for breath.

Several cops were standing around in case we needed help. I yelled at the closest one. "Get a paramedic."

Charlie was hugging his chest. "No, no. It's just an anxiety attack," he said gasping for air. "I get them. I'm okay. I'm okay."

"You're not okay," Kilcullen said. "You can't breathe. Sit down."

Charlie let us ease him down to one of the white marble steps leading up to Nora's house. Two EMS workers came running. We gave them some room.

"Can you guys take it from here?" Kilcullen said. "I've got BUTA, all the way up to the Top Cop waiting to talk to me."

"No problem," I said. "Thanks for staying. It helped."

He grunted something that sounded positive, then made his way toward the sea of flashing lights, where the brass was waiting to crawl up his ass.

Five minutes later the same paramedic who was first on the scene gave us the report on Charlie. "His BP is high, rapid heartbeat, and I don't have a Breathalyzer, but I recommend taking his car keys."

"What about the chest pains? He says it's just an anxiety attack."

"Famous last words," the paramedic said. "Look, he may be right. His wife was just killed, he's way hyper, and his heart's in normal sinus rhythm, but he needs more than a field cardio checkup. I want to take him to Cedars."

"Keep him there overnight," I said. "We'll have two of our guys follow you, just to make sure he doesn't decide to check out early."

Terry and I walked over to talk to Charlie. He was sitting quietly inside the tail of the ambulance.

"I can't begin to tell you how sorry we are," I said.

"I know," he said. "Terry, I wasn't kidding. Marilyn is a partner. Make sure she's okay."

"Thanks. I will."

"Charlie, you need to get to a hospital," I said.

He nodded. Total acceptance.

"Stay overnight. Terry and I will be there to talk to you in the morning."

"Is there anything I can tell you guys now," he said, "besides I didn't kill them?"

"We know you didn't. Do you have any idea who did?"

He put his hand over his eyes and shook his head. His body started shaking. The paramedic tapped me on the shoulder, then drew his finger across his neck. The interview was over.

We helped Charlie into the ambulance and sent him off to the hospital. But first we took his gun.

This time we didn't even have to ask.

CHAPTER TWENTY-FOUR

"Biggs!"

It was Kilcullen.

"The chief agrees. The motive on this case looks like it's about this real estate business. If we issue a department-wide warning that our wives are all a potential target, every one of them will wind up armed to the teeth."

"Did you tell him it was my idea?" Terry said.

"I was going to, but then he said, 'That's real smart thinking, Brendan,' and the moment passed."

Two squad cars came around the corner and pulled as close to the house as the helter-skelter of vehicles would allow. Tony's white Escalade pulled in behind them.

"Our dates for the evening have arrived," Terry said.

Marilyn is not the hysterical type, but she was as close to it as I've ever seen. She got out of the car, saw Terry, and ran toward him. He met her halfway, wrapping his arms around her. He rocked her back and forth, while she buried her face in his chest and sobbed.

Diana seemed calm by comparison. She kissed me as if we'd

been separated for months, and before you could say, "Don't forget about that double homicide, Detective," I was hard as a crowbar.

She responded with a gentle pelvic thrust and a series of tiny kisses that went from my ear to my lips and radiated south. "You don't have to buy me the house," she whispered. "Just take me home and fuck me." *yEA!*

This is probably why LAPD discourages cops from bringing dates to crime scenes. All those flashing lights, guys in uniform, and the drama of a cold-blooded murder can get a girl as horny as a teenager on prom night. *Gale Worthington, 1951.*

I pulled out of the clench as Marisol came toward us, her heels machine-gunning their way up the walk. Tony was right behind her, but all eyes, and there were lots of them at the scene, focused on the hot little Latin package wrapped in black and bronze. The black was a slinky piece of fabric that started halfway down her boobs and ended in mid thigh. The bronze was all Marisol. Not your traditional real estate lady look, but, hell, this is LA.

Her makeup was perfect. The loss of two more business partners had not evoked any emotion that might smear her mascara. In fact, she looked pissed. Or at the very least, inconvenienced.

She walked right at me. "Let me see the note, Lomax," she said.

I gave her a blank look. Before I could ask her to explain, Tony came up behind her and put his hands on her bare shoulders. "There is no note," he said.

Marisol whirled around at Tony. *"Cabrón!"* she yelled.

Tony went right back at her. "I made it up, because you're such a *perra terca*, that was the only way I could get you out of that goddam house." He turned to Kilcullen. "She didn't want to shut down the party, so I told her the killer left a note saying she's next."

"If you had given me ten more minutes I would have had an offer from that dentist and his wife," she said.

"It doesn't matter what offer you'd have gotten tonight," Tony said. "When word gets out that Nora was murdered, the price is going to go sky high."

"Sounds like a motive," Kilcullen said.

"A motive?" Marisol said, turning her fury on him. "Kill an author who could have written ten more books and sold ten more houses, just to drive the price up on this one? *Pendejo!*"

I didn't know what it meant, but Tony did, and he winced. "Boss, I'm sorry," he said. "She's upset. This was supposed to be her big night. . . ."

"We're all upset," Kilcullen said. "Charlie showed up with chest pains. We had to ship him off to Cedars."

"Jesus," Tony said. "What have we got so far?"

"Same basic M.O. Lomax and Biggs are still working the scene. Then they're going to want to talk to you all individually. In the meantime, I'll authorize round-the-clock protection for both Marisol and Marilyn."

"You think we're next?" Marilyn said.

"Nobody's next," Kilcullen said. "It ends here. But just to be on the safe side, I'll have a female detective spend the night with each of you."

"Forget it, Lieutenant," Marisol said. "I have a male detective who is spending the night." She poked a finger in Tony's chest. "If he stops lying to me."

"And I've got two cops living with me," Marilyn said.

"How about if I post a squad car in front of each of your houses," Kilcullen said.

"I accept," Marilyn said.

Marisol held up both hands. "Not me. Putting some cop in front of my house isn't going to do shit. And then he's going to follow me wherever I go? No thanks."

"Are you sure?" Tony said. "I'm not going to be home all the time."

"Like I need you to baby-sit? I spend six days a week with a bunch of nasty-ass illegals. They got knives, they got power tools, they got shovels, and they all hate my guts, but I'm not afraid of them, and they know it," Marisol said. "Don't worry. I can take care of myself."

Nobody argued the point.

A FEMALE jERK

CHAPTER TWENTY-FIVE

"How can I help?" Big Jim said, after the crime lab took his prints and relieved him of his bloody shoes.

"You can start by taking me off your speed dial," I said.

"I'm not talking long term. I mean tonight."

"Actually, I've been looking for a three-hundred-pound control-freak teamster to help me with logistics."

He patted his belly. "Look no further."

"I just spoke to my boss and got official dispensation to let Marilyn and Diana stay here until Terry and I finish. We'll drive them home, but their cars are still at the flip house on South Cherokee."

"No problem," Jim said. "I'll get a couple of drivers to run the cars over to Terry's house. They'll be in the driveway before you get home. What else?"

"Marilyn is worried about Sarah and Emily. They're each staying with a friend. I want you personally to pick them up and bring them home."

"Tell those kids Big Uncle Jim is on the way with the limo. What else?"

"Stay with them till Terry and I get home."

"Duh," he said. "Do you think I'm so dumb I would just drop off a couple of teenage girls and leave them?"

"Hey, I didn't think you were dumb enough to track blood through a crime scene, but I'll be damned if you didn't manage to do it."

He held up the three middle fingers on his right hand. "You're a detective," he said. "Read between the lines."

Jim recruited his wife, Angel, and his best driver, Dennis Hoag. By 8:00 P.M., I was able to assure Marilyn that her daughters were safe at home, being looked after by three bodyguards and an equal number of watchdogs.

"Plus Dennis is an ex-cop, and my father has a serious gun collection," I reminded her, "so they're safe."

"Thanks," she said. "Nothing makes a soccer mom feel more secure than knowing her little girls' babysitters have plenty of firepower."

Because Marilyn was a possible target, we talked her and Diana into waiting in a squad car outside the crime scene perimeter, while we went back to work.

Jessica estimated the time of death between 4:00 and 6:00 P.M. Once again, she doubted if we'd get usable ballistics on the small-caliber bullets. Chris High and his team were canvassing the neighborhood, but so far no witnesses.

Not that we needed permission, but we politely asked Tony if we could talk to Marisol in private.

"Does she need a lawyer?" he said.

"No," I said. "What she doesn't need is to be arguing with her husband while we're trying to ask questions."

He gave us his best vote-for-me smile. A lot of cops have

second-career plans. I haven't made mine yet, but Terry's dream is to become a stand-up comic. Tony's plan for life after LAPD is to run for office. I have no doubt that he can get elected to city council in his district. He's smart, he's Spanish, and if dark eyes and white teeth can get votes, the man is a shoo-in.

"You know there's a reason Marisol and I fight so much," he said. "The make-up sex is fantastic."

"In that case," Terry said, "we'll do our best to keep her real ~REALLY~ pissed off."

We interviewed Marisol in the backyard, so she could smoke.

"Anything you want to add that you didn't want to say in front of Tony and everyone else?" I asked.

"No. Except that this house-flipping business, with Nora's books driving up the price, was the best gig I ever worked. And now it's over. Whoever did it might not have killed me, but he killed the goose that was laying the golden eggs."

"Are you really sure you don't want police protection?" Terry said.

"You don't know me," she said, lighting up a cigarette. "I come from a small border town in Mexico. I grew up hating cops."

"Why'd you marry one?"

"Because he's hung like a donkey, and marrying him got me a green card. So what if he's with LAPD. Two out of three ain't bad."

"What's your beef with cops?" Terry said.

She inhaled deeply, and I had a pang of envy. I quit smoking almost ten years ago, but every now and then, I see someone under stress sucking on that tobacco crutch, and I think to myself, *I could do that. Just one or two Marlboros a day.* Sure. And by the end of the first week I'd be buying cancer by the carton.

She exhaled long and slow, and the smoke, backlit by the floodlights in the trees, wafted upward. Within seconds the nicotine pleasure molecules had reached her brain, and a calm spread over her face.

"Where I grew up, the cops broke more laws than they enforced," she said. "They were corrupt. They were sadistic. One Sunday morning when I was eight years old, my brother Joaquin was taking me and my brother Manuel to church. Manuel was eleven. Joaquin was sixteen. We were poor, so he did what lots of poor kids did. He worked as a runner for one of the local drug dealers. Three cops pulled up in a car and started to shake him down. I'm not sure if they wanted drugs, or money, or names of people he worked for, but Joaquin spit in one of their faces. They started beating him, so Manuel jumped in to protect his big brother. They beat him too, and when the two of them were lying on the ground, the cops handcuffed them together and started kicking them. In the head, in the balls, everywhere. I screamed and screamed, until one of them took out his gun, pointed it at me, and pulled the trigger."

"Jesus," Terry said.

"The bullet bounced off the house behind me, and pieces of cement and glass were flying everywhere. Then the others took out their guns and started shooting. Some of the bullets came real close. Some they just fired in the air or at my feet. They could have killed me, but they didn't want to. They were just trying to scare the shit out of me. And they did. It ran down my legs. I fell to the ground crying, my little white church dress covered with shit, and they just laughed."

Tears ran down her cheeks. This was much more painful for her than the murders that happened earlier this evening.

"That's horrible," I said. "What happened to your brothers?"

"Joaquin never regained consciousness. A week later he died from a brain hemorrhage. Manuel lost a spleen, and he's got so much nerve damage on his left side, he'll walk with a cane for the rest of his life."

"I'm sorry," I said. "Not all cops are like that."

She shrugged. "The fact that I married one is proof that God has a sense of humor. But I'll tell you boys, I'd rather have some *cabrón* with a gun stalking me, than be followed around the clock by LA's finest. Any more questions?"

"One," Terry said. "These illegals who do a lot of the work for you at the flip house—you got names?"

She laughed. "Yeah. Names, home addresses, social security numbers . . . you want photo IDs along with that? C'mon Terry, which part of *illegal immigrant* are you having trouble processing?"

"Which part of 'I'm trying to find the person who killed three of your partners and might be looking to do you next' are *you* having trouble processing? They're illegal, not invisible. Do you know where to find any of them?"

She looked away and exhaled two lungs full of smoke. "Jesus, you guys live in LA. You know how it works. I drive down to the parking lot at Home Depot or one of the other day-laborer pickup spots, and I grab a bunch of guys. Most of them still have border dust in their boots. I pay them cash, and when they make enough money, they go back to the wife and four kids, and they live like Mexican royalty."

"You said they've got knives, and shovels, and hate your guts. How did they feel about the three victims?"

"You don't get the same workers every day, but we had our

regulars. They liked Nora. Even the most illiterate among them knew she was a famous writer. Plus she spoke a little Spanish. Julia was *la silenciosa*, the silent one. I don't think they saw much of Jo. They don't like me because I'm *el jefe del infierno*, the boss from hell. If one of them was going to commit murder, he'd get drunk and put a screwdriver through my heart. He's not going to make house calls and cut off locks of hair."

"How'd you know about the hair?" I said. "We didn't release that."

"Tony released it. He told me what the killer did to Jo. I'm betting he did it to the other two."

"Tony told you more than he should have," I said. "What happened to Jo's hair is something we're keeping under wraps. You may be right about the illegal workers, but they may know something. You mind driving down to Home Depot with us and picking out a few that you recognize?"

"Sure. How's tomorrow morning?"

"Make it Monday," I said. "We have to see Charlie in the hospital first thing tomorrow."

"Chest pains." She said it like she doubted it.

"And half a bag on," I said. "He must've gotten to the party and started drinking early." *oh, oh.*

She shook her head. "Charlie wasn't at the party. I don't know where he got drunk, but he never showed up at the flip house."

"The obligatory question," I said. "What time did you get there?"

"I got to the house at seven in the morning, and I was working like a crazy woman, prepping the place for the party all day. But I understand that you have to ask." She took another drag on her cigarette.

"Thanks," I said. "We'll meet you Monday morning at the Home Depot parking lot. Which one and what time?"

"The one on Sunset near the station. Six A.M."

"We'll see you there," I said. "Thanks."

"In the meantime, do us a favor," Terry said. "Stick close to Tony. There's still a killer out there, and you really may be on his list."

"I have a gun at home," she said. "I learned how to use it when I was eight and a half."

We watched her walk away.

"Hell of a story," Terry said. "No wonder she hates cops."

"Yeah," I said. "I just wonder if she hates them enough to kill their families."

CHAPTER TWENTY-SIX

Reggie Drabyak showed up ten minutes later, drunker than Charlie and more pissed off than Marisol.

He slurred a bunch of trash talk about how he and Charlie would get the muhfuhs who shot their wives. Kilcullen took his car keys, tossed him in the back of a black and white, and shipped him home.

"The fun never stops here in Margaritaville," Terry said. "Who's next? Lindsay? Paris? Nick Nolte?"

By 10:00 P.M. Terry and I had done as much as we could at the scene. After about half a dozen tries Terry finally convinced Marilyn that the girls were safe and sound and that they'd be much happier if their parents came home calm, collected, and well-fed. He suggested we all go out to a late dinner. Terry wanted Chinese, I wanted Italian, and, as usual, Diana was flexible.

"I think whoever is under the threat of death gets to pick," Marilyn said. "I vote for Doughboys."

Doughboys started out as a bakery. Their red velvet cake is a magnet for locals and tourists alike. They expanded into a café, and I've never walked out of there without having to loosen my belt a notch.

Marilyn is one of those people who eats when she's under stress, and nothing makes you hungrier than thinking someone is planning to shoot you in the back of the head.

"This may be my last meal," she said when we sat down. "In which case I want a stack of pineapple, coconut, and macadamia nut pancakes, swimming in hot caramel sauce."

"Hey, add a side of sausage," Terry said. "That way if the shooter doesn't kill you, your dinner will."

"It's not your last meal," Diana said. "Nothing's going to happen."

"Especially if you and the girls leave town for a few days," Terry said. "Maybe you could fly to—"

"No," Marilyn said. "Absolutely, positively, definitely not. And if I'm being too vague, allow me to add, 'No fucking way.'"

"Do you mind if I ask the logic behind your decision?" Terry said.

"Sarah just started college. Emily just started tenth grade. You want me to pull them out of school? *For a few days?* Are you telling me it will be solved in a few days?"

"Fine," Terry said. "Just wait till this maniac pops you, then the girls can take off school for the wake and the funeral."

"Maybe he's not killing off our little real estate cartel," Marilyn said. "Maybe he's just killing random cop wives."

"Then you're still a target."

"But it wouldn't be down to me and Marisol. He'd have thousands to choose from."

"Jesus, I hope you're wrong," Terry said.

"You're *hoping* I'm next on the hit list?"

"No, dammit. I just convinced Kilcullen not to issue a

department-wide warning. What if I'm wrong? What if this killer is after all cops' wives and families?"

"Well, if he is," Diana said, leaning over and stroking my cheek, "that's another good reason not to marry you."

"I don't remember asking," I said. My cell phone rang. "Can we discuss this some other time?"

"Sure," she said. "Marilyn, don't let me forget. Discuss marriage with Mike some other time."

I answered the phone. "Hello."

"Sorry to bother you so late, mate, but I've been interviewing Nora Bannister's neighbors, and I've got something you and Biggs might fancy hearing."

It was Chris High.

I glanced around the table. Marilyn and Diana were chatting it up about weddings. Terry was sitting quietly, focused on me.

"Chris, if you've got something, mate—anything—it's never too bloody late to call."

Terry nodded. He was locked in to my half of the conversation.

"It may be nothing," Chris said.

"Try me."

"Well, it's a quiet neighborhood. Not too many people around. And the folks who are home are locked up in these big houses, completely isolated from the outside world. Nobody hears or sees anything because they're either at the pool, or watching Dr. Phil, or working on their next martini. But this one woman who lives two houses up the road from Bannister said that she left a FedEx package at her front door for pickup at three, and it was gone when she checked at five. So I thought, maybe the FedEx driver saw some-thing."

"And you tracked down the FedEx guy," I said.

"It took a bit of time," High said. "FedEx was cooperative, but I still had to jump through hoops before I found someone who could give me his name and home phone number."

"And?"

"The driver's name is Joe Price. According to FedEx he picked up the package at 4:04 P.M., and according to Price, that's when he saw a black BMW convertible pull out of Bannister's driveway, and take off in a big hurry."

"Did he see the driver?"

"Nothing we can use," High said. "Back of a head through tinted windows. But he did get a partial on the plate. He says it caught his eye because his name is Joe, and it was a vanity plate that started with *JO*."

"It started with *JO*," I repeated, and Terry's eyebrows went up.

"Right. And there's only one car in the state that's a match. It's registered to our boy Tony Dominguez's wife, Marisol."

"Chris, that's damn good police work. Why do you say it may be nothing?"

"As I recall from our little go-around on Monday, Tony's wife works with Nora Bannister. One writes the books, the other sells the houses. So it wouldn't be unusual for Marisol to be parked out-side Bannister's house."

"Except for one thing," I said. "She just told us she was at the flip house all day. You just put her at the victim's house at the time of the murders."

A, ha!

"Well, then, I guess you were right, mate," Chris said. "It looks like I have been doing some damn good police work."

I hung up. "You get all that?" I said to Terry.

"Yup," he said. "It's a two-way street, mate. She doesn't trust us. And now we don't trust her."

CHAPTER TWENTY-SEVEN

It was almost midnight by the time we got back to Terry's house. As the car pulled into the driveway, Emily came running out the front door, followed by Sarah and three barking dogs. The girls threw their arms around their mother, and Terry quickly ushered them into the house, stopping in the doorway just long enough to shake hands with Big Jim.

Jett followed the family inside. Houdini, the black Shepherd, and Skunkie, the shaggy-haired mutt, stood at the front door waiting for a cue from Big Jim.

"Dad, I'll be right there," I said. Then I went over to the squad car that was parked in front of the house.

There were two young white male patrol officers in the front seat. Emphasis on young. My guess was that I was as old as the two of them put together. "You guys here for the night?" I asked.

"All night, all day, twenty-four seven, sir," the one on the passenger side said. "There's a team covering your wife till the shooter is caught."

"I'm Detective Lomax," I said. "My partner, Detective Biggs, lives here. It's his wife you're protecting."

"Is that her over there?" he said, pointing toward Diana.

 she

"That's my girlfriend. We're staying with Detective Biggs and his wife. They're the ones who went inside."

"No problem, sir," the cop said. "We've got your back. Have a good night."

"Thanks, boys," I said. That's pretty much what they were. Boys. Young, eager, and relatively inexperienced. They were here to serve and protect, but they weren't even sure who they were pro-tecting. I was beginning to wonder if Marisol was right. *Putting some cop in front of my house isn't going to do shit.*

I put my arm around Diana, and we went inside. Jim locked the door behind us.

I gave Angel a hug and thanked Dennis for his help. I could feel Big Jim looming behind me.

I turned around. "What?"

"Don't shoot the messenger," he said, "but your contractor quit."

"What are you talking about?"

"Hal Hooper, your contractor—his wife called here."

"She called Terry's home phone?"

"She couldn't find any of your numbers," Jim explained, "but Hooper told her you were staying with Mr. and Mrs. Biggs in Sherman Oaks, so she dialed information, got Terry's number, and called here."

"And you answered Terry's home phone?"

"Of course I answered. I was on guard duty."

"IPB, Dad. Improper Personal Boundaries. Why would you answer Terry's home phone?"

"It was for you, numb nuts. Talk about improper personal boundaries. Why would you get a call on Terry's home phone?"

"I live here, dammit."

"So I answered a phone call for my own son. Is that crossing a boundary? Do you want the message or not?"

I was tired and cranky. But Diana was sitting back on the sofa, enjoying the show. Laughing, actually. "He can't wait for the message, Jim. Give it to him."

"Hal Hooper fell off the roof and broke his leg. He's out of commission for at least eight weeks."

"You've gotta be kidding me," I said.

"So first you don't want me taking your messages, and now you don't think I can get them right."

"Hooper fell off my roof? Did his wife threaten to sue?"

He dismissed the thought with a wave of his hand. "Don't worry, he can't sue you."

"How can you be so sure?"

"He fell off somebody else's roof."

Diana was now laughing out loud. I, on the other had, was not amused. "That son of a bitch. He's supposed to be at our place. He was working at someone else's house?"

Jim shrugged. "Lucky for you. If he fell off your roof, he'd be suing your ass."

"This is bullshit," I said. "I don't believe he fell off anything. It's just another excuse to delay the job for a couple of months."

"That's what I thought," Jim said. "So I told Mrs. Hooper we want to send him flowers. I asked her what hospital he's in. She said Good Samaritan on West Sixth."

Diana got up from the sofa. "Good Sam? I can check it out." She looked at her watch. "In fact, I have a friend who works the night shift in the ER. I'll call her."

I put my arm around Jim and did my best to direct his massive body toward the front door. "Dad, it's after midnight, and I've been going since dawn. Thanks for watching out for Emily and Sarah. Now take Angel and Dennis and the dogs and go home."

"No problem," he said. "You tell Marilyn if she doesn't feel safe with those two kiddy cops out there watching her house, I'll get some teamsters up here. A lot of them got licenses to carry."

"Truck drivers with guns," I said. "It doesn't get any more reassuring than that. I'll tell her."

I said good night to Dennis and Angel, and a minute later, the entire Lomax Security Force piled into the limo.

Terry came from the kitchen carrying two beers. He offered me one.

"No thanks. I'm going to bed."

It was the first time we'd been alone since Doughboys.

"So Marisol was spotted pulling out of Nora's driveway around the time of the murders," Terry said. "I guess she was so busy getting the flip house ready, she forgot all about it."

"Should we remind her?" I said.

"Why bother? She'll just have some lame excuse for being there. She's not going to say, 'Oh, silly me, I did go over to Nora's house this afternoon, and I shot her and her daughter. It completely slipped my mind.' Let's give her a little more rope and see if she hangs herself."

Diana came back in, even more bubbly than when she left. "I just spoke to my friend Nina Bernard. She's a nurse at Good Sam. You're going to love this."

"Oh, God, I need something good tonight," I said. "Lay it on me."

"Hal Hooper *is* a patient. He came into ER this afternoon. Nina read me his entire chart."

She was beaming. I was beginning to believe that I might actually enjoy what she had to say.

"You realize that telling you what's on a patient's chart is a violation of some kind of privacy act," I said.

"That's the problem with Nina," Diana said. "Pretty face, beautiful figure, fantastic personality, and yet she has this glaring character defect. She will actually seek out private information about contractors from hell, and pass it on to those of us who hate them."

"I'm sure there's a twelve-step program for that," I said. "So, did Mr. Hooper really break his leg?"

"In six places," she said.

"And did he fall off a roof?"

"Two stories."

"So now I don't have a contractor," I said. "How is this supposed to bring me joy?"

Her eyes were dancing now. "Ask me how he fell off the roof."

"Consider it asked."

"He shot himself with a nail gun. He screamed in pain and went crashing to the ground."

"It couldn't happen to a bigger asshole," Terry said.

"I'm not finished," Diana said. "Ask me where he shot the nail."

"I'd guess his brain, but he doesn't have one."

"Go lower," she said.

"His stomach?"

"Lower."

"His thigh?" I said.

"Go higher."

I was all smiles myself now. It was too much to hope for. "His . . ."

"Yes, yes, yes," she screamed. "Hal Hooper shot himself in the dick with a nail gun and fell off the roof." *ouch!*

"There is a God," I said. I checked my watch. "It's too late to call Kemp, but I'll call him first thing in the morning."

Kemp Loekle is a good friend who gave up being a carpenter in LA to pan for gold in Oregon. He had e-mailed me to let me know that after six months of eating freeze-dried beef stew, shitting in a spackle can, and sleeping on a cot with a .44 magnum at his side, he was ready to come back home and start swinging a hammer.

"Even if we lose a couple of grand from the advance we gave Hooper, it'll be worth it," I said.

"We're not losing anything," Diana said. "Tomorrow morning while you're calling Kemp, I'll be calling my friend Liz Corrado. She's a lawyer. And if Hooper is lucky, he'll only wind up with one nail in his dick."

CHAPTER TWENTY-EIGHT

Before he became a cop, Charlie Knoll was a crook. He grew up in foster care, and by the time he was fourteen, he'd been arrested for shoplifting, vandalism, and breaking and entering. One night he decided to swipe a couple of bottles of sacramental wine from the storage room of a Catholic church.

Luckily, the priest who caught him believed in redemption and gave Charlie a chance to do penance. But instead of giving him an Our Father to say, the priest gave him a bucket and a bottle of Mr. Clean. Charlie spent the next six months cleaning up the floors, the toilets, and his act. His juvey records were sealed, and eventually, his benefactor, Father Bill Leydon, gave him the reference he needed to get into the Police Academy.

After a few years as a beat cop, Charlie made detective. Once again he gravitated to robbery, only this time he wasn't the perp.

Terry and I were in an elevator at Cedars-Sinai on our way up to interview him.

"This is not going to be fun," Terry said.

"It's a homicide investigation," I said. "Where is it written that we get to have fun?"

"And yet, we so often do." Terry said. "But this is different.

The poor bastard's wife and his multimillionaire mother-in-law got iced. If he didn't do it, he's probably devastated. If he did do it, we have to nail one of our own. Either way, where's the fun?"

"I'm sure you'll come up with something," I said.

The door to Charlie's room was closed. I knocked. No answer. I opened it, took one look, then closed it again.

"Are visiting hours over already?" Biggs said.

"Father Bill is in there with him. They're praying."

"Maybe he's confessing. If you open the door a smidge, we might be able to hear him. It would save a lot of time."

"I know you're determined to have fun, but the guy's wife just got murdered. Give it a rest."

Much to my surprise, he actually did. We waited in silence for five minutes. Then the door opened, and the priest came out. Father Bill is short, white-haired, with a cherubic face and rimless glasses. If someone called central casting and said, "Send over a guy to play a priest," he'd be perfect.

"Mike, Terry," he said, shaking our hands. "It's been too long. Charlie said you'd be coming. I guess we're both here under the worst of circumstances."

"How's he holding up, Father?" I said.

"It's one of those times when someone asks me to explain God's will, and all I can say is don't try to understand the ways of the Lord; just accept it. We were praying for that strength."

"Charlie's a trooper, Father. I know he'll get through this, especially with you praying for him."

"I'll be praying for you boys too. I hope you find the bastard who did this."

"We'll do our best, Father," I said, and Terry and I stepped into

Charlie's room. There were two beds. Charlie was in one. The other was vacant.

"How you doing?" I said.

Charlie shrugged, then coughed up a half-hearted laugh.

"We're really sorry about your loss," I said.

Terry nodded. "We both are."

"Thanks," Charlie said.

"How are the chest pains?" I said.

"They gave me some pills. Come on, Mike, cut the crap. This ain't a social call. You're here on business. Ask me what you've got to ask."

"Where were you yesterday afternoon, say from around four until Sergeant Bethge called you at six forty-five?"

"I was having a few drinks."

"At the book launch party?"

"Come on, guys. By now you talked to half the people who were there. You know I never made it to the party. I was with a friend."

"What's her name?" I said.

"None of your business," he said.

"Actually, it is our business," I said.

"Why? Do I need an alibi? Are you charging me?"

"Take it easy," Terry said.

"Don't tell me to take it easy. I'm taking it hard. I loved Julia. And her mother. What I've never loved are those big splashy parties where Queen Nora is the center of attention, and everyone knows she's making a mint, and they all come up to me and tell me I stepped in shit when I married Julia. Like maybe I'm getting a piece of every book she sells. I wasn't looking forward to the party, so I drowned my sorrows with a very understanding, very sympathetic, very compassionate friend."

"Is she a cop?" Terry said.

Terry must have hit it on the head, because Charlie's face went flush. "Which part of *none of your business* didn't you understand?"

"Okay," I said. "So you were having a drink with another woman at the same time your wife was murdered, which is not something you're anxious to share. And she's probably married, so you don't want to drag her in unless you're charged. Understood."

"Thank you."

"What time did you and this compassionate, sympathetic friend start drinking?"

"Five. Maybe a little before."

"In a bar?"

"It was a little more private than that. Next question."

"Where were you between four and five?"

"I left work at three, went home, put on my party clothes, drove to meet my friend."

"Anybody see you?"

"Not between three and five," he said. "Did the crime lab establish the time of death?"

I nodded. "Between four and six."

He smiled. "So even if I gave up my friend's name, I'd only have half an alibi."

"Did you kill your wife and your mother-in-law?" I said.

"No."

"Do you have any idea who did?"

"Not who, but maybe why."

"You know something?" Terry said.

"Nothing specific," he said. "It's just my best take as a cop. Three women dead, all part of the same real estate venture. I didn't know much about who invested what, or what the details of the business deal were, but if I were working this case, I'd follow the money."

"And where would we pick up the trail?" Terry said.

"Her publisher and her accountant will have all kinds of financial records, but nobody's going to just pop open their books unless you guys find a judge, get a warrant, the usual crap."

"The Justice Prevention Department," Terry said. "We've been there."

"Your best bet is to just ask Martin," Charlie said. "He'll know."

"Martin Sorensen," I said. "Her assistant."

Charlie nodded. "He's a pretty okay guy once you get to know him."

"You know him well?"

"We're not shopping for furniture together, but sometimes after one of those book parties, he and I would take it across the street and toss down a few beers. I gotta tell you, in another life, I wouldn't have wound up friendly with this guy, but we've got a common pain in the ass."

"Nora," I said.

"Yeah. I mean, she was kind of all right as a mother-in-law, but as a person, it was a whole other story. She's one of those people who knows it all and wants to make sure you know she knows it. You should hear Martin go off on her after he's had a couple of drinks. Poor guy, he was working for her, sleeping with her . . ."

"Maybe killed her?" I said.

Charlie laughed. "Hey, you're thinking like a cop. I've been there, but no. If Nora was the only victim, I'd put him high on the list, but Jo, and . . ." He took in a breath and let it out slowly. His voice dropped and his eyes went to the ceiling. "Could Nora have driven Martin to shoot her? Sure. But he never would have killed my wife, Reggie's wife . . . where's the upside? What's the motive? Like I said, if this was me on this case, I'd follow the money."

/ were I

"Does Martin have access to her financial records?" Terry said.

"Martin knows everything about Nora's business," Charlie said. "He was with her every day." He paused. "And a hell of a lot of nights."

CHAPTER TWENTY-NINE

We were on Wilshire, driving to Martin's apartment on South Cochran, about five minutes away.

"I'm confused," I said.

"We could put in a call to Father Bill," Terry said. "He seems to do well with troubled cops."

"I'm not troubled. I'm confused. I don't understand why these people are getting killed."

Terry crossed himself. "It's God's will, my son."

"Quit dicking around. I'm serious. You heard what Marisol said last night. Nora's books are what's driving up the price of these houses. So even if it is about money, why kill the cash cow? Did Marisol hate her partners enough to kill off her own income stream? As for Charlie, I believe he loved Julia. So why would he kill her? Why would he kill Nora?"

"Money. It's your basic age-old motive. With Julia dead, maybe Charlie inherits Nora's estate."

"Then why kill Jo Drabyak?"

Terry made the turn onto Cochran. "Good question. Now I'm confused," he said.

Martin's apartment was a lot like the man who lived there—neat, orderly, and efficient.

He greeted us at the door, a copy of the *LA Times* in his hand.

"I wonder how Nora would feel if she saw that her book launch party made page one of every paper in America," he said. "How's Marilyn?"

"Totally spooked," Terry said. "I'm surprised you're not a little nervous yourself."

"I locked my front door, but I just can't see how I'd be a target. I'm just Nora's lowly assistant."

"Cut the bullshit," Terry said. "This is a homicide investigation, not a book party, so let's skip the social amenities. You were a lot more than her lowly assistant. You've been banging her for years."

"It's part of my job description," he said. "Arranging her travel, getting her coffee, giving her multiple orgasms. Gentlemen, I'm a relatively good-looking, thirty-seven-year-old assistant working for a sixty-four-year-old money-machine. This is La-La-Land. Fucking goes with the territory. And for the record, she was damn good in the sack. It was a hell of a lot more fun than filing."

Terry and I had never seen this candid side of Martin, but of course, we had never seen him without Nora lurking nearby.

"What do you know about Nora's financial picture?" I asked.

"Everything. I see her contracts, I deposit her royalty checks, I pay her bills—there's not too much I don't know. She was completely open with me."

"What would you say she's worth?"

"Twenty million. But that was before she went from the arts section to the front page. A violent death is a big boost to any artist's career. People who never heard of her will buy her books now. The money will be pouring into her estate for decades."

"And speaking of her estate, who's the beneficiary?"

"Nora only had one living relative. Julia."

"So what happens now that her one living relative is no longer living?"

"You mean does it all go to her lowly assistant?"

"The thought did cross my mind that maybe you could be next in line for the twenty mill."

"If only," he said. "But alas, Detective Biggs, the University of California at Santa Barbara has that enviable position. Nora's alma mater is going to have themselves one generous fellowship fund. Perhaps you should interrogate them."

"We're not done with you," Terry said. "When was the last time you saw Nora alive?"

"We worked from nine till noon yesterday. Then Julia came over and they went shopping."

"And where were you from noon till six?"

"I was here in my apartment. I arrived at the book launch party precisely at five forty-five."

"So nobody saw you from noon till the time you got to the party."

"Please, Detective, tell me you aren't seriously considering me as a suspect," Martin said. "Allow me to refresh your memory. I don't inherit her money."

"Not a penny?"

"A year's salary. Hardly enough to kill for."

"I've seen homicides for a lot less," Terry said. "Tell me something. Who inherits Julia's money?"

"Julia didn't have any money," Martin said.

"Sure she did," Terry said. "She just didn't have it for long. It appears that Nora was murdered first, which means Julia automatically inherited her mother's estate. Unfortunately for her, she wound up dead a minute later. So now the question is, who gets Julia's money?"

"Probably her husband, but he'd only get Julia's money. He has no claims to Nora's estate."

"Why not?" Terry said. "If the crime lab proves that Nora was dead first, her money would legally go to Julia, not to the university. So technically it's Julia's estate that will get passed on. Am I right?"

"No, Detective Biggs, you are wrong. A person does not get to be a multimillionaire for half a minute then pass it along. Have you ever heard of the simultaneous death clause?"

Terry looked at me, and I shook my head. "Enlighten us," he said.

"It's a common clause used in most wills. It states that if Julia were to die within sixty days of her mother, it's considered that they died at the same time."

"Keep enlightening."

"Let's say a mother and a daughter are in a car crash. Mom dies at the scene. Without that clause the daughter would immediately inherit Mom's estate, and Uncle Sam would automatically be entitled to an estate tax. Now suppose the daughter dies on her way to the hospital. Then somebody in her will inherits the money. The IRS can now collect a second estate tax. The purpose of putting in the simultaneous death clause is to avoid double taxation."

"So what you're saying is Charlie doesn't get any of Nora's money."

"It's not what I'm *saying*. It's what I *said*. Several times. All Charlie can inherit is whatever money Julia already had, but I've known her for years, and she writes poetry."

"I heard there's big bucks in poetry," Terry said. "Didn't Dr. Seuss make a killing?"

"The only money Julia ever earned came from being part of the LA Flippers. I assume Charlie will wind up with her share of the real estate profits, but it's not going to be a ticket on the retirement express."

"Speaking of real estate," I said, "did any of the partners have any major arguments with any of the contractors working on this house?"

"Marisol tangled with a few," he said. "She fired two plumbers before she finally found one she could work with. But let's face it, if contractors shot everyone who was pissed off at them, they'd be building houses for each other."

We talked for ten more minutes. Martin acted a bit self-important, but he was comfortable, not guarded, and if he did have anything to hide, he was hiding it well. We thanked him, and I gave him a business card, with the usual call-us-if-you-think-of-anything parting words. He walked us to the door.

"One last question," I said. "What are your plans, now that you're out of work?"

"I'm not out of work just yet," he said. "It could take me six months to straighten out all of Nora's business affairs. The estate will pay my salary."

"And after that?"

"Maybe I'll write a book about my seven wonderful years with Nora," he said, "but I'm going to need your help."

"Us? For what?"

"You can't write a murder mystery without telling the reader who the killer is," he said, giving us a smug grin. "Unless you solve it, I won't have an ending."

CHAPTER THIRTY

Kilcullen called and told us to meet him for lunch.

"Barney's Beanery in West Hollywood," he said. "It's more private."

West Hollywood is under the jurisdiction of the sheriff's department, so we were less likely to run into anyone from LAPD at Barney's. But knowing Kilcullen, he picked it because they've got killer chili.

He was already sitting at a table when we got there. He looked at his watch just in case we didn't know we were two minutes late.

"I ordered," he said. "Hope you want chili." He didn't wait for an answer. "The deputy chief called me. We've had an outbreak of blue flu."

It's illegal for cops to go on strike, so one of the few actions we can take is a sick-out. The blue flu.

"A lot of cops called in sick today. Twice as many as on a normal Friday," Kilcullen said. "But it's not a job action. These guys are staying home and babysitting their wives."

"Do we know that for sure?" I said.

"We don't know shit for sure, but Nora Bannister's murder is all over the TV this morning, and some reporters have put two and two together, and they're asking if there's a guy with a gun out there targeting cops' families. This is exactly why I told the chief not to issue a department-wide warning. We've got the makings of a panic. We need answers. What have you got so far?"

The food came and we filled him in on our meeting with Charlie.

"Charlie had a babe on the side?" Kilcullen said with a mouthful of chili, cheese, and onions. "Do you know who she is?"

"No," Terry said. "We're guessing she's a cop, but he's not giving her up, because even with an alibi, there's still one hour he can't account for."

"Well, then he didn't do it," Kilcullen said. "He wouldn't murder his wife and mother-in-law, then leave himself hanging without an alibi. He's too smart a cop."

"Right," Terry said. "Plus I saw him reading a copy of *Perfect Crimes for Dummies*, so he couldn't possibly have made any mistakes."

"You think Marisol had anything to do with it?" Kilcullen said.

"I wouldn't put it past her," Terry said. "She's one tough chick, and she lied about not being at Nora's house yesterday afternoon. Her car was spotted around four o'clock. The big question is why would she do it. She doesn't have a motive. Martin Sorensen, on the other hand, has two. Fame and fortune."

"He wants to write a book about Nora," I said. "And he reminded us that nothing sells like a dead celebrity."

"He's right," Kilcullen said. "You should see how many Elvis CDs my wife owns. What do you know about this Sorensen guy?"

We gave him everything we knew about Martin.

"Dig deeper. Check his bank records, credit cards, phone calls, whatever you can find," Kilcullen said.

"We've already got Muller on it," I said.

"Tell him to make it priority one. You know me, boys. I don't like to tell you how to work your case, but until this guy is caught, there's going to be an epidemic of cops staying home to protect the wife and kids."

"Speaking of which," Terry said, "can you do any better on Marilyn's protection detail?"

"What wrong with what we've got?"

"Nothing, if she was an old lady who needed two boy scouts to help her cross the street," Terry said. "The guys you had last night were a little green."

Kilcullen doesn't take criticism well. "What are you talking about?" he said. "They're smart, they've got guns . . ."

"And they're as low on the pay-grade scale as you can go without sending the cleaning crew," Terry said. "How about I pay for lunch and you milk the budget for a few more bucks, so I can focus on this case without having to worry about who's looking after my wife and kids?"

Kilcullen held up both hands. "All right, all right. I'll upgrade. I'll do whatever it takes to take care of them."

"Good," Terry said. "And I'll do whatever it takes to take care of myself." He sniffled. "Because I was starting to feel a little touch of the flu coming on."

CHAPTER THIRTY-ONE

"Do you know what today was like?" Terry said as we were headed home on the Ventura in bumper-to-bumper Friday night traffic.

"A day without sunshine?"

"No."

"One of those bad dreams where you show up to take the final exam, and you realize you never went to class all year, and you didn't even buy the book?"

"You're getting warmer, but no."

"I give up," I said.

"Today was like the worst part of a romantic comedy movie."

"I'm from the school of thinking that romantic comedies suck from beginning to middle to end," I said, "so you'll have to fill me in on which part actually qualifies for the worst."

"The failure montage."

"I still give up."

"In every romantic comedy, there's always some dork like Ben Stiller, and they want to show you that he's a total loser at love, so what do they do? A two-minute montage of him striking out on seven different blind dates. That was our day, Mike. A montage of failure in living color, without the sound track."

"Ben Stiller's not a dork," I said. "He's kind of cool."

"Okay, so he's cool in a dorky way. My point is that the highlight of all our police work today was watching our boss chow down a bowl of beans."

"And if that doesn't say romantic comedy, I don't know what does."

"Right. But if this were a movie, and if I were Ben Stiller, the boss would call and tell me that his wife kicked him out of the house, and he'd invite himself to spend the night in my claustrophobic little one-room apartment. And then . . ." He started laughing. "And then those damn beans would kick in."

"We could call the movie *Love's a Gas*," I said.

For the next five minutes we regaled ourselves in how shitty our day had been.

When you work homicide, you have to find the laughs or you'll blow your own brains out. It's not a job for the faint of heart. You start with some grisly murder. Then you have to break the bad news to the victim's loved ones and watch them go through shock, pain, and anguish. Then comes the investigation, which is basically a series of blind alleys, dead ends, and other letdowns.

Today was a perfectly good example. After getting nowhere with Charlie and Martin, we spent two hours trying to track down people on the enemies list Nora had faxed us. The few that we reached either wouldn't talk without a lawyer or laughed at the idea that they might even be considered a suspect.

"What did the old bitch do?" her ex-publisher asked. "Leave the names of people who wanted her dead? I didn't do it, but I'd feel great if you told me I was at the top of her list."

Later that afternoon we pissed away more time with Anton Areizaga. Anton is one of our informants, a street hustler whose motto is, "Information is like pussy. You can always find somebody to pay for it." He's been a semi-reliable source in the past, but he's also been known to use us to put the squeeze on someone he's pissed at.

"Billy Shoes killed that cop's wife," Anton told us.

Billy Shufeldt, aka Billy Shoes, is a Hollywood pimp who rotates in and out of the justice system.

"Detective Drabyak is always busting him and his girls," Anton told us, "so Billy decided it's payback time, and he shot Drabyak's old lady."

"And you know this how?" I asked Anton.

"Shoes was bragging about it. Even showed me the gun he popped her with."

"A nine-millimeter Glock, right?" Terry said, pulling a couple of twenties out of his wallet.

Anton eyed the cash. "Exactly," he lied. "I seen the murder weapon."

"I'm sorry," Terry said. "Did I say Glock? I meant a pearl-handled derringer."

"Yeah, that's more like it. I think I seen a pearly handle." Anton reached for the money. His fingers were delicate and neatly manicured.

Terry whacked them hard and yanked the money back. "How

would you like a pearly handle up your ass, you lying son of a bitch?"

"Shit," Anton said, massaging his damaged hand. "Wrong gun?"

"Wrong gun, wrong day, wrong cops," Terry said. "Get your weasely little ass out of here, and stop wasting our time."

The only glimmer of hope in our montage of failure came at the end of the day. Muller did a thorough check on Martin Sorensen.

"Nothing unusual in his background," Muller said. "Finances, phone records, they all seem pretty straightforward. There is one thing that's kind of interesting, but you may already know about it."

"We don't have a lot on this guy except for a possible motive," I said. "What's interesting?"

"Over the past three years he took half a dozen criminology and criminal justice courses at two local colleges. Forensics, weapons, profiling, stuff like that. There's no record of him being enrolled in a degree program, so I'm guessing Nora had him doing research for her books, and it was probably part of his job to learn as much as he could about homicide."

"That's funny," Terry said. "Martin mentioned filing and fornicating as part of his job description, but he never said anything about becoming an expert on how to kill people."

"So he not only had motive," I said. "He had means."

"Why don't we pay him another visit," Terry said.

We drove back to Martin's apartment, but in keeping with the rest of our unproductive day, he wasn't home.

"It's Friday night," Terry said. "He's probably out hunting for cougars. Let's come back tomorrow."

Kilcullen had authorized OT, so working the weekend wasn't an issue. In fact, *not* working wasn't even an option. At some point during our chili-fest, the boss had let us know that we'd be working long shifts, seven days a week, until we caught the killer.

It was after eight when we got off the 405 at Sherman Oaks and headed up Sepulveda toward Terry's house.

"So about this failure montage," I said. "Once it's over, things start to get better for the hero, right?"

"Oh yeah," Terry said. "It's all part of the formula, and by the end of the movie he gets the promotion he's been waiting for, he marries the girl of his—" He braked the car hard. "What the fuck?"

We had just made the turn onto Terry's street, Alana Drive. There were at least ten cop cars scattered in front of his house, lights strobing, radios squawking. A paramedic unit was parked in the driveway.

Terry and I jumped out of the car and ran toward the house.

CHAPTER THIRTY-TWO

We ran past a dozen cops who were casually milling about outside the house. Apparently, whatever the emergency was, it had passed, and now they were waiting for orders.

There were two uniforms in the living room, along with Marilyn, Diana, Emily, Sarah, and a third teenage girl I'd never seen before. Emily was on the sofa, sobbing.

"What happened?" Terry yelled.

"It's okay," Marilyn said. "We're all fine."

"What went on? What happened." Terry looked around for an answer.

Sarah held up both hands. "I had nothing to do with it." She pointed a finger at her younger sister.

"Emily?"

"I'm sorry, Daddy," Emily choked out through her tears. "I'm really, really sorry."

Terry sat down on the sofa and put his arm around the girl. "It's all right. Just tell me what happened."

She wiped her nose and ran her arm across her eyes to dry the tears. "I wanted to go to the mall, or a movie, or anyplace, but Mom wouldn't let me. She said I have to stay home till you catch the asshole who's shooting everybody. Do you know how bad it sucks to be quarantined to your house on the weekend?" She looked at Terry for sympathy.

"That's a family discussion. We'll talk about it later," he said. He turned to the cops. "You were on watch?"

The male cop stepped front and center. He was big, burly, about thirty years old. His female partner was smaller and older, with intense dark eyes. Kilcullen had kept his promise. They were definitely more experienced than the kids who had been on duty last night.

"Tim Kaczmarek, sir," he said. "This is my partner, Jane Lester. We were parked outside. We heard a girl scream, followed by three gunshots."

"Jesus," Terry said. "Did you get the shooter?"

"There was no shooter, sir. Your daughter Emily and her friend over there . . ." He stopped to check his notepad. "Her name is Heather Gore."

"Yeah, I know her," Terry said. "What did they do?"

"They downloaded some sound effects off the Internet. A scream and three gunshots. My partner and I heard it, we called for backup, and ran to the house."

"And that battalion of cops out there," Terry said. "That's the backup?"

"We radioed in a 246. They know we're watching your house, Detective," Kaczmarek said. "Everyone scrambled. Code 3."

Terry turned back to Emily. "So you were stuck at home on a Friday night, and you thought, What can I do to have some fun? How about rousting up every cop from here to Ventura County?"

"It's not what we wanted to happen," Emily whined.

"What were you hoping for? Fire engines? Media coverage? Ryan Seacrest? What?"

"Heather started it," Emily said.

"Did not," Heather said.

"You're somebody else's problem," Terry said. "I want to know what my daughter was thinking."

Emily had stopped crying. "Dad, we were sitting upstairs with nothing to do. My entire social life was completely ruined," she said, sliding comfortably into surly-teenager mode. "I was trapped in my room like a rat."

"A rat with a high def TV, hundreds of video games, and a brand new sound system that she got for her birthday," Terry said.

"It doesn't matter. I was still trapped with the cops guarding my life like I was the king's daughter or something."

"I got the picture. Princess Emily locked in the palace tower. Get to the part about the gunshots."

Emily tossed her hair back and threw Terry a grown-ups-just-don't-understand-anything look. "So we're bored to death, and Heather said, 'What can those cops do to protect you anyhow? They're parked in front, and your room is in the back. The killer could climb that tree out there, bust your window, smoke you, then split before the cops even know what's happening.'"

Terry looked at Heather. "You said that?"

Heather shrugged. "It's true. You ever watch 24 with Kiefer Sutherland? He could sneak past fifty cops."

"True," Terry said. "But usually it's to save the planet from imminent danger, not to smoke sixteen-year-old girls." He turned to Emily. "So you thought you'd test Heather's theory."

"Why should I live in a bubble if some guy with a gun can

sneak past the cops and kill me anyway?" she said. "I might as well go to the mall. I'd have a better chance of escaping if I was at the Galleria."

"Absolutely," Terry said. "They should post signs. When you're life is in danger, head for the nearest shoe department."

Sarah laughed, and Emily threw her sister the finger. "Dad, you're making it sound like I'm an idiot."

"Sorry," Terry said. "Let's get to the genius part where you downloaded a scream and three gunshots and blasted it to see if the cops would actually be able to save you."

"We only downloaded the gunshots," Emily said. "Heather did the actual scream."

"We wanted it to sound authentic," Heather said.

"Had I but known," Terry said, "I would have left you girls an actual gun."

"Those shots sounded real enough, sir," Kaczmarek said.

"And how fast were these officers up here?" Terry said to Emily.

"Very fast," Emily said. "If it was real I would have been dead, but they'd have caught the guy who did it."

"Thank you, Officers," Terry said. "You're everything a cop dad could hope for."

Kaczmarek looked a little pained. "I'm afraid we did some damage to your back door," he said. "The frame is all splintered, and it's gonna need some new hinges. I'm really sorry about that."

"Don't apologize," Terry said. "You did what you had to do. I can only imagine what kind of damage that size-thirteen boot did to it."

"Actually, Detective, it was my size six," the female cop said.

Kaczmarek grinned. "Officer Lester is a lot tougher than she looks. But I'm a pretty good carpenter. I can come over tomorrow and fix it."

"No need," Terry said. "The Biggs family has inconvenienced LAPD enough, and we apologize, don't we Emily?"

"Sorry," Emily mumbled.

"No problem," Kaczmarek said.

"Got room for one more cop in here?"

We turned to the front door. It was Kilcullen.

"I heard the 246," he said. "Shooting at the Biggs house on Alana Drive. I came running."

"Thanks for coming," Terry said. "False alarm."

"But you're happy with the department's response," Kilcullen said.

"More than happy, sir."

"Good, because after our little talk this afternoon, I upgraded your level of protection."

"Thank you. The officers on duty did the department proud, Lieutenant. They were right to call out the cavalry."

"God only knows what it cost the taxpayers," Kilcullen said. "But we do what we have to do to take care of our own."

Terry just stood there and let Kilcullen have his fun.

"I'll be going now," Kilcullen said. "Glad your family is safe."

He left. Kaczmarek and Lester said good-bye and followed him out the door.

The rest of us stood there in silence. Finally Terry looked at Emily. "How do you feel about all this?" he said.

"Terrible. Especially about the way your boss just treated you. Like it was your fault. I'm sorry, Dad. How do you feel?"

"Me?" Terry said. "I feel like Ben Stiller."

CHAPTER THIRTY-THREE

Saturday morning. Serenity had returned to the Biggs household. Sort of.

Marilyn insisted that we have a big family breakfast, which didn't sit well with her two teenage daughters, who rebelled against the very thought of "getting up before noon to eat food that's only going to make us fat, Mom."

Marilyn's response was plain and simple. "This is not a democracy. And, even if it were, after what Emily pulled last night, she doesn't get a vote for at least a year."

Sarah came back at her with, "What did I do to get punished?"

"First of all, breakfast with your family is not punishment," Marilyn informed her. "And second, you ratted out your sister. Next time don't point the guilty finger at her and proclaim your own innocence. It's not cool. It's certainly not sisterly."

"Does that mean you expect me to lie for her?"

"No, I expect Emily to tell the truth. It's not your responsibility to drop a dime on her if she doesn't."

And so, we all sat down for a big breakfast of Marilyn's four-cheese omelet, raspberry-lemon French toast, fresh fruit, and figgy scones.

"What do I look like?" Sarah asked. "A lumberjack?"

"Stop moaning and eat," Marilyn said, "because this is the most exciting thing you're going to do all day."

"Am I grounded too?" Sarah said.

"No. You're just quarantined till Mike and your father catch this crazy person."

"That cop from last night," Sarah said. "Tim. Will he be back tonight?"

"Why?"

"No reason."

"He's thirty years old if he's a day," Marilyn said. "You're eighteen."

"I'm not marrying him," Sarah said. "I'm stuck in the house. He's cute. Maybe I just want to hang with him while he's on duty."

"Cops aren't allowed to hang with the people they're protecting," Terry said. "Besides, he's got a girlfriend."

"You don't even know him. How do you know he has a girlfriend?"

"All good-looking cops have girlfriends. It's part of LA police procedure. Look at Mike. He's a cop. He's good-looking. And guess, what?" he said, pointing at Diana. "Girlfriend."

"And not only is she a girlfriend," Diana said, "but last night she was promoted to carpenter's helper. While the four of you were sorting out family matters, Mike and I found some plywood in the garage and nailed it over the back door."

"How are we supposed to get in and out?" Emily said. "Are you and Mike gonna put in a doggie door?"

"Don't be fresh, young lady," Marilyn said. "You're on thin ice as it is."

"It's okay," I said. "This is what happens to the youth of America when you let them hang around with Terry Biggs. Actually, my good buddy, Kemp Loekle, who is a world-class carpenter but a lousy gold prospector, is driving down from Oregon as we speak, and he'll be glad to build you a new doorjamb. But first, he has to renovate our house, so we can move out of your way as soon as possible."

Emily stared at me. "Who said you're in our way?"

"Duh," Sarah said. "We're in *their* way. He's just too polite to say it."

"If Mom and Dad would let us out of jail, we wouldn't be in anybody's way," Emily said.

"Don't hold your breath," Marilyn said. "You're under this roof for the weekend. When it's time to go to school, Big Jim will drive you."

"I have a better solution," Emily said.

"I can't wait to hear it," Terry said.

"Okay, listen to this. Rebecca is free to come and go as she pleases, right?"

"That's because Rebecca is in St. Louis," Terry said. "The killer has a pattern, and we don't expect him to fly halfway across the country for his next victim."

"So how about if I stay with Rebecca in St. Louis?"

"That's a fair question," Terry said. "But no."

"Why not?"

"This is difficult," Terry said. "But the truth is, we think the killer is actually focused on getting you, so if you fly to St. Louis, you'll be putting Rebecca in jeopardy."

"Ha, ha, ha," Emily said. "You just better catch him fast. I'm wasting away the best years of my life." She turned toward her mother. "Why did you make this fancy breakfast anyway? Two more of your friends got shot. It feels like we're celebrating."

I've never had kids, but even if I had years of practice, I wouldn't have been able to handle a crack like that as well as Marilyn did.

"We *are* celebrating," she said, her voice calm and even, although I could see that her breathing was much more pronounced. "We're celebrating life."

Emily came right back at her. "Whose?"

"Mine. A few days ago there were five women in my little partnership. This morning only two of them woke up alive. I'm thrilled to be one of them, so I decided to mark the occasion by making breakfast for some of the people I thought would be just as thrilled. I was working under the assumption that you were one of them. But even if you're not, suck it up, and eat your figgy scone."

Breakfast went very well after that, and for the next twenty minutes we were one big happy family.

Our plan was to drive back to Martin Sorensen's apartment after breakfast and ask him about those criminology courses he had taken. We were getting ready to leave when my cell phone rang.

"Wendy Burns," I said, looking at the caller ID and flipping open the phone. "This is Lomax. What's up?"

Wendy wasn't supposed to be working the weekend, so I knew that whatever was up wasn't going to be good.

"Tony Dominguez was shot," she said.

I repeated it for Terry, and Marilyn let out a loud gasp.

"I don't have any other details," Wendy said. "Meet me at the scene."

"We're on our way," I said heading toward the door. "Where are we going?"

The answer stopped me cold in my tracks. "611 South Cherokee."

"Holy shit," I said. "That's the flip house."

CHAPTER THIRTY-FOUR

A new team of cops was parked outside Terry's house. He ran over, and within seconds their doors swung open, and they headed for the house.

"I told them to get their asses inside and watch the girls from in there," he said as he peeled out of the driveway. "Give your father a call. Until we know what's going on, I want some backup."

We flew along the 101, and I called Big Jim. It was one of those rare times when he followed orders without asking questions.

We were on Cahuenga just a few minutes from the scene, when Wendy called back.

"We've got two dead," she said. "Tony took a bullet, but the paramedics say they've seen worse."

"Can you ID the two victims?"

"Yeah. Bad news. One is Tony's wife, Marisol. The other is Martin Sorensen."

"Are you sure?"

It was a dumb question, but the information was so impossible to digest that dumb was the best I could do.

"Mike, I knew them both," Wendy said. "I'm sure."

As soon as we rounded the corner onto Cherokee I thought

about the last time Terry and I were at the flip house. One lone cop car, the house cordoned off with tape—all for the theatrics built around Nora's book. But it was nothing compared to the real thing. Uniformed officers were rolling out an even wider yellow perimeter. The street was a logjam of cruisers, EMS units, and a growing convoy of media trucks. We were bombarded with lights, cameras, radio chatter, and the organized chaos of TV reporters yelling unanswered questions into microphones. I'm sure Marisol would have reveled in the drama.

"Murder at 611 South Cherokee," I said.

"It's got bestseller written all over it," Terry said.

"Lomax. Biggs." It was Wendy Burns. She was standing by as the paramedics lifted a cart into the back of an EMS bus.

"He's in a lot of pain," she said, "but they say he'll make it."

The paramedic was about to shut the doors. "Give me ten seconds," I said, and without waiting for an answer, I climbed in.

Tony Dominguez was strapped to a stretcher, his left shoulder covered in a field dressing. Bags of fluids were hanging from an IV tree running down to his arm. His face was contorted, and he was looking up, moaning something in Spanish.

"Tony, it's Mike. You're gonna be okay."

"Bastard . . . killed . . . my wife," he said.

"I know. I'm so sorry."

"I got here . . . heard a shot . . . ran in . . . Martin running out. He fired twice. Second one nailed me. I shot back." He started sobbing. "My fault she's dead . . ."

"Don't blame yourself, TD."

"I'm a cop . . . I couldn't protect my own wife. . . ." He let out a yelp of pain, and started coughing.

The paramedic outside yanked on my pant leg. "In or out, Detective. This bus is rolling."

I jumped out, and within seconds, the ambulance was blasting its way through Saturday-morning traffic.

"Clue me in," Terry said.

"He's in shock, but the bottom line is, Martin shot Marisol, then he got into a shootout with Tony. Tony won."

Terry just nodded. I knew exactly what was running through his brain. This could have been Marilyn.

"Let's go see the others," he said.

The crime lab people had already gotten started. We put on gloves and shoe covers and followed Wendy into the master bedroom.

There, just a few feet from the chalk outline of the fictional Stephen Driscoll was the very real, very dead Marisol Dominguez. She was wearing a pale blue T-shirt, covered in blood at the neckline, and a pair of skin tight jeans. Jessica Keating was kneeling beside her.

"Another cop's wife," Keating said, skipping the usual happy-to-see-you-boys banter. "COD looks the same. A small-caliber bullet to the back of the head."

"Back of the head?" I said. "And she fell face up?"

"Tony rolled her over," Wendy said. "After he took the bullet he managed to get in here, but she was dead. That's when he called 911. He was on the floor with her head in his arms when I got here."

I knelt down beside Jessica. "Did the killer take a lock of her hair?"

"Not that I can see," she said, "but I haven't really given her a thorough."

"I don't think he had time," Wendy said. "Tony heard the shot and came running in. Sorensen headed for the front door, but he didn't get very far. He's in the living room."

Martin Sorensen was lying face up on the living room rug. His chest and the carpeting around him were soaked with blood. There was a .22-caliber pistol on the floor near his right hand. One of Jessica's people was taking pictures of both the body and the weapon from every angle.

"This bastard was going to kill my wife next, wasn't he?" Terry said.

"We don't know that," I said.

"Mike, it's me. Who are you bullshitting? Marilyn is the last partner. Of course she was next."

"Fine. She was next. But now she's not."

"What I don't get," Wendy said, "is why. Sorensen had such a good thing going with Nora. Why would he kill all these people?"

"Money," Terry said. "Nora was making a bundle, and part of Martin's job was to watch it pour in. He must've decided he wasn't getting his fair share."

"But what's the payoff for killing the moneymaker?" Wendy said. "Is he in the will?"

"Not for much. That would be too obvious," Terry said. "I think he figured he could make a fortune on his own if he wrote a book about his life with Nora, including all the juicy stuff that happened between the sheets."

"Wow," Wendy said. "I can think of ten people who would buy that book. And I'm one of them."

"The problem is, he never would have been able to write it if Nora was still alive," I said.

"Or Julia, for that matter," Terry added. "She would have at least tried to stop him."

"So he killed the two people who were standing between him and the bestseller list," Wendy said. "Why did he kill Reggie Drabyak's wife?"

"I don't know," Terry said. "Maybe he was thinking more bodies sell more books."

"You guys interviewed him," Wendy said. "What was your take?"

"He wasn't at the top of our suspect list," I said, "but he was starting to move up the ladder. Last night Muller told us that Sorensen had been taking forensics and other criminal justice courses that would make him a lot smarter than your average murderer."

"How did he explain that?" Wendy said.

"I'm sure he would've said it makes him a better resource for Nora, but we never got a chance to ask him. We were planning to pay him a surprise visit this morning."

"Yeah," Terry said, staring down at the body. "But we got all involved in this big family breakfast, and Tony Dominguez got to surprise him first."

CHAPTER THIRTY-FIVE

If you want to assemble a bunch of politicians in a big urban area like LA, there are two words that will get their attention in a hurry.

Officer down.

By 11:00 A.M. there were more windbags on Cherokee than you'd find at a party caucus in Iowa. Council people, assembly people, and a gaggle of wannabes who were gunning for their jobs in November showed up in droves. At the center of it all was the mayor himself.

He arrived, buoyed at first, because LAPD had caught and killed the guy who had murdered Nora Bannister and the two cop wives. He was probably thinking he'd bask in the limelight of the capture, then do a photo op at the hospital with the wounded hero cop.

Unfortunately, his entourage had neglected to tell him that Marisol was dead too. Within minutes of his arrival he was taking heat from reporters, Hispanic activists, and political snipers of every persuasion, all of whom demanded to know why the police hadn't put poor Mrs. Dominguez into protective custody.

His Honor didn't have a good answer.

So he told Deputy Mayor Mel Berger to get one. Our handsome mayor is the face of city hall, but Berger is the brains. Rail-thin and brutally ruthless, the man is all guile and no body fat. He's the mayor's liaison to the Jewish community and the Hollywood studios, and because he's fluent in Spanish, he knows how to reach out to the Latino voters.

Right now he was reaching out hard to an Irish lieutenant by the name of Brendan Kilcullen. Berger is not the type to bitch to the chief of police and hope that his outrage and disappointment are communicated with the same intensity right on down the chain of command. Mel Berger doesn't trust middlemen. If he wants somebody's ass kicked, he makes sure it's his size 9 inside the wingtip.

Terry and I were standing in the front yard, watching the interchange between the two men from fifty feet away. We couldn't hear a word, but the body language was clear. Berger's right index finger was wagging rapidly in the direction of Kilcullen's chest. Never touching, but causing our boss to lean back defensively.

Finally, Kilcullen started walking in our direction.

"Five dollars says he's not inviting us out for another afternoon of chat and chili," Terry said.

"I'm in deep shit," Kilcullen said, as soon as he got us alone.

"Today hasn't exactly been a slice of heaven for Marisol Dominguez either," Terry said.

"The mayor is blaming me for Marisol," Kilcullen said. "Why didn't I protect her?"

"You offered," I said. "She turned you down."

"No excuse."

"Of course it's an excuse," Terry said. "She's a private citizen. You heard what she said about putting some cop in front of her house not doing shit. Remember 'Don't worry. I can take care of myself'?"

"Well, obviously she couldn't."

"And that's LAPD's fault?" I said.

"Not all of LAPD," Kilcullen said. "According to Berger, it's mine."

"And by extension, ours," I said.

"Don't flatter yourselves," he said. "If city hall decides to look for a scapegoat, it's my head that'll roll. I'm the one who authorized protection for Biggs's wife, but I didn't take care of Mrs. Dominguez. According to Deputy Mayor Berger, I should have been smarter."

"There's not going to be a scapegoat," I said. "Marisol made her own choice. Besides, Sorensen was her business partner. He had access. If he was hell-bent on killing her, ten teams of cops couldn't have protected her."

"Debatable point," Kilcullen grunted. "Were you on to this guy Sorensen?"

"He was starting to look good," I said. "We were going to pay him a visit and push him a little more this morning, but then we got the call from Wendy to come here."

"Did you figure out his motive?"

"Money, fame, glory," Terry said. "Basically, he helped run Nora Bannister's empire, and he wanted it for his own."

"Why did he kill all those other women? I thought they were just small players."

"They were," I said. "We assume he killed Julia Knoll because she was Nora's daughter. As for the others, we don't know what was going on in Sorensen's head. We need some time to pull it all together. We'll start by searching his apartment."

"Start now," Kilcullen said. "According to Berger, the mayor wants a full written report."

"By when?"

"The usual deadline. Day before yesterday."

"If we'd have had the answer then," Terry said, "Marisol wouldn't be dead."

"Right," Kilcullen said. "And my ass wouldn't be in a sling."

CHAPTER THIRTY-SIX

Jessica helped confirm what we had started to piece together.

"I did a GSR test on both bodies," she said. "Marisol was clean. Sorensen had gunshot residue on his right hand. The .22 we found next to his body appears to be the murder weapon. Even if the bullet is too obliterated to give us usable ballistics, you'll still have Detective Dominguez's testimony. That ought to clinch it."

We knew the who, what, when, and where. Our job now was to figure out the why.

"We should have been smarter," Terry said, as we headed for Martin Sorensen's apartment. "And faster. If we had driven out to see Sorensen early this morning instead of wasting our time on breakfast, we might have tripped him up before he went over to the flip house and shot Marisol."

"So it's our fault," I said. "You think because we sat down to a family breakfast, Marisol wound up dead."

He hit the back of his palm on the steering wheel. "And why did we have breakfast this morning? Because Marilyn was using food to compensate for Emily's dumb stunt the night before."

"So it's Emily's fault that Marisol is dead," I said.

"In a convoluted, indirect way, yes."

"How old was Emily when you married Marilyn?"

"The twins were seven. Emily was five."

"But if you *hadn't* married Marilyn, she wouldn't have needed police protection, and Emily wouldn't be your daughter, and you wouldn't have wasted the morning eating figgy scones," I said.

"So it's my fault that Marisol is dead," he said.

"In a convoluted, indirect way, yes. Of course, since I'm your partner, it's half my fault."

"Thank you for clearing that up. I feel better already."

I knew he still felt like crap, but I've learned that when something is gnawing at Terry, he needs the time to let it chew. We didn't talk until we arrived at Martin's apartment.

We informed the building super that his tenant in 3-B was deceased. He extended his condolences as if we were the next of kin, then let us in the apartment without even looking at the warrant.

We searched the place. There were eggshells and warm coffee grounds in the garbage can, which indicated Martin had eaten a hearty breakfast before heading out to kill Marisol. But there were no dirty dishes in sight, and the coffee pot had been washed, dried, and put away. Even the bed was neatly made.

"Neat as a pin," I said. "Not exactly your basic bachelor apartment."

Terry shrugged. "It is if the bachelor is an anal-retentive mass murderer."

Martin's appointment book was on top of his desk. These days, a lot of searches turn up a Blackberry, a Treo, or a Palm Pilot, which means that Terry and I have to take it in for a techie to help us crack. Martin was one of those people who still used one of those old-fashioned week-at-a-glance paper calendars.

"Good news," Terry said. "We won't be needing a decoder ring."

The book was bound in black vinyl, and a quick thumb through it showed that Martin Sorensen had a busy schedule. I flipped ahead to a few weeks from now.

"According to his calendar, he expected Nora to be around for a while," I said.

"Of course he would write that in," Terry said. "The guy took all those criminology courses. He's not stupid. But just for the heck of it, check out today's entry. See if it says, *Go to 611 South Cherokee, kill Marisol.*"

There were no entries for Saturday or Sunday. But Monday morning got my attention. It said *Call Mike Lomax* and had my office number written below it.

"I wonder what he was going to call about," I said.

"I have no idea," Terry said. "But I'll go out on a limb and take a guess that it wasn't fashion advice."

We spent another two hours going over the apartment. It was basically benign. Most murderers aren't like the madmen portrayed by Hollywood, who cover their walls with newspaper clippings of their kills. Real murderers are not that blatantly obvious, so not finding anything incriminating came as no surprise.

We were just about ready to take Sorensen's computer and bring it back to Muller when my cell rang. It was Jessica Keating.

"We just went over Sorensen's car," she said. "It was parked outside the house and the keys were in his pocket."

"Did you find anything?"

"A gun case, complete with a box of .22 shells and some gun-cleaning equipment."

"I'm glad," I said. "Because there's no gun paraphernalia in the apartment. We figured he had to keep it hidden somewhere."

"He had it tucked away in the wheel well under the jack," she said. "You want to know what else we found inside the case?"

"The way you're asking, I think I definitely do."

"Three plastic baggies, each with a lock of hair," Jessica said. "I haven't done a DNA on them, but under a microscope they would appear to belong to Jo Drabyak, Julia Knoll, and Nora Bannister."

"Good job," I said. "Did you find anything else?"

"What more could you ask for?"

"Well, in a perfect world," I said, "it would really help if he left us a written report explaining why he killed all those women. Preferably neatly typed—something that Terry and I could drop off at the mayor's office."

CHAPTER THIRTY-SEVEN

"I guess the siege is officially over," Terry said as we pulled into his driveway at 7:00 P.M. "No more cute cops in squad cars parked outside the house. Sarah will be devastated."

"Emily, on the other hand, will be thrilled," I said.

"Let's not tell her till she's thirty. It couldn't hurt to keep her locked up for a while longer."

The house was quiet. Diana was working late at the hospital. Marilyn was lying on the sofa reading a book. Jett was curled up next to her head. Neither of them looked up.

"Where are the girls?" Terry said.

"Out enjoying their newfound freedom," Marilyn said. "I didn't even know Emily knew the word *emancipation,* but she used it a dozen times this afternoon. I called Rebecca at school and told her it was over." She hesitated. "It is over, isn't it?"

"Everything but the paperwork," Terry said.

Marilyn sat up on the sofa. Jett perked up. Marilyn on the move usually meant food. The dog was poised for a trip to the kitchen.

"Sit. Stay," Marilyn said.

"You talking to me?" Terry said.

Marilyn ignored him. "I still can't believe Martin would murder someone," she said. "Especially Nora. She loved him. She took such good care of him."

"Apparently not good enough. You ever get a hint that he was angry enough to kill her?"

"Kill her? No. But I knew he had a beef. When I first joined the LA Flippers, I was over at Nora's house. She was on a conference call, so I just hung around and talked to Martin. Sort of a getting-to-know-you conversation."

"And what did you get to know?" Terry asked.

"According to Martin, the *House to Die For* series was all his idea. Nora loved it, and immediately decided that Julia should be a partner. Of course, Julia was totally inept, so Nora brought Marisol in. Eventually, she added me and Jo, but Martin never got his piece of the pie. As far as Nora was concerned, pitching ideas was part of his job."

"So Martin came up with this gold mine of an idea, Nora took on four partners, and he got nothing?" I said.

"Not nothing," Marilyn said. "But not much. I think she gave him a Christmas bonus. A trip to Hawaii."

"And she tagged along," Terry said.

"Of course," Marilyn said. "She wasn't going to let him go off by himself. They were . . . you know."

"So he has the big idea. She cuts other people in on the action, and all Martin gets is a ticket to bang Nora on Waikiki Beach. Talk about a motive," Terry said. "No wonder he killed the others along with Nora. He must have hated everyone in the group."

"Thank you for reminding me, Terry," Marilyn said. "Because I haven't thought about the fact that I was next for at least two minutes."

"Sorry." He sat down next to her. "What are you reading?"

"Murder at 611 South Cherokee." She closed it, so we could see the cover. "I read the advance copy six months ago, but this has the acknowledgment page. She mentions me and all the other partners, and she thanks you, Mike, Charlie, and Wendy Burns for helping her get all the cop stuff right."

"Well, we got the cop stuff wrong this time," Terry said. "We suspected Martin, but we didn't go after him fast enough."

Marilyn put a hand on his knee. "Are you upset that Tony will get all the credit for solving the case?"

"No. I'm upset that we didn't solve it before Tony's wife got killed."

Jett sat up and barked. Marilyn jumped.

The front door opened. "It's only us," Emily yelled.

She and Sarah came into the living room. They each gave Terry a quick kiss. "How you doing, Mom?" Emily said.

"I'm in shock," Marilyn said. "What are you doing home so early?"

"The mall is boring."

"And the guy she has the hots for was hanging with another girl," Sarah said.

"I do not have the hots for him," Emily yelled.

"For the record," Terry said, "you're too young to have the hots for anyone."

"This is embarrassing," Emily said. "I'm going to my room."

"I don't get it," Marilyn said. "Last night you called out half the cops in LA because you were tired of being stuck in the house. Now that you're free to go, you're not going anywhere."

"It's my call," Emily said, tossing one hand in the air. "And that, Mother, is the beauty of emancipation."

CHAPTER THIRTY-EIGHT

The next morning we were on the 101 headed for Cedars-Sinai to talk to Tony Dominguez. Terry was in a pissy mood.

"You haven't said a word since we left the house," I said. "What's your problem?"

"I was just wondering if we can find a Hallmark store open on a Sunday morning," he said. "I'd like to get Tony one of those Sorry If My Lousy Police Work Caused the Death of Your Wife cards."

"It's probably in the section next to the Your Wife Should Have Taken Us Up on Our Offer of Police Protection cards. Lighten up on yourself. Marisol called her own shots. What's done is done. Let's just talk to Tony and wrap this up. You okay with that?"

"I'm fine," he said, sounding anything but.

"As long as we're at Cedars," I said, "we should stop in and talk to Charlie and get his take on Martin Sorensen."

"How about your contractor with the nail in his dick? Isn't he in the hospital too? Why don't we pop by Good Samaritan and spread some cheer his way? We can make a day of it."

"My contractor," I said. "We've been so crazy, I forgot all about it." I dug into my jacket pocket and pulled out a sheet of paper.

"What's that?"

"Liz Corrado, our lawyer, has been talking with Hal Hooper," I said. "He flat out refuses to give us back the advance we gave him."

"On what grounds?"

"On the grounds that he's an asshole. He said his injuries won't slow him down that much."

"I thought his leg was broken and he couldn't work for eight weeks."

"Yeah, well, he changed his tune when we asked for a refund. He said he would pick up where he left off in a few days."

"By pick up where he left off, does he mean keep the money and not show up?" Terry said.

"Right, and by a few days, he means when hell freezes over. So, Liz is threatening to sue. She sent me a draft of a letter she's working on."

"I got a good opening for you," Terry said. "How about, 'Dear Dickwad, we don't mean to be *hard on* you, but we really need to *nail this down.*'"

"Hard on. Nail down," I said. "Liz is a little more artful."

"I'll be the judge of that. Read on."

I unfolded the piece of paper. "Dear Mr. Hooper. My client's roof was supposed to be finished two weeks ago, but with your recent unfortunate injury, it is apparent that *it will be a long time before you can get it up.*"

Terry laughed out loud.

"Unless you return my client's advance payment of seven thousand dollars within forty-eight hours of receipt of this letter, we will proceed with litigation."

"That's not a believable threat," Terry said. "These contractors get sued eight days a week. Lawsuits don't scare them, because it would cost you more in legal expenses than you can win in court. He knows you'll never go through with it."

I smiled. "Don't bet on it. Listen to this. 'My client is determined to see this through, no matter what the legal costs. We intend to subpoena your medical records, and while a jury may be sympathetic to a man who mistook his genitalia for a roofing shingle, you are at risk of your little private matter becoming public fodder for the media.'"

Terry slammed his palm on the steering wheel. "Little private matter. If I weren't doing eighty, I'd get up and give Liz Corrado a standing ovation. That's the kind of twisted thinking that restores my faith in our legal system. Kudos on finding a lawyer who uses her powers for good instead of evil."

He had a smile on his face all the way into Cedars.

We parked at the South Tower and took an elevator to the seventh floor. When Charlie Knoll checked into the hospital with chest pains, they put him in a double room. But when hero cop Tony Dominguez took a bullet protecting the citizens of our fair city, he was gratefully bedded down in a private suite usually reserved for the rich and celebrated.

The mahogany-paneled hallway leading to Tony's room looked more like a European hotel than a hospital. We knocked on Tony's door.

"Come in."

It was one of those rooms that most patients will never see, or even dream of. More wood-paneled walls, antique furniture, and a muted Persian rug that definitely had not come from Carpet City. The Old World feel was offset by twenty-first-century amenities like a high def plasma TV and a home theater system. Tony was sitting in a leather armchair, wearing a dark blue silky robe. His left arm was in a sling.

There was a second chair and a second man. He was in his mid-sixties, silver-haired, impeccably dressed, and noticeably handsome. He looked like a Hollywood star. In a way, he was.

"Guys, thanks for coming," Tony said. "This is my friend, my mentor, and most important, my shrink, Ford Jameson."

Dr. Ford Jameson, legendary psychiatrist to the rich and crazy, smiled, stood up, and shook our hands. He was tall and trim, with the kind of warm, caring eyes you want in a TV dad, or a therapist you're going to trust with your innermost secrets.

"Nice to finally meet you," I said. "Tony's told us a lot about you."

"The question is," Terry said, "has he told you a lot about us?"

The doc laughed. "I can't break doctor-patient confidentiality," he said, "but I'll go out on a limb and say that based on what I've heard about you, Detective Biggs, I wouldn't want to go up against you in a poker game."

We all laughed at that one, then the room grew uncomfortably quiet, and I was reminded that this was as much a condolence call to a friend as it was a police investigation.

"Tony," I said, breaking the silence, "we can't tell you how sorry we feel about Marisol."

"Yeah," Terry said. "We were looking at Sorensen, and we only wish we could have—"

Tony held up his good right hand. "Stop. I've been blaming myself for Marisol's death, and Ford has just spent the last half

I think Tony is the killer.

hour helping me understand that she was a strong woman who made her own choices. What happened is not my fault, and God knows, it's not yours."

"Gentlemen," Jameson said, "survivor's guilt is incredibly common in situations like this. If either or both of you would like to spend some time talking it through with me, I'd be glad to help. There's never a charge for LAPD."

"We appreciate it," I said.

"Thanks," Terry said. "At those prices, I'd like to bring my sixteen-year-old daughter and leave her with you till she's forty."

Been there.

Jameson laughed again and handed each of us a business card. "Anytime. I mean it."

"Anytime but now," Tony said. "We were in the middle of a therapy session. Can you guys give us a half hour?"

"No problem," I said. "We'll stop in and see Charlie."

"He's downstairs," Tony said, sweeping his hand across his outrageously expensive hospital suite. "In the poor people's wing."

That, of course, got another laugh all around.

We didn't know it at the time, but as it turned out, Charlie Knoll was not quite as poor as we all thought.

CHAPTER THIRTY-NINE

Charlie was in bed reading the *LA Times*.

"There's half a dozen different stories about us in the paper, and we're all over the TV," he said. "How much of this shit is the truth?"

"Which part don't you believe?" I said.

"All of it. Last Sunday the five of us were on the boat drinking beer and playing cards. A week later two of us are in the hospital, three wives and my mother-in-law are dead, and a guy I knew and trusted turns out to be a maniac serial killer. How did this all happen?"

"Charlie, if you're looking for someone to blame, I'll own a lot of it," Terry said.

"Thank you, Detective Martyr, but I'm not looking to point the finger. I just can't believe that bastard killed four women. It's surreal."

"Still, it was our job to catch him, and we didn't."

"You guys did what you could do," Charlie said. "And if you ask me, nobody *caught* him. Tony brought him down, but not through brilliant detective work. He just showed up at the right place at the right time."

Neither do I ...

Too many pages

(100 +) to go.

"Almost the right time," Terry said. "Five minutes earlier and Marisol would still be alive."

"Did you visit him in his lah-dee-fucking-dah suite?"

"Yeah, but we have to go back," I said. "He's with his shrink. Speaking of which, how's your mental health?"

"Oh, you know that five-stages-of-grief thing—denial, anger, bargaining, depression, and acceptance. I'm stuck at extremely pissed off."

"Dr. Jameson treats cops for free," Terry said.

"No thanks. I'm allergic to shrinks," Charlie said. "They mess with your head. What I really need is a doc who will release me from this place. They did an echocardiogram, and they didn't like what they saw. So then they did a stress test, and they gave me some shit about a problem with my left main coronary artery. You know what the cardiologist calls the left main? The widowmaker. I told him it's too late for me to die and leave a widow. He wants to do an angiogram tomorrow. I told him he better keep me alive, because I've got funerals to plan."

"Did you know that Martin Sorensen claimed to be the brains behind the house-flipping concept?" I said.

"It's true," Charlie said. "Julia told me a few years ago when the whole thing started. But I never thought about it as a motive. I figured Nora was paying him well."

"He told us he was planning to write a book about his relationship with Nora," Terry said.

"Good for him," Charlie said, not sounding particularly impressed. "He'd make some money on it, but it's a dead end, a one-book deal. No, I don't think writing a tell-all book about Nora was the motive. Now that I have the benefit of hindsight, I think I know what Martin was really planning."

Terry and I exchanged a look.

"Charlie," I said, "there is a big blank section in the final report we're writing. If you actually know what Martin was planning, that would go a long way to filling that hole."

"I'll give it a try."

"Go ahead."

"I think Martin was planning to become Nora Bannister."

"Meaning what?" I said.

"I told you—me and Martin, we'd sometimes go out for a couple of pops together."

"Yeah."

"Well, one night, maybe a year ago, we're both at a bar, a little shit-faced, and we're talking about plan B. Martin asks what am I gonna do when I retire from the force. I have no idea. I mean, Reggie's gonna make fishing rods, or maybe open a bait and tackle shop, and get as far away from LA as he can. Me, I haven't even thought about it. So I ask Martin what's he gonna do. He says when Nora is ready to pack it in, he could easily take over writing her books."

"How?"

"It's not that complicated," Charlie said. "There are plenty of writers whose estates are still churning out books. Ian Fleming has been dead for about forty years, but James Bond lives on with new stuff all the time."

"And Martin thought he could write Nora's books?"

"By now, I could probably write them." He laughed. "Maybe not, but hell, a guy as smart as Martin could crack the code."

"But even if Martin wrote them," I said, "wouldn't the money go to Nora's estate?"

"The estate would get the bulk of the dough, but with Julia gone, the university would be the executor. If you were them, who would you turn to for help in managing all of Nora's intellectual property?"

"The guy who worked with her for the past seven years," I said.

"No question. Martin could literally take over Nora's ideas, her books, her life. He could make a ton of money for the university, plus he'd get paid as the writer, which would be a hell of a lot more than he made as an assistant." Charlie smiled. "Plus he'd be banging a lot younger broads."

"It makes sense," Terry said. "But . . ."

"But what?"

"He killed Nora so he could take over her books. He killed Julia so she wouldn't stand in his way. But why did he bother to kill Jo and Marisol?"

"For the same reason he would have killed your wife next," Charlie said. "Everybody was cashing in on Martin's real estate idea but him. This was payback time. Get rid of all five partners, and he'd have the house-flipping business all to himself."

Terry exhaled loudly. "Whoa."

"Not pretty," Charlie said, "but what goes on inside the head of a mass murderer is never pretty."

"Charlie, this has been a big help," I said. "Thanks."

He shrugged. "It would have been a bigger help if I'd have figured this all out after Jo Drabyak got killed. But I gotta tell you, Martin Sorensen wasn't even on my radar. I really liked the guy."

"How much time are you going to take off before you come back to work?" I said. "I only took a few weeks when Joanie died. I probably should have taken more. I was totally useless the first month or so."

"Not totally useless," Terry said. "But a lot more useless than usual."

"Fellas," Charlie said, "I'm not going back to work."

"It's too soon to make a decision like that," I said. "Take some time . . ."

"Mike, I'm turning in my tin. So is Reggie. We talked about it."

"What are you gonna do?" Terry said.

"Fish."

"You?"

"Not off the Santa Monica pier, for Christ's sake. Reggie and I are going to sail around the world."

"In a houseboat?"

"He's going to upgrade to a sailboat. Reg has been planning for years to chase the big ones down in Australia, Japan, the South Pacific. He was going to go with Jo once he got his twenty. But with her dead, he's not waiting, and he's going with me."

"You and Reggie?" Terry said.

"You think you and Mike are the only happy couple living together?" Charlie said. "So, yeah, me and Reggie. We're friends. We're both going through the same shit. I wasn't sure at first, but I thought about it, and I decided that catching fish can be a lot more fun than catching scumbags."

"You and Reggie are both gonna chuck your pensions?" I said.

"I got a little money to keep me afloat for a while. And you know Reg. He's a saver, and he's got that side business making fishing rods and selling them online."

"What about that very understanding, very sympathetic, very compassionate friend you were with the other night?" Terry said. "You got a rod for her, or does she stay behind?"

"Jesus, Biggs, you never let anything go, do you?" Charlie said. "That part of my life is none of your goddam business."

"I'm sorry," Terry said. "I had to ask."

Charlie laughed. "No you're not, and no you didn't. But if anybody would have the balls to ask, it would be you."

"When are you and Reggie leaving?" I said.

"The funerals are Thursday. It'll take a few days to process me out of the department. Then I'll put the house on the market. Hopefully, we can leave by November and spend Christmas on the Great Barrier Reef."

"We'll miss you," I said. "Send us a postcard."

"Even better," Terry said, "send us a fish."

CHAPTER FORTY

AVID

We still had time to kill before going back to see Tony, so we went downstairs to the cafeteria. The place was basically deserted. I got a container of orange juice and a bagel. Terry bought coffee. We sat as far away from the counter people as possible.

"Charlie and Reggie?" Terry said. "Sailing around the world? Catching fish? You were a little nuts when Joanie died, but these guys have taken it to a new level."

"I was braced for Joanie's death. For these guys it came out of the blue. I guess they just really want to get away from it all."

"Not to sound like a detective, but since that's what they pay me for, I've got a question. Don't you think it's sounds a little—I don't know—suspicious?"   *INDEED!*

"You mean the fact that they're both leaving town?"

"Town? Mike, they're leaving the fucking hemisphere. Does that set off any alarm bells in your head?"

"Like what?"

"I don't want to pollute your mind with what I'm thinking about. Just free associate and see where it takes you."

I gnawed on my bagel. "Well, if Charlie and Reggie were a man and a woman, and both their spouses were murdered, and suddenly they announced that they're going to sail off into the sunset, I'd think they're having an affair and they were involved in the murders. But they're two men."

"And two men can't have an affair? Catch a movie, Mike. They have gay cowboys now. I hate to break it to you, but there are cops who like to ride bareback too. For all we know, Charlie's compassionate, understanding friend could turn out to be Reggie."

"That's brilliant," I said. "Why didn't I think of it? Two married men we've known for years are suddenly struck gay. They don't know how to deal with it, so they murder their wives, and go sailing off to Australia. You're grabbing at straws—Charlie and Reggie are not gay."

"Is that your final answer?"

"Even if they were," I said, "Charlie is sooooo not Reggie's type."

We both laughed hard enough to get the handful of people who were in the cafeteria to look up.

"Okay, let's assume they're not gay," Terry said. "Look at the money angle. With all this publicity, the price of the flip house is going sky-high, and they each stand to inherit their wife's cut."

"I don't know how much money is involved, but it doesn't seem like enough to murder your wife. How much would it take for you to kill Marilyn?"

"There are days when I'd do it for twenty bucks and a six-pack of Heineken, but stop giving me straight lines. What if it's the money, plus something else?"

"Something else like what?"

"I don't know. They each have a mistress . . . or . . ."

"Look, Terry, I know what you're trying to do. Even if you

can't figure out their motive, this news about the two of them retiring in a hurry and moving to the other side of the world makes it look like they were involved. But let's look at the facts. We know they didn't kill Marisol. Martin did."

"And Martin probably killed the others," he said. "But what if Reggie and Charlie paid him to do it? They knew he wanted to take over Nora's empire, so they came up with a plan to . . ."

He stopped, and let out a long slow breath. Then he gulped down several swallows of his coffee.

"I'm sorry," he said. "I don't know what the hell I'm talking about. I don't even know why I went off like this."

"I know why," I said.

He leaned back in his chair. You don't have to be a student of body language to understand what that means.

"You want me to tell you?" I said.

He held up one hand, shook his head no, and finished off his coffee. Then he folded his arms across his chest, and still sitting far back in his chair he said, "Fine. Go ahead, tell me."

"Guilt," I said. "Good old-fashioned, lapsed-Catholic guilt. You've been beating up on yourself that we didn't solve this sooner. You feel bad about Nora and Julia, but you're totally devastated about Marisol. We were starting to like Martin for these murders, but we didn't get to him fast enough."

I've known Terry a long time. I'm one of the privileged few who occasionally gets to see his serious side. This was one of those rare occasions. He was staring at me, not thinking ahead to the next joke, but listening hard.

"Go on," he said.

"The reality is that his next victim was Marisol, but in your mind, it wasn't." I paused for a few seconds. He knew what I was going to say next. "It was Marilyn."

"Could have been," he said softly. "It was just luck of the draw."

"I don't think it was luck. I think Marisol made herself an easier target than Marilyn did."

"We'll never know."

"Maybe . . . just maybe," I said, "if we had been more aggressive, we could have nailed Martin before he killed Marisol, and that's hard for you to deal with. But if you turn this into something bigger and more complicated, then whatever we did won't matter. I think you're trying to make the guilt go away by changing the case into something we couldn't have solved."

"Wow."

"Here's the bottom line," I said. "Martin Sorensen killed Tony's wife, not yours. And it is not your fault. Now get past it."

He unfolded his arms, reached across the table, and tore off a piece of my bagel. He chewed on it, and we just sat there quietly. Finally, he smiled.

"You're scary good at this analysis shit," he said. "Thanks."

"Anytime," I said. "There's never a charge for LAPD."

CHAPTER FORTY-ONE

Tony was still sitting in the leather armchair, his feet propped up on an ottoman. "How's Charlie holding up?" he asked.

"They're keeping him another day for some tests," I said. "You up for answering a few questions?"

"Is this an official visit? I've got enough painkillers in me to make my answers qualify as somewhere between stupid and unreliable."

"It won't be as invasive as the one you're going to have to go through with IA, or as mind-numbing as the one you'll do with the department shrink," I said, "but we do need some answers, so we can fill in the blanks on our report. If you're too doped up we can come back."

"No. Even if my shoulder wasn't killing me, the subject is so painful, I'm glad I'm on the drugs."

"What happened yesterday morning?" I said. "You both knew she could be a target. How did she happen to be alone in the house with the killer?"

"Dr. Jameson made me promise I would do this interview without blaming myself," he said. "So I won't, but you can draw your own conclusions."

He closed his eyes and rubbed his forehead. We waited for him to refocus and get to the facts.

"I went out for a run about six thirty. Marisol was still in bed. When I got back she was showered, dressed, and on her way out the door. I asked where the hell she's going by herself, and she said, 'The flip house—the same place I go to every day, and I don't need a police escort.'"

"Did you ask why she was going?" I said. "Do you know if she was planning to meet Martin?"

"Marisol doesn't deal well with questions about where she's been and what she's done. Whenever I ask, she backs off like I'm grilling her."

"So you offered to go with her, and she said no."

"Yeah, but I told her she didn't have a choice. She turned down police protection from Kilcullen, but she couldn't turn it down from me. I told her to sit tight while I shower, and we'll go together. She says, 'Fine, just move your ass.'" He smiled. "I loved her, but she could be a real bitch."

"So I went upstairs to take a quick shower. I'm stripping down, and my cell rings. It's Ford—Dr. Jameson. We had talked the day before, and I had told him all about the first three murders. He knew I was worried about Marisol, and he also knew that she would rather walk through South Central LA on her own than accept help from a cop."

"Even her husband?"

"Especially me. She grew up around some real badass cops in Mexico. It left her with some old wounds that never healed."

I nodded.

"Anyway, I did phone therapy with Dr. J. for maybe fifteen minutes. Then I yelled downstairs to tell Marisol I needed another five, and we could go. No answer. She had left without me. So I threw on some clothes and I drove to the flip house."

"You didn't shower?"

He shook his head. "No, I'm embarrassed to admit it, but I wanted to show up all hot and sweaty and read her the riot act. I was really pissed. Then when I got to the flip house I saw her car and Martin's."

"And what did you think?"

"I figured they were working out what to do about the business now that Nora was dead."

"So you thought it was strictly business?" I said.

His eyes ignited, and he bolted forward in his chair. "Jesus, Mike, I know you have to go into dark places, but give me a fucking break. If you're asking do I think there was anything going on between my wife and Martin, the answer is no. She was a bitch on wheels, but I loved her, and we were happy, and if you go down that road again, the interview is over."

"Tony, I'm sorry, but it's part of—"

"I know, I know, it's part of the job to treat the husband of the dead woman like he's guilty of something . . . anything."

"Hey, Tony," Terry said. "We went through this with Reggie, and then Charlie, and now you. We're just asking what we've got to ask, and believe me, Mike was lobbing them in as easy as he could. IA won't be that gentle. Now, get back on track. What happened once you got to the house?"

"I was agitated." He smiled. "Like I am now." He eased back

in his chair. "So I sat in the car for a minute trying to calm down, doing my best not to run into the house and have a domestic dispute in front of Martin."

"And then what?"

"I heard a shot from inside the house."

"Just one?"

"That's all I needed. I jumped out of the car and ran for the house."

"Did you call for backup?"

"My wife was a target and I heard a gunshot. No, I didn't stop to call a cop. I couldn't wait for backup."

"Had you heard anything from the house before the shot?" Terry said. "Like arguing?"

"No."

"What happened once you got to the house?"

"I threw open the door and ran in, screaming, 'Police. Drop your weapons.' A guy comes running out of the bedroom with a gun in his hand. It's Martin. I couldn't believe it. He shoots. It misses. But the second one hits me. I go down, but I managed to return fire. Three shots."

"From the looks of it, you only needed one," I said.

"Yeah," Terry said. "Nice shot group."

"Thanks. You know what they say . . . the only difference between the good guys and the bad guys is that we spend more time at target practice."

"What happened next?" Terry said.

"I crawled into the bedroom. Marisol was face down on the carpet. I turned her over, but she was dead. I just laid there, held her in my arms, and called 911."

"Do you have any idea why Martin would kill your wife?"

"Same reason he killed all the others. I don't know what that is, but Marilyn is lucky. She had to be next."

"You're probably right," Terry said. "Thank you for preventing that from happening."

"You're welcome, amigo, but a thank-you is not really necessary. It's what we do for each other."

"I know," Terry said. "I only wish I could've done it for you."

I don't believe Tony's account.

CHAPTER FORTY-TWO

Terry and I returned to the scene of the latest crime. We walked through the flip house one more time to see if the physical evidence jived with Tony's account of what happened. It did.

"We have everything we need to start writing up all this paperwork," I said.

"Everything but the stomach," Terry said. "Do you really want to go back to the office on a beautiful Sunday afternoon in September and spend the rest of the day hunched over a keyboard? Or would you rather go home and hunch over the woman you love?"

"As long as you put it that way," I said.

"Besides, the perp is dead. All we have to do is crank out a report for the mayor."

"Which Mel Berger said is due the day before yesterday."

"So we've already missed the deadline. One more day won't make a difference."

"Except for the fact that the later we are, the more we'll piss off Berger."

"There you go. Yet another excellent reason to put it off. Look, the case is wrapped up. We're not the guys who cracked it, but we can still celebrate."

No!

"On one condition," I said.

"You name it."

"We don't celebrate together."

I called Diana and told her about my sudden availability.

"Thanks for the warning," she said. "That gives me time to get rid of the other guy. Did you eat?"

"I had a bagel at ten o'clock."

"How about I pack some sandwiches and take you on a picnic?"

"Where?"

"It's a surprise."

"Knowing you," I said, "I'll bet it's quiet and serene and romantic."

"It's not," she said. "That's the surprise—it's a construction site."

We drove out to our new house. It's a sweet little three-bedroom on Hill Street in Santa Monica. It's in a perfect spot—close enough to the ocean so we can walk there, but far enough away that we can still afford the house. At the moment, it was suffering from a bad case of urban blight. Hal Hooper had left construction debris from one end of the property to the other. We found a clean patch of lawn and some late afternoon sunshine in the backyard, and spread out a blanket.

"Enjoy the rubble while you still can," she said. "Kemp starts the transformation tomorrow morning." She unpacked the picnic basket. "I have sandwiches, chips, and beer."

"I'll have the beer."

She handed me a bottle of Amstel Light.

"That's girl beer," I said.

"Maybe you can get your feminine side drunk, and take advantage of yourself." She pulled two sandwiches out of the cooler. "Do you like ham and Swiss?"

"What's my second choice?"

"Swiss and ham," she said handing me a sandwich. "Look, there's something you should know before we move in together. I'm not as domestic as Marilyn Biggs. I'm quite adept at putting packaged meat on presliced bread, and I'm relatively competent at applying heat to frozen items or certain cuts of beef. But fair warning—once we start living together there will be no fresh-baked figgy scones in your future."

"I'll settle for a roof, indoor plumbing, and a backyard that doesn't look like springtime in Fallujah."

"Are you nervous about buying this house together?"

"Totally," I said.

"Me too. Thank you for being honest."

"Actually, I'm lying. I'm not nervous at all, but I didn't think you'd believe me if I said no. Why are you nervous?"

"It's a girl thing."

"Try me," I said. "I'm drinking girl beer. Maybe I'll understand."

"I'm afraid of losing you."

"I cosigned the mortgage. Where would I go?"

"These murders really got to me. Three of the men you work with lost their wives. I spent a couple of hours listening to Marilyn the other night. She was petrified."

"She's safe now."

"I know, but my mind is filled with images of couples who get ripped apart. I haven't been this happy in a long time, so there's a little voice inside me that says something terrible is going to come along and destroy it."

"That's not a girl thing. It's called fear. Even manly-man cops get it. Can I give you three words of advice?"

"Carry a gun?"

"Let it go."

"That's easy for you to say. You have a gun."

We talked, drank two beers apiece, split a brownie for dessert, curled up on the blanket, and fell asleep. When we woke up, the sky was dusky, and the air was chilly.

"Want to go home?" I said.

"Yes," she said. "Our home. Grab the blanket. I have a key."

We went to the bedroom and spread the blanket on the floor under a section where Hooper had not yet gotten around to finishing the roof. Moonlight spilled gloriously through the beams.

"Our very own moonroof," I said. "I guess there are times when it pays off to have a bungling idiot for a contractor."

Diana stretched out and stared up at the sky. "Wow, this is some fantastic view. I can see a star."

"Make a wish," I said, wrapping my arms around her.

"Don't have to," she whispered. "I've already got everything I need."

CHAPTER FORTY-THREE

Terry and I got to the station at seven on Monday morning. Eileen Mulvey was sitting at the front desk.

Mulvey is one of the good guys. She knows everybody, hears everything, and goes out of her way to protect the detectives' asses. She also enjoys busting our balls.

"You're late for church, boys," she said. "Father Kilcullen has been looking for you since the crack of dawn."

"Good morning to you too, Officer Mulvey," Terry said. "My weekend was excellent. How was yours?"

She leaned forward across the desk. "Oh, I'm sorry, Detective Biggs. I didn't realize you wanted foreplay with your messages." She blew him a kiss. "This is the best I can do when I'm on duty. Maybe later we can hook up for pizza and a Coke."

"Thanks," Terry said. "And for the record, we're not late. He's early."

At 7:01 we were in Kilcullen's office. "It's about time," he said. "How're you doing on the mayor's paperwork?"

"Moving right along," Terry said. "We interviewed Tony yesterday."

"I'm putting him up for a Medal of Valor."

Neither Terry nor I said a word.

"No comment, Biggs?" Kilcullen said.

"No sir. I'm just grateful my wife no longer has to wear Kevlar to the supermarket."

"How about you, Lomax?"

"Lieutenant, I think it's a smart move for the mayor to offset the murders of three cop wives and a famous author by anointing a public hero."

"Very astute," Kilcullen said. "Mel Berger had the same thought."

"We've always thought of Mr. Berger as an ass-toot kind of guy," Terry said.

"Get the hell out of here and finish the paperwork," Kilcullen said.

Terry and I grabbed some coffee and sat down at our desks. He yanked open a drawer, rifled through some papers, and pulled one out. "Listen to this. It's from last year's medal ceremony. 'The Medal of Valor is awarded to officers who distinguish themselves by conspicuous bravery or heroism above and beyond the normal demands of police service.' Conspicuous bravery? Above and beyond? The guy's wife was in the house, he heard a shot, he ran in."

"You sound jealous," I said.

"There's more. 'To be awarded the Medal of Valor, an officer would have performed an act displaying extreme courage while consciously facing imminent peril.' Am I missing something here, Mike? How extreme is it for a cop to enter a house when he hears a gun go off? Do firemen get a medal every time they run into a burning building?"

"You're beyond jealous," I said. "Excuse me, but the message light on my phone is blinking. Kilcullen probably left it just in case Mulvey didn't catch us at the door."

I dialed the code to access my voice mail.

"You have one new message," the robotic phone-mail lady informed me.

I tapped the play key. The next voice I heard made the hairs on the back of my neck stand up.

"Good morning, Detective Lomax. This is Martin Sorensen."

For a split second I thought it might just be a lame joke, but this was not the kind of case the office pranksters would rag us about. I pressed the phone to my ear, and Sorensen continued.

"You told me to call you if I thought of anything else. It's almost midnight, but I figured this is your office phone, so I won't wake anybody up. I hope you're sitting down, because I found something that could crack this case wide open."

And then the phone went completely dead. There was no background noise, no hum, no Martin. All I could hear was the sound of my own breathing. I whispered into the silent phone. "Talk to me, dammit, talk to me."

And then he laughed. It was the evil cackle of a cartoon villain, except Martin's laugh was laced with alcohol.

"I guess I got your attention," he said. "I pushed the mute button, and gave you ten seconds of silence to build the suspense. Works every time."

Charlie once told me that Martin had a reputation for drinking and dialing, so I knew I wasn't his first victim, but I'd bet I was his last. He stopped talking again, but this time I could hear ice clinking as he sipped his drink.

"Anyway, I remembered that Nora left her laptop in the trunk of my car, so I decided to do a little digging, and guess what? It looks like Charlie Knoll will be getting a payday after all. And a pretty big one at that. That's all I'm going to say over the phone. I figure you won't get this message till Monday morning, so why don't you give me a buzz then? If I don't hear from you by around noon, I'll call you. Cheers."

This time he really did hang up, and the automaton message taker droned out the day and time of the call. *Friday, 11:49 P.M.* About eight hours before he killed Marisol Dominguez.

"You won't believe the voice mail I just got," I said to Terry.

"You look like you just heard from a Nigerian government official who will give you thirty million dollars if you help him transfer the funds of a deposed African leader out of the country. I get that all the time. Usually e-mail, but a phone call would be a refreshing—"

"Turn off the Comedy Channel and listen to this," I said.

I redialed my voice mail, put the phone to his ear, and watched his expressions. Surprise, followed by anticipation, then a scowl during the ten seconds of silence. When Martin started talking again, Terry mouthed the word asshole. When it was over he hung up.

"Holy shit," he said. "Dead man talking."

CHAPTER FORTY-FOUR

Muller, our resident computer genius, was at his desk tinkering with a Blackberry. He gave us the usual greeting.

"What's happening, dudes?"

"Rush job," I said. "We need you to hack into a computer for us."

"This is a treat. You guys don't usually generate emergencies till five minutes before I'm ready to go home."

"Can you drop what you're doing now?"

He held up the Blackberry. "Irv Ziffer in narcotics took this off a drug dealer. I'm cataloging everything in it. Names, numbers, e-mails, and some really piss-poor video game scores. It's totally tedious, and if one of you guys would call Ziff the Sniff and tell him that homicide trumps drug trafficking, yes, I'll drop what I'm doing."

"Deal," I said.

He dropped the Blackberry on his desk.

We filled him in on the details as we drove to Martin's apartment.

Nora's laptop was on his desk. Muller booted it up. "Sorensen said it was about a big payday. I'll start with her Quicken file."

He double clicked on the application. A window popped up and asked for a password.

"How long will it take you to figure that out?" Terry said.

"Normally, I'd say let's take it back to the office, and I can hack it in a couple of hours. But if you're in a hurry, I may have a faster way."

"Fast is good," Terry said. "Do it."

"Okay. It's experimental. I haven't done this before, so bear with me and try not to talk."

Muller closed his eyes and rested his fingers on the keyboard. And then he sat there.

He didn't move for nearly a minute. Finally, Terry couldn't keep quiet any longer. "What the hell are you doing?"

"Channeling," Muller said. "I'm getting in touch with Nora."

"Are you on crack?"

"No. I've been studying paranormal phenomena."

"You're yanking my chain."

"Really, I've been working with a medium. Don't knock it. If I can channel Nora, it's the fastest way to get her password."

"You're gonna conjure up the dead? What kind of bandwidth do you need for that? Mike, talk to him."

"I'm fascinated," I said. "Give him a minute. This is cool."

"You're both nuts," Terry said.

"I can tell you one thing," Muller said. "Nora is not happy about being a murder victim. She definitely wants to help."

"I can't believe this," Terry said.

Muller opened his eyes. "Dude, police departments all over the world hire clairvoyants and people with ESP. Is it so hard to believe that maybe one already is a cop? Trust me, it's gonna happen. Just give me some room."

He sat rubbing his fingers on the keyboard. Finally, he said, "the password is *crime pays*. No space between the two words."

"You sure about that, Kreskin?"

"I'd bet a dollar on it, Detective Biggs," Muller said.

"How about ten?" Terry said.

Muller came right back at him. "Make it twenty."

Terry, as smart as he is, is a lot less smart when he gets frustrated. And Muller had really pissed him off. He bit.

"It's a bet, geek boy," Terry said. "Move over. I'll type."

I tried not to smile, but I already knew the outcome. My grandfather once said to me, "Mike, if you're watching raindrops roll down a windowpane, and somebody bets you that one drop will beat the other to the bottom, you've got a fifty-fifty chance of winning. But if the same guy bets he can cut a deck of cards, turn over the jack of spades, and that jack will jump up and spit in your eye, don't get suckered, because, boy, that guy knows something you don't."

Terry poked at the keys, then hit return. Quicken welcomed Nora in.

"Son of a bitch. How the hell did you do that?"

"Ancient geek boy secret," Muller said. "Pay up."

Terry handed him the money.

"Fun's over, boys," I said. "Let's find something that looks like payday. Try starting with the last stuff Martin looked at."

"How about this?" Muller said. "On June thirtieth Nora Bannister gave her daughter Julia a million dollars. And since Julia is now deceased, I think that qualifies as a payday for Charlie."

"Are you sure?" Terry said.

"A one with six zeroes? Yeah, I'd bet a dollar on it, dude."

Terry ignored the dig. "Do you know what the rest of this crap means?"

The words *OTO gift* and *file form 709* were typed in the memo field.

"*OTO* is one time only," Muller said. "The IRS has a rule that says that once in your lifetime you can give away a million dollars, and nobody pays taxes. Not the recipient. Not you. All you have to do is file a gift tax return, which in case you haven't figured it out yet, is a form 709."

"I can barely afford the twenty bucks I just lost," Terry said. "How do you know about million-dollar gifts?"

"My wife's uncle is an accountant. I do computer trouble-shooting for him."

"So Nora gave Julia a million bucks, and it's tax free?"

"That's what it looks like. Actually, you can give the entire million to one person, or you can split it up, like give a hundred thousand apiece to ten people—whatever you want."

"Who do I have to know to sign up to be on the receiving end?" Terry said.

"At this point, I guess you could start sucking up to Charlie Knoll," Muller said.

"Funny, he didn't mention the million bucks yesterday when we talked to him," Terry said. "I think we should go back to Cedars and have another little chat with Detective Knoll."

"Drop me off at the office first," Muller said.

"Take the laptop back with you," I said. "Spend a few hours seeing what else you can find."

"Or maybe I can just conjure up Nora and save time," Muller said laughing.

"Kiss my ass," Terry said.

"Deal with it, Biggs. Today I'm the dog, and you're the hydrant."

"Okay, you conned me, but for my twenty bucks, are you at least gonna tell me how you came up with the password?"

"When Nora was working on a new murder mystery, did she ever ask for help?" Muller said.

"Constantly. She'd call or e-mail or even come to the station and bombard me with questions about guns, interrogation techniques, homicide procedure, you name it. Mike and I were always helping to make sure she got her facts straight."

"Yeah, Nora asked a lot of people for help," Muller said. An impish grin spread across his face. "Who do you think installed all the software on her laptop?"

CHAPTER FORTY-FIVE

We weren't ready to tell Kilcullen about Martin's voice mail from the grave or Charlie's million-dollar windfall. So we dropped Muller off at the station, told him to dig deeper into Nora's computer files, but to keep it under the radar. Then we drove toward Cedars-Sinai.

A few blocks shy of the hospital Terry pulled into Tully's, a Starbucks clone. We not only needed the caffeine, we needed to regroup before we met with Charlie.

The morning rush was over. Half a dozen loners were reading the paper or working on laptops. We ordered coffee and sat down in the back.

"What do you think?" I said.

"I think it was really nice of Martin to give us a lead after the case was solved, but he was totally dicking us around. Charlie didn't have a solid alibi for Julia's murder. Martin was making sure we knew Charlie also had a motive."

"There's only one small flaw in his logic," I said. "Why call and leave a message pointing the finger at Charlie, if he was planning to shoot Marisol the next morning while Charlie was still in the hospital?"

"Because he was drunk? Because he was a wannabe mystery writer who thought he was smarter than real cops? Because he was hoping to earn a special place in our Really Dumb Fucking Criminals file? Stop me when you hear something you like."

"Okay, I expect a mass murderer to lie to us," I said. "But why did Charlie lie? Remember what he said? If it was his case he'd follow the money, and he told us to start out by talking to Martin. What about the million dollars he's inheriting from his wife?

"Technically, he didn't lie about it," Terry said.

"No. He just left out a shitload of truth."

"This is getting messy," Terry said. "Charlie is a poker buddy, a fellow cop, someone we trusted. And now we find out that he was boning some chick, probably at the very same time his wife gets murdered. On top of that, Julia is a starving poet who suddenly comes into a million dollars right before she gets whacked, and Charlie collects that. And as soon as her funeral is over, he's going to get on a boat and sail to the other end of the world."

"What's your point?"

"Do you really want all that incriminating shit in a report that Mel Berger is going to use to kiss some political ass?"

"If it's not relevant to the case," I said, "we can leave it out."

"Of course it's not relevant. Charlie's innocent. He didn't kill anybody."

"Not Marisol, but are you convinced he didn't kill any of the others?"

"I'd bet a dollar on it, dude."

"Would you bet your reputation on it?" I said.

Terry sat back in his seat and mulled over the question. "I

don't have a reputation," he finally answered. "We do. And if you're not sure, then I'm not sure."

"Thanks," I said. "You may be right that technically Charlie didn't lie to us, but we're investigating a multiple homicide, and he held back two major pieces of information. Let's try to find out why."

Terry bought a cappuccino to go. "For Charlie," he said. "It feels less adversarial if you have coffee with a guy before you interrogate him. It's a little technique I learned from the mafia."

The cappuccino was still hot when we got to Charlie's hospital room. Unfortunately, his bed was cold.

"He checked out a few hours ago," the nurse said.

"I thought he was having an angiogram this morning," I said.

"He did," she said. "They took him at six. They didn't find anything wrong, so he left. Is there anything I can do for you?"

Terry handed her the cappuccino. "Here," he said. "Hold this till a cop comes."

We walked back to the car, and I dialed Charlie's cell phone.

"I'm out on Reggie's boat," he said.

"Can we get together and talk?"

"Can you swim?"

"Come on, Charlie."

"Look, Mike, my wife's murder is solved. I'm free to roam. So I'm out here where I can clear my head. What's so important you need talk about?"

"The million bucks."

He took a few seconds before he answered. "What about it?"

"You never mentioned it."

"It was a gift from Nora to Julia on her fortieth birthday. There was no reason to mention it. How'd you hear about it anyway?"

"Martin Sorensen."

"I thought he was dead."

"His anal-retentive legacy lives on," I said. "Living or dead, he's very efficient. Apparently you're going to inherit the million Nora gave your wife."

"I only inherit half a mill. One half is already mine. It's jointly held—invested in the market. You think I killed my wife for money we already had? You're way off base, Lomax."

"I didn't say that."

"I'm waiting for Julia and Nora to be released from the morgue, so I'm spending the day with Reggie because I've got funerals to plan, and he's got a lot of experience."

"Look, Charlie, I just want to—"

"I'm losing the signal, Detective Lomax. If you want to arrest me, I'll be back tonight. You can meet me at the dock."

He hung up.

"From what I could hear," Terry said, "that didn't go well, did it?"

I shook my head and closed my eyes. I remembered how I felt almost two years ago when my wife was newly dead. Angry. Non-communicative. Not willing to reach out for help, even when it was offered. If anyone could appreciate what Charlie was going through, it was me. I'd talk to him some other time.

But damned if I'd bring him cappuccino.

CHAPTER FORTY-SIX

We drove to the morgue. Eli Hand, our favorite pathologist, was assigned to do the autopsies on Marisol and Martin.

As a young man Eli trained as a rabbi, but he quickly realized he was missing one of the key qualities of an effective spiritual leader. He couldn't stand people.

At least, not the live ones. So he went to med school and has spent the last forty-plus years working with the dead.

"I don't understand why more doctors don't work with dead patients," he tells every new detective who steps up to his autopsy table. "They don't call you at home in the middle of the night. They don't have a shit fit if you show up late to cut out their vital organs. And they never ask for a second opinion." Then he gives one of those borscht-belt comic shrugs. "Sure, they smell bad, but it's a small price to pay."

He's a total curmudgeon, but a very funny one. The public would be horrified to hear how much laughter comes out of his autopsy room. He's known around the morgue as the Jewish Cutup.

"It's going to take most of the day to do both of them," Eli said. "You guys need to stay for the whole thing?"

Normally, Terry and I are in the room for the entire autopsy, in case we have to testify in court. But there would be no trial for Martin Sorensen, at least not here on Earth.

"We've got a lot to do," I said. "Why don't we stay long enough to get a top line. We can read the rest of the gory details in your report."

"Fine by me," Eli said, walking us to the steel table where Marisol was waiting to be dissected.

For all his crustiness, Eli still has the compassion of a rabbi.

"Such a beautiful young woman," he said after he confirmed that Marisol was shot in the head with a low-velocity hollow-point .22. "Same basic wound that killed the others. Such a tragedy. It's a *shonda*."

Then his lips moved silently. It was a Hebrew prayer for the dead. He never says it out loud. I once asked him why.

"You know what happens if someone who works for the county gets caught drinking on the job?" he said. "They send you to rehab. But if you get caught praying, they fire you on the spot, because they know there's no cure."

His initial findings on Martin Sorensen confirmed Tony's story. "Talk about overkill," Eli said. "Any one of these bullets would have done the trick. But, in this guy's case, I'm glad Detective Dominguez made triple sure."

To his credit, Eli also mouthed a prayer for Martin. His philosophy: let God sort them out.

We got back to the office at 4:00 P.M.

"The lieutenant told me to remind you about the paperwork," Wendy said.

"Where is he?"

"He's out at an antiterrorist meeting, but he'll be back. He's been getting pressure from city hall to close up this case."

"City hall?" Terry said. "That's where all the real terrorists hang out."

We checked in with Muller.

"Just the cops I wanted to see," he said.

"You've got 'interesting news' written all over your face," I said.

"Maybe. You know Gaffney McDonough, right?"

McDonough is a baby-faced detective who retired from LAPD and took the path of least resistance. He became a PI. Now he spends most of his time peeping through windows watching middle-aged rich guys get their knobs polished by girls with a chest full of silicone and a head full of dreams. LA is full of opportunities. You just have to find your own special niche.

"The Gaffer?" I said. "He's a good guy. Terry and I have been known to reach out to him every now and then. Especially when we need to dig up some sensitive information, and the judge won't cooperate unless we can show cause. A private cop has a lot more latitude."

"Right," Terry said. "McDonough bends the law, they call it free enterprise. We do it, and it's a felony."

"Tell me about it," Muller said. "Hacking into the Pentagon's mainframe is cake. Getting a warrant is the bitch. Anyway, Gaffney McDonough's name pops up a bunch of times on Nora Bannister's Quicken file. She was paying him a literary consulting fee."

"Paying?" Terry said. "Nora picked our brains for free, but I guess Gaffney does nothing for nothing. How much was he charging?"

"Most of the payments are small," Muller said. "He got six consults in the past year. Five hundred, seven-fifty, four and a quarter, ten thousand . . ."

"Run that last one by us again," I said.

"That's what I thought," Muller said. "The last check was for ten Gs. Nora cut it two weeks before Jo Drabyak was murdered. Unless Nora's next book stars Gaffney McDonough, Private Investigator, I'm wondering what kind of literary consulting he was doing for ten thousand bucks."

"We should definitely give him a ring," I said.

Muller handed me a piece of paper. "I just happen to have his number handy."

I called.

"We can do it in a couple of hours," McDonough said. "I'll call you back with a time and place."

There was no sense driving back to the Valley, so we decided to hang out and work on our report.

Kilcullen came back at seven.

"You guys got the paperwork wrapped up?" he said.

"Almost. We're waiting for one last autopsy report," I lied. "Plus there are a few loose ends."

"This case is locked up tighter than a witch's butt crack," Kilcullen said. "What do you mean by loose ends?"

"Martin Sorensen left me a middle-of-the-night voice mail. I picked it up this morning. Julia's murder is going to leave Charlie a much richer man. A million dollars richer."

"His wife dies, he gets her money," Kilcullen said. "Who gives a shit? Sorensen was yanking your dick. The case is done, finished, kaput. We've got a killer. We've got a hero cop who put him out of business. Are you jealous because Tony is front page, and you're staying late to crank out the paperwork? Get over it."

"There are a few things we'd still like to look into," I said.

"Perhaps you didn't get my drift. Let me spell it out for you," he said. "N-O."

"No?"

"As my good friend and classmate from the academy, Frank Faluotico, is fond of saying . . . and I quote . . . 'When dead bodies stop piling up in LA, you can go back and take another look.' But since we've got fresh ones coming in every day, finish the paperwork and move on to the next assignment."

He turned around and walked out the door.

"Do you realize that he only came back here to check up on us?" I said. "He walked in, got in my face, tore me a new one, and walked out."

"I couldn't believe it," Terry said. "All these years I thought he only had a hard-on for me."

CHAPTER FORTY-SEVEN

Twenty minutes later Gaffney called. "There's an Italian restaurant on Melrose between Alta Vista and Poinsettia. It's called Angeli."

"You buying?" I said.

"Sorry, guy," he said. "We're not eating there. We're just sitting in a van half a block away, gathering incriminating evidence on some lying, cheating bastard husband who is eating there."

"Where are you parked?"

"Northwest corner of Poinsettia. It's a white Chevy Express tricked out to look like one of those cable TV vans."

It was easy to find. But even if there had been a dozen white vans parked on that corner, we could have picked out Gaffney's. The logo on the side said it all: *Fidelity Communications.*

Inside, the van was part living room, part CNN control booth. Gaffney and an assistant were at a command console, staring at a cluster of monitors. He took off his headset and pointed to two leather chairs. "Have a seat. It's not easy to stand up in this place. Good to see you guys."

"What are we watching?" Terry said, pointing at one of the monitors.

"Same old soap opera crap. Rich Hollywood asshole, cheating on his devoted wife, who will in the very near future wind up with all of the children, half of the money, and none of the asshole. We've got one camera in the van pointed at the restaurant window. You can't see much detail, but I still get a clean picture of the couple I'm tailing."

"You're lucky they sat at that table," I said.

"Let's just say the hostess is lucky I paid her a hundred to sit them at that table." He smiled. "But then you knew that, didn't you?"

"Actually I did, but I don't know how you're getting that close-up on the other monitor. Where's the second camera?"

"There's a couple at the next table. Friends of mine, Matt and Daniella Smith. She use to work vice for LAPD, but she left to become a pastry chef."

"Vice and pastry," Terry said. "Your buddy Matt is a lucky guy."

"Anyway, Daniella's purse has a pinhole camera and an omni-directional mic. We just sit in the van and record it for posterity. When the target and the bimbette leave drunk and horny, they'll go back to her apartment, which we've already wired."

"How do you know ahead of time where they're going?"

"Cell tap," he said. "Did I mention that Matt is a supergeek? So, how can I help you boys?"

I pointed at the young guy sitting at the console listening to the dinner chatter at Angeli on his headset.

"That's my assistant, Todd Hoza," McDonough said. "You can trust him. His nickname is Iwazaru."

"If only we spoke Japanese," I said.

"You know the three monkeys—see no evil, hear no evil, speak no evil? They have names. Iwazaru is the one who speaks no evil. Todd sees and hears a lot of funky shit, but his lips are sealed."

"Even so, Gaff . . ."

"I get it," he said. "This is hush-hush police business. Top secret."

"Actually, this is not a department call. Terry and I are flying under the radar, which make it hush-hush personal business."

"No problem," he said. He pulled the headset away from Hoza's right ear. "Hey, desk monkey, what's happening?"

"He's starting with the grilled eggplant. She's having the roast beet salad."

"Besides that. Any friction? Any bickering? Any anything?"

"No sir. They're happy as clams," Hoza said. "Which is what I would have ordered."

"You'll have to settle for pizza. Albano's is across the street. Bring us back a large pie. You guys okay with mushrooms and extra cheese?"

"That's fine," Terry said. "Just tell Iwazaru to speak no pepperoni."

"All right," McDonough said, once Hoza was gone. "It's just the three of us under the Cone of Silence. You want to talk about that multiple homicide you just cracked, right?"

"You knew most of the principals," I said.

"That Sorensen dude always struck me as weird," Gaffney said. "Kinky weird, but not shoot-you-upside-the-head weird."

"We have a few questions about Nora Bannister," I said.

"Nice woman. Damn shame."

"Why did she pay you ten grand?"

"She didn't."

"Gaff, according to her financial records—"

"Mike, I know the money came from Nora's checking account, but she wasn't the client. Marisol Dominguez was."

He blindsided me. *"Marisol* was your client?"

"She hired me to tail her old man."

"You were following Tony? Why?"

"The usual. WD̲S̲." He smiled, knowing I'd never figure it out. "Wandering Dick Syndrome. It's my bread and butter."

"There's an unfortunate metaphor," Terry said. "Question: if Marisol hired you, how come Nora paid you?"

"Lot of wives want to spy on their hubbies, but they don't want to get tripped up by writing checks from the joint checking account. So they funnel the money from an outside source. In this case, Martin Sorensen worked it out with Marisol. The way I understand it, she was going to pay Nora back from her profits in their real estate deal. It happens a lot. Somebody hires me, somebody else makes the payments. Whatever. If the check clears, the van rolls."

"What reason did Marisol give you for following her husband?"

"You gotta understand that some of these angry babes don't always tell you the whole truth and nothing but the truth when they hire you," he said. "But in her case she told me he asked for a divorce. She had no idea why, so she hired me to find out who he's banging."

"And?"

"As far as I could tell, nobody."

"Nobody?" Terry said. "Maybe you just didn't catch him."

"Hey, Detective, I can smell sex from a hundred yards away."

"There's some more imagery I could do without," Terry said. "I wasn't saying you couldn't catch him. I'm just saying Tony is smart. Maybe he saw you shadowing him."

"He didn't. Ever. And I dogged that guy on and off for a full month. Tony Dominguez wasn't banging anyone," Gaffney said. "Including his old lady. Which, between you and me, was his loss. She was one hot tamale."

"Do you know the other two cops whose wives got murdered?" Terry asked. "Drabyak and Knoll."

"No," Gaffney said. "The only cops' wives I worked for were Marisol Dominguez and yours. But I gave your old lady her money back, because I followed you for a week, and I realized you couldn't find your dick with a flashlight and a pair of tweezers."

"All right, all right," Terry said. "I take it back. You're the world's greatest hound dog hunter."

"I'm glad you came around to my way of thinking," Gaffney said. "I'd bet my license that Tony Dominguez wasn't having an affair. That said, he was up to a lot of strange shit, but him being a cop, I could never tell if it was personal-peculiar or just the kind of covert ops you gotta do on the job."

"Strange shit like what?"

"Like meeting people on the sly. But who knows? It could be cop stuff. Like when you go out to pump a CI, you don't sit down for coffee at Starbucks. You sneak off and talk in private."

"Can you give us a specific?" I said.

"I can do better than that. I can give you a pound of specifics." He opened a drawer in the console and pulled out a folder.

"This is a log of all the places I tailed Tony to. It's an interest-

ing collection of venues," he said, "but none of them look like a romantic tryst."

He swiveled in his chair, tapped on a keyboard, and a printer
started humming. "I'll run you off a copy. If it helps you guys,
good. I'm not one of those guys who gets all hung up on that
client-confidentiality shit. Especially since my client is dead."

He reached into a drawer and came up with a handful of
DVDs. "And if you really want to knock yourselves out, I've got
video on Tony Dominguez." He handed them over to Terry. "You
watch him, Detective Biggs, and tell me if I missed any secret girlfriends."

"All this plus pizza," Terry said. "We should come here more
often."

"Thanks, Gaff," I said. "You've been a big help."

He smiled, and I could make out the wrinkles that were slowly
encroaching on his baby face.

"I don't think so," he said. "I saw your reaction when I told
you Marisol hired me to tail Tony. You're trying to dot your i's and
cross your t's for the department, but for some reason you're off the
clock tonight and flying solo. Now I give you this new information,
and instead of tying things up in a neat little package, it opens up a
whole new can of oh shit. But whether I helped or not, it's always a
pleasure to work with you guys. Plus, you know what they say in
the surveillance biz: one hand washes the other."

Terry pointed at the monitor. The guy Gaffney was tailing had
dipped his finger in his wine and touched it to the girlfriend's lips.
We watched as she leaned in and sucked it off.

"And seeing the kind of sleaze you have to deal with," Terry
said, "I'll bet your hands need a lot of washing."

CHAPTER FORTY-EIGHT

"Gaffney is right," Terry said, as we drove home.

"You mean that crack about you not being able to find your dick with a flashlight and a pair of tweezers?"

"Cute. No, our boss is pacing the halls with a Case Closed stamp in his fist, and we keep coming up with new information that says something stinks, keep it open. First, Charlie tried to get over on us, now it looks like Tony was lying through his teeth about being the happiest married man in the kingdom."

"And if you go back over your notes, I'm sure you'll find Nora lied, Marisol lied, and Martin lied. That's what people do," I said. "They lie to cops. Didn't we just lie to Kilcullen? Hell, I do it every time I tell you you're funny."

"You're right," he said. "Those DVDs of Gaffney following Tony will take us forever to wade through. Why don't I just toss them out the window?"

"That's one option," I said.

"You got a better one?"

"We could run them over to Muller's house and get him started on looking at them."

"Call him, and tell him we're on the way."

I called Muller's home number. His wife, Annetta, answered.

"Robert's not home," she said. "He's got a gig tonight. He's playing at Spazio on Ventura Boulevard."

When he's not hacking computers or pretending to conjure up the dead, Muller plays jazz piano. He's not just good, he's good enough to play at Spazio, one of the top jazz supper clubs in the Valley, maybe even all of LA. As luck would have it, it's in Sherman Oaks, about two minutes from Terry's house.

He was finishing up a set when we got there. We told him what was going on, gave him the DVDs, then ordered a couple of beers and sat through his next set. It was a great way to unwind from the day.

We got home at eleven. Marilyn and Diana were in the kitchen eating ice cream. Actually, Marilyn was eating. Diana was keeping her company.

"You okay?" Terry said.

Marilyn waved a spoon at him. "Nothing a half gallon of Rocky Road can't cure."

"What's bothering you—I mean, besides the obvious?"

"Do you think Martin would have killed me next?"

"I don't know, baby. I don't even know why Martin killed Marisol."

"Maybe she figured out that he killed the others," Marilyn said. "And once he realized she was on to him, he had to shut her up."

"Her husband is a cop," Diana said. "If she suspected Martin, she would have told Tony."

"Don't bet on it," Marilyn said, getting up and putting her empty bowl in the dishwasher.

"What is that supposed to mean?" Terry said.

Marilyn hesitated. "Well, seeing how she's dead, it's not going to hurt anyone to let the cat out of the bag. Marisol was having Tony followed."

Terry and I both came up with the same knee-jerk response. "You knew about that?"

"Well, that sure hit a nerve," she said. "Yes, I've known it for a while." She went back to the table and ate another spoonful of ice cream direct from the container.

"How did you know," Terry said, "and why didn't you tell me?"

"Martin told me, but he swore me to secrecy. Marisol suspected there was another woman."

"There wasn't," Terry said. "We just talked to the PI she hired. Marisol claimed that Tony wanted out of the marriage, but there was no other woman."

"Ha!" Marilyn said. "There's always another woman."

"I wish we could find her," Terry said. "Ninety-nine percent of the guys who ask for walking papers have another woman to walk to. And since there doesn't seem to be one, the question is, why was Tony leaving her?"

"I don't like to speak ill of the dead," Marilyn said, "but in case you hadn't noticed, Marisol was a total bitch."

"Or maybe she just had her own reasons for tailing him," Terry said, "and she invented the affair as a cover."

"If only I actually cared," Marilyn said. She put the lid on the Rocky Road. "Are you coming to bed, or do I have to take this ice cream with me for emotional support?"

"Give me five more minutes with Mike, and I'll be in."

"I'm putting a clock on it," Marilyn said. "Any longer than five minutes, and the two of you can sleep with each other."

"I'm going to bed too," Diana said to me. "I don't have a five minute rule. Just show up."

The two women left.

"I'm going to bed too," I said.

"You don't want to talk this through just a little more?"

"Terry, we're not going to resolve anything in five minutes. And I'm not sleeping with you."

"The case is closed, but there are still a lot of unanswered questions."

"I think they had the same problems with the Kennedy assassination."

"I'll make you a deal," he said. "If you look me straight in the eye and tell me to drop the case and stop being such an obsessive-compulsive asshole, I will."

"Fair enough," I said, looking him straight in the eye. "I want you to drop the case and stop being such an obsessive-compulsive asshole."

He looked hurt. He hadn't expected me to give up that easily.

"Then tomorrow morning, when you wake up," I said, "you can reopen the investigation, because if you weren't such an obsessive-compulsive asshole, I'd start looking for a new partner. Good night."

CHAPTER FORTY-NINE

"I feel human again," I said to Terry as we got into the car the next morning. "Six hours' sleep, a hot shower, and two cups of coffee work wonders."

"It's all part of the service at Chez Biggs. Picking up where we left off last night, how much longer do you think we can stall Kilcullen on the paperwork?"

"Actually, Diana had an interesting idea last night," I said.

Terry smirked. "So did I, but by the time I got my clothes off and climbed into bed, Marilyn was snoring like a bull moose with a deviated septum."

"I'm being serious."

"Me too. Do you know how much sexual tension builds up after spending the day talking about how hot Marisol was?"

"Diana made me realize that we're swimming in uncharted waters, and we can't see the forest for the trees."

Terry put on his tough cop voice. "Back away from the metaphors, Lomax. I'm with the Logic Police. Plain English, or I'll shoot."

"Think about it," I said. "The pressure is always on us to close a case. This time, we're slow dancing, hoping to keep it open. But what if we finished the report real fast? What would happen next?"

"We'd get assigned another dead body. It's kind of what we do, and like the boss said, there's never a shortage."

"But what happens to the paperwork we turn in?" I said.

"The DA's office reads it, blesses it, closes up the case, and feeds the report to the political piranhas."

"Exactly. Cops don't close cases. District attorneys do. Unless . . ." I stopped and let it hang.

"Give me a break, Mike. Dramatic pauses are worse than metaphors. Spit it out."

"Unless the DA who is assigned to the report zeroes in on the same inconsistencies that bother us. The case would stay open."

He didn't say anything, which with Terry is always a good sign.

"Of course, we'd need a real smart deputy DA," I said. "Someone we can trust, who will send us back to dig deeper, instead of accusing us of sloppy police work."

"Someone like Anna DeRoy," he said.

"Now you're getting the hang of this uncharted-waters thing," I told him.

Five hours later we walked into Kilcullen's office with the good news.

"The report is done," I said.

"About time," he said. "Let me take a quick look."

"Anne Batchelor is typing it up as we speak."

Anne is a civilian employee and the fastest typist in the department, maybe even on the planet.

"Good call," Kilcullen said. "That'll move it along. Last night I thought you were going to start dragging your heels on me."

"We were just trying to be totally buttoned up," I said. "With all these politicians looking over our shoulder, we didn't want anything to come back and kick us in the ass."

He snorted out a laugh. "*My* shoulder. *My* ass."

We laughed along with him.

"As soon as it's typed, we'll hand-carry it over to the DA's office," I said.

"Let's just hope they assign it to someone good," Terry said.

Kilcullen looked up. The possibility that the DA's office could somehow assign it to the wrong lawyer and screw up the process had never crossed his mind. "You would think those guys know this is a hot potato," he said.

"I'll tell you who would be right for this," I said. "Anna DeRoy. She's fast, she's smart, and she won't let you give the mayor anything less than perfect. If we're lucky, she'll catch the case."

"Fuck luck," Kilcullen said, picking up the phone. "I'll call ahead and make sure they assign it to DeRoy."

A half hour later we were standing outside Anna's office. Her door was shut. Terry knocked. "It's your two favorite cops," he yelled in.

"Cagney and Lacey?" Anna yelled back.

"Wrong gender," Terry said.

"Batman and Robin?"

Terry opened the door. "Oh, you were so close," he said. "We're the other ambiguously-gay dynamic duo."

"I've been expecting you," Anna said. "Your boss just called my boss, and I've been told to put this on the fast track. Congratulations on solving it."

I handed her the report. "We didn't solve it," I said, "and we're not sure it's really solved."

"In that case," she said, handing the report back to me, "come back when it's *really* solved."

"It's not that simple," I said, shutting the door. "One of the victims hired a PI to spy on her husband. Her business partner, Martin Sorensen, helped her pay the fee, so that hubby wouldn't catch on. But it turns out Sorensen is the killer, and now he's dead."

"Who's the wayward husband?" DeRoy asked.

"Tony Dominguez, the hero cop who shot and killed Sorensen."

"Well, isn't that nice and messy," she said. "Does your report get to the bottom of that little triangle?"

"No. Last night the PI gave us the video he shot when he tailed Dominguez, but we haven't had time to go through it."

"There are a bunch of other red flags," Terry said. "Like one victim's husband suddenly inherited a million dollars from his wife. He and one of the other husbands are planning to take a one-way trip to the other side of the world."

"I'm missing something," she said. "Explain to me why you're rushing to close this case."

"We're not. Everyone else is."

"You bastards," she said. "You don't have the balls to stand up to your boss, so you come over here and make me the heavy?"

"Standing up to Kilcullen won't work," I said. "There's a shortage of testicles going all the way up the chain of command. Nobody is willing to tell city hall that we need more time, so we decided to finish the report and put it into the system. That'll keep the bureaucrats at bay for a day or two while we try to dig up some more information."

"So even though you know the case is full of holes, you want me to spend time wading through it, write up my decision, and then bounce it back."

"It's not what we want. It's the way the system works. Four members of cops' families got killed. One of those cops shot and killed the bad guy." I held out the report. "It's all nice and tidy, ready to be signed, sealed, and archived."

"And what makes you think I won't just sign off on it?" she said.

"Because, Deputy DA DeRoy, you're one of the few people in this flawed fucking system who actually has balls."

She took the report from my hand. Terry and I left without saying another word.

CHAPTER FIFTY

We spent the afternoon catching up on some of the paperwork we had let slide for ten days since Jo Drabyak was murdered. Around four o'clock Charlie Knoll showed up.

"I'm turning myself in," he said. "I tried to escape on that houseboat, but it doesn't navigate too good once you get past Redondo Beach. If I'm ever going to sail to Australia, I'm gonna have to help Reggie buy something a lot more seaworthy. Especially now that I'm rich."

"How you feeling?" I said.

"The good news is my heart is okay. The bad news is my wife is still dead. You schmucks really thought I killed her?"

"You inherited a lot of money," I said. "All I did was ask."

"You didn't ask. You accused."

"Sorry," I said. "But once we found out about the money, we had to wonder why you never mentioned it."

"You're a cop, Charlie," Terry said. "Didn't you ever ask an innocent person a question that pissed them off?"

"It happens all the time," he said. "I'll be working a burglary, and I'll say to the victim, 'Are you insured for that?' And they'll look at me and say, 'Are you accusing me of stealing my own diamond ring for the insurance money?' Usually that's not what I'm getting at. But sometimes, that's what's actually going down."

"So tell us why you never mentioned the million," Terry said.

"God's honest truth, Thursday when it all happened, I was in shock. It never crossed my mind. The next day in the hospital, it finally dawned on me that I had all this money, but I felt like I had it before Julia was killed. We shared everything. It wasn't half mine, half hers. It was all ours. We weren't even thinking about spending it. It was tucked away, invested. I knew it wasn't relevant to the case. But I also knew if it got public that I had a million bucks, everyone would look at me different."

"Different how?"

"Different like maybe old Charlie Knoll killed his wife for the money," he said. "And then even after you found out Martin killed her, I was still worried about people saying, 'Hey, Charlie is rich. Maybe I can hit him up for a few bucks.' All I was doing was protecting my privacy. It's none of anybody's business how much money I have."

"Does your girlfriend know?" Terry said.

"That's low, Biggs."

"Charlie, you were with another woman the night your wife was killed. We have a right to ask."

"No you don't," he said. "You had a right to ask, before you had the killer. But now, who I was with that night is none of your business. The case is closed."

"The case is not officially closed," Terry said. "It's being reviewed by the DA's office. What if they call and say, 'Charlie Knoll had a motive. Maybe he paid Martin Sorensen to kill Julia and Nora.'"

"And Jo? And Marisol?" Charlie laughed loud and long. It took a good fifteen seconds till it petered out to a chuckle.

"What's so funny?" Terry said.

"You're supposed to be half of the hotshot homicide team, and you're asking dumb questions that make you sound like a rookie. Let's me ask you a question, Biggs. If you were going to kill your wife and all of her partners, would you hire Martin Sorensen? He was a cocky son of a bitch who thought he was better than everyone he associated with, and once he started drinking, you'd have to worry that he'd try to impress people by telling them he was a gun for hire. So if the DA's office calls, just tell them that Detective Knoll might be stupid enough to kill his wife for the money he already had, but he's not that dumb that he would hire Martin Sorensen to help him."

"I think we've had enough questions," I said.

"Good, because I didn't really come back to turn myself in," he said. "I'm here to clean out my desk."

"You a hundred percent sure you want to quit?" I said.

"No. Did you know what you wanted five days after Joanie died?" he said. "The only thing I'm sure of right now is that Nora's and Julia's funerals are on Thursday. That's about as far ahead as I can plan."

"We'll be there," I said.

"Don't come as cops," he said, his voice cracking with emotion. "Come as friends."

CHAPTER FIFTY-ONE

Around five o'clock Muller stopped by my desk. "I'm going to catch an early movie," he said, holding one of Gaffney's DVDs in his hand.

"Is it any good?" I said.

"A lot of it is boring, but there's one part that is definitely worth the price of admission. Would you and your friend Detective Biggs care to join me?"

"Where?" I said.

He looked around the squad room. "Anywhere but here. Do you have a DVD player over at your place?"

"I don't even have a place," I reminded him.

We decided that Muller would follow us to Terry's house, so we could watch Gaffney McDonough's video without anybody watching us. We were crawling along on the Ventura Freeway when Big Jim called my cell.

"Mike, I've got good news," he said. "You officially have a roof over your head."

"And how do you come to know this?" I said.

"Kemp and I just finished."

"Kemp and *you?*" I said. "Dad, what the hell were you doing on my roof?"

"If that's a crack about my weight," he said, "I don't think it's particularly funny."

"It's not a crack about your weight. It's a crack about your meddling. What are you doing helping Kemp?" *I hate Jim.*

"I had some free time."

I could feel my blood pressure rising.

"For your information," he said, "I didn't climb on the roof. I hauled a lot of the roofing material for him. Saved him hours. Then I got my buddy Pete to come over."

"Who the hell is Pete?"

"You know Pete Estes. He and his wife Karen sometimes go bowling with me and Angel. Pete's an excavator, so I got him to bring over his Kubota."

"His what?"

"His Kubota. It's a skid steer, you know, like a tractor. I can't believe I've been in the transportation business all my life, and I have a son who has no idea what a Kubota is."

"Well, I can't believe I've been in law enforcement all my life, and I have a father who has no idea what a boundary is. Dad, why did you get involved?"

"Because the renovation has been going slow, because you and Diana want to move in, and because I'm the kind of father who thought his son might appreciate a little help."

"Dad, I do appreciate it—"

"Don't mention it," he said. "That's what fathers are for."

"Let me finish. I appreciate it, but in the future—"

He cut me off. "You don't have to finish. I get it, I get it. Your father tries to help you out, lend you a hand, and it pisses you off. No good deed shall go unpunished, right, Michael?"

"Dad, it's not a good deed if you get involved in my life without an invitation. When I want your help, I'll ask."

"No you won't," he said.

"What is that supposed to mean?"

"I know you. You're proud, just like your mother. You don't like asking for help. And me, I don't like sitting around waiting to be asked. That's why when I found those two dead women the other night, I called you straight out. I didn't wait for an invitation."

"You're comparing apples and—"

"Okay, okay. Spare me the lecture. I just want you to know that Pete cleaned up all the rubble in the backyard, and we took it to the dump. Why don't you tell Diana? I'm sure at least she'll have a little gratitude."

"I'm sure she will," I said.

"Do you want Pete Estes's phone number?" he said.

"What for?"

"To thank him. He did the work as a friend. No charge."

"Dad, I'm busy. Thank him for me."

"Now you're talking. I'd be glad to thank Pete for you. You see how easy it is to ask me for a favor? Call me if you need anything else."

He hung up.

I looked at Terry, who was grinning.

"That was my father," I said.

"I could tell," he said. "But if I hadn't heard you call him Dad, I'd swear you were back on speaking terms with the contractor from hell."

CHAPTER FIFTY-TWO

The house was quiet. Emily and Sarah were both in their rooms, Diana was working late, and Marilyn was out shopping for something to wear to Nora's and Julia's funeral.

"Don't ask me why she won't wear the same black dress she wore last week to Jo's funeral," Terry said. "She shops like she's going to a prom."

Muller brought a laptop, and we locked ourselves in Terry's office with a bag of chips and a six-pack.

"Before we get started, I'd like to propose a toast," Terry said, raising a beer can. "We've bent a few rules in our day, but this is a new plateau, even for us. Here's to exploring uncharted waters, and not getting caught."

The three of us drank to operating outside the department's authority.

"What we have here," Muller said, holding up the DVDs McDonough had given us, "is two weeks in the relatively uneventful personal life of Tony Dominguez. McDonough tailed him mostly nights and weekends, and it's basically a snore. Except for this."

He put one of the DVDs in the computer and jumped to the chapter he wanted. "You ever been to the Roadium?"

"I was raised in the Bronx," Terry said. "We didn't have too many cowboys."

"Roadi*um*," Muller said. "It's a monstrous open-air market on Redondo Beach Boulevard in Torrance. They've got hundreds and hundreds of merchants, spread out over God knows how many acres."

"I've never been there either," I said. "What do they sell?"

"Food, clothes, electronics, hardware, everything, and any-thing," he said. "If you've got crap to sell, they rent you a booth, and presto, you're in retail."

"It sounds like Wal-Mart without the charm," Terry said.

"Not the kind of place Tony would go to," I said.

"And yet," Muller said, "this is where Detective Dominguez's life gets real interesting."

He hit play and there was a very clear image of Tony wearing jeans, an unbuttoned flannel shirt over a black T-shirt, and a Dodg-ers baseball cap. The camera followed him as he wandered aim-lessly from one booth to another.

"He's not shopping," Terry said. "He's blending in."

"And he's checking to see if anyone is watching him," Muller said.

"McDonough is damn good," I said. "Tony has no idea he's be-ing taped."

"Neither did you," Muller said. "One of the other DVDs has footage of Tony and you guys on Reggie's boat. Okay, pay attention to what's coming up."

We watched Tony stroll from one booth to the other.

"He's not even pretending to check out the merchandise," Terry said. "He's only looking up at the booth numbers. B-5, B-6, B-7."

Tony weaved through the crowd a little faster. And then he stopped.

"B-14," I said.

Terry raised his hand. "Bingo."

The booth was cluttered with racks and tables filled with CDs, tapes, and albums. Tony went to a bin, pretended to browse, then pulled out a CD. He took it to the vendor, and reached in his pocket to pay for it.

Muller froze the image on the screen. "Check it out," he said.

Tony was handing the vendor a thick white envelope.

"A lot of places don't take American Express," Terry said.

Muller released the pause button, and the vendor deftly took the envelope and stuffed it in his pocket. He put the CD in a bag, handed it to Tony, and walked out of frame. The camera panned to the right and caught up with the vendor as he approached a large gray van parked just outside the booth. He knocked on the side door. It slid open, and a young man cautiously stepped out.

"Freeze it again," I said.

He did, and we studied the two men. They were both Mexican. The vendor was so out of shape, he could have been anywhere between forty and sixty. His face was covered with a week's worth of gray stubble, and his body was evidence of a lifetime's worth of bad eating habits. The other guy was in his mid-twenties, wiry build, dark skin, dark hair, and dark eyes that telegraphed fear. He had a knapsack on his back and a snake tattoo on his right arm.

"If you're interested, that's Quetzalcóatl, the feathered serpent," Muller said. "He's some kind of an Aztec god."

"That's good to know if we ever go out looking for the snake," Terry said. "Who's the kid?"

"Don't know," Muller said. "Let me grab a screen shot."

"Grab a few," I said. "Including the guy who took the payoff."

Muller captured the images, then hit *play*. Tony and the young Mexican exchanged a few words, then they started walking.

"Watch this," Muller said.

Tony walked casually through the flea market, with the kid just behind him. They were heel to toe, pretending not to be together. At one point they passed a trash can, and Tony tossed the bag with the CD in the garbage.

"I guess he's not that into music after all," Terry said.

"This picture is crystal clear," I said. "Why don't they have surveillance cameras this good at 7-Eleven?"

"Or the women's dressing rooms at Nordstrom," Terry said.

"McDonough is working with a top-of-the-line digital camera," Muller said. "Based on the angle, I'm guessing it's at about six feet, maybe inside a baseball cap."

We watched as Tony and the kid entered the parking lot.

"Big finale coming up," Muller said.

"Don't ruin the ending for us," Terry said.

They walked for another thirty seconds, then stopped at a late-model Lexus sedan. The young Mexican got in the back. Tony shut the rear door, and watched the car drive off, as the camera zoomed in tight on the license plate. Muller froze the picture, and I wrote it down.

"That's basically it," Muller said. "There's another minute of Tony walking back to his car and driving off in a different direction."

"And Gaffney made it sound like there was nothing interesting on the tape," Terry said.

"From his perspective, there really isn't," I said. "He was looking to catch Tony shacking up with some woman. As far as he could tell, this was police business."

"I went through Gaffney's notes," Muller said. "He logged it in as 'Target paying off an informant.'"

"Since when does LAPD pay off CIs by slipping them envelopes and picking them up in sixty-thousand-dollar cars?" Terry said.

"Did you trace the license plate?" I asked.

"Umm, that was a little dicey," Muller said. "Since we're supposed to be flying under the radar, I didn't want to do it from the office."

"No problem," Terry said.

He took out his cell and dialed. "Yeah, good evening dispatch, this is Detective Terry Biggs. My partner and I are in this real nasty neighborhood in Compton, and there's a car parked here that costs more than any of the houses on the block. It might be stolen. Can you run the plates for me?"

He pushed the speaker button on the phone, and we waited.

The dispatcher came back a minute later. "Well, you're right about one thing, Detective," she said. "It doesn't belong to anyone in Compton. But so far, it's not reported stolen. You might want to check with the owner to see if it's missing."

"Good idea," Terry said. "You got a name?"

"The car is registered to a Dr. Ford Jameson, Beverly Hills."

the shrink!

CHAPTER FIFTY-THREE

The next morning we called Wendy and told her we needed to take a personal day.

"Just stay in touch in case all hell breaks loose," she said.

We agreed, and by 9:00 A.M. we were headed south on the 405 toward the Roadium.

Gaffney's video didn't do it justice. It was much more vibrant and energetic than he had captured on tape—a sprawling street bazaar with commerce happening in multiple languages, all of them loud.

We parked and went to the main office. Mike Romo, the director of operations, was eager to cooperate.

We gave him the date and the booth number where Tony had exchanged the envelope for the young Mexican with the snake tattoo.

It only took him a few seconds to type it into his computer and come up with a hit. "The vendor's name is Raoul Castaneda," he said. "I'll be right back."

A few minutes later he returned with a folder and handed it to us. Inside was a photocopy of fat Raoul's driver's license.

"Jeez, he's only thirty-eight years old," Terry said. "He could use a couple of salads and about a year and a half on the treadmill."

"Did you do a background check on him?" I asked Romo.

A woman sitting at a nearby desk blurted out an involuntary laugh. She quickly turned around and apologized.

"We'll take that as a no," Terry said.

"It's more like an impossibility," Romo said. "We have seven thousand different vendors selling here over the course of the year, so background checks are out of the question."

"Is Castaneda here today?" I asked. "We'd like to talk to him."

"No. It looks like he mostly rents on weekends," Romo said. "And by the way, you're not the first to come looking for him. According to the memo in his folder, an agent by the name of Deborah Aronson was here asking about him six months ago."

"What kind of an agent?" I asked.

"She's with Immigration and Customs Enforcement. She left her business card." Romo handed it to us, and we copied her name and number.

We thanked him, went back to the parking lot, and I called ICE Agent Deborah Aronson.

She was not as quick to cooperate as Romo.

"Are you looking at him for an immigration or a customs violation, or is this something else?" she said.

"Agent Aronson," I said, "we barely have time to solve all the homicides that get thrown our way, so LAPD is happy to leave immigration and customs issues to ICE, CPB, USCIS, and the rest of the Homeland Security alphabet soup. Castaneda may or may not have information on a case we're working on, and once we heard you were asking about him, we thought we'd check and see what you have on him that you might be willing to share with your local underbudgeted, overworked law enforcement partners."

That softened her up. She laughed. "Okay, Detective Lomax, how can I help you?"

"What do you have on Castaneda? And hopefully, it's more interesting than he's been peddling illegal copies of Britney's latest CD."

"He's a coyote," she said. "Correction, he's only an alleged coyote, because we've never been able to convict him, but we know that he's part of a thriving business smuggling people across the border. He was born in Mexico, moved here thirty years ago, and became a US citizen. He still has plenty of friends and family on the other side who drive the illegals across. Castaneda waits on this side of the fence, picks them up, and helps them find work here in the Land of Opportunity."

"And then they just blend into the fabric of LA?" I said.

"Only for about a year or two," Aronson said. "He traffics in a lot of young men who are looking to earn mucho American dollars, then go back to the wife and kids with enough money to live extremely well. So not only does he pick up these border jumpers after they sneak across, he drives them back to Tijuana, and they walk back across the bridge to Mexico with a fistful of dollars."

"You have all this on him, but you can't convict him?" I asked.

"He's smart. The one time we thought we nailed him, his lawyer beat the charge. Said that Castaneda just drove down to the border town, met an old friend, and gave him a ride to LA. The judge let him go."

"What happens if you convict?"

"His US citizenship wouldn't save him," she said. "He'd wind up doing some jail time, or at the very least get slapped with a fine, and then it would be *adios amigo*. We'd deport his sorry ass. Of course, he'd probably wind up operating his coyote business on the other side of the border, but that would be the Mexicans' problem, not mine. Does any of this help?"

"All of it helps," I said. "Thanks, Deborah. Crime-fighting is a two-way street, so if I can ever reciprocate the favor, just ask."

"Well, I do have one question," she said. "You have a very charming way about you. In the interest of interdepartmental relations, how would you like to get together for a drink after work some evening?"

"Wow, that's not the question I expected," I said. "But I can't. I'm in a serious relationship."

"That's not the answer I was hoping for, but it eliminates the need for any future questions. Nice talking to you, Mike. I hope you get your man."

"Thanks, Deborah. And I hope you get yours."

She hung up, and I stared at the phone, a little dumbfounded.

"Y'know, Lomax," Terry said. "I only get to hear one side of a lot of your phone conversations, but I've got to tell you something. They are a hell of a lot more interesting than both sides of mine."

CHAPTER FIFTY-FOUR

Even though we knew Castaneda's address in East LA, finding his house required some basic math skills. Most of the front doors had their numbers removed.

"Don't these people know that stripping off their house numbers makes it hard for the cops to find them?" Terry said. "Not to mention the fact that it's totally confusing to your average gang member on a drive-by shooting."

We finally zeroed in on a small olive-drab house on the corner of Hubbard and Sadler.

"Looks like the cover of *Better Dumps and Gardens*," Terry said.

We locked the car and headed up the walk. Before we could ring the bell, Castaneda opened the door. He was wearing a stained tank top and skivvies.

"You cops?" he said.

"No," Terry said. "We're the Publishers Clearing House Prize Patrol. Congratulations. You're our big winner."

"Fuck you, I didn't do nothing," he said.

"Then you won't mind answering a few questions about someone who did," Terry said. "Get in the house, or get in the police car. Your choice."

Castaneda backed in the door, and we followed.

Even when you expect a pigsty, you can still be amazed by the creativity of some pigs. We stepped into what was probably meant to be a living room, except that it was furnished with four beds, all at odd angles. One of them had a table and a bunch of chairs on top of the mattress. The other three were covered with dirty linens, pizza boxes, beer cans, and on one bed, a partially inflated basketball. There were dozens of plastic milk crates filled with CDs and albums on every inch of floor space, and the entire room smelled of rancid food that probably didn't smell all that terrific when it was fresh.

"I see you're a big fan of Martha Stewart," Terry said.

Like most slobs, Castaneda felt the need to defend the mess. "A friend of mine crashed here," he said.

"And what's your friend's name?" Terry asked. "Amtrak?"

Castaneda sat down on a bed and took a can of Hormel chili off a makeshift cinder block nightstand. "I was in the middle of breakfast. What do you want?" he said, shoving a spoonful of brown glop into his face.

Terry reached into one of the crates and pulled out a CD. "What are you selling besides the finest musical entertainment that ever fell off the back of a delivery truck?" he said.

"*Nada*," Castaneda said. "And it ain't stolen. They're all promotional shit that the music companies throw away." He took another spoonful of chili.

Terry whirled around and smacked the spoon and the can out of his hand. "Put the fucking dog food down and get off your fat, greasy ass, or we'll be back with a warrant, and the music companies will throw you away for three to five."

Castaneda stood up. "What do you want?"

Terry showed him a screen shot of the young Mexican with the snake tattoo. "Who is he, and don't tell me you never saw him, because the next picture I've got is you and him standing as close as prison shower buddies." *he*

"Keep cool, man. I didn't say I don't know him," Castaneda said. "That's Esteban."

"Last name?"

"That I really don't know. I swear."

"You turned him over for a fistful of cash, and you don't know his name? Last chance to tell the whole truth and nothing but, Raoul. Otherwise, you'll be trading in all these luxurious accommodations for a triple-XL orange jumpsuit and twenty miles of barbed wire."

"Okay, bro," Castaneda said. "Chill. It just come to me. Benitez. Esteban Benitez."

"Now let's hope that the details of that little business transaction just come to you also," Terry said. "Why did you get paid to deliver him?"

"It's for medical science," Castaneda said. "Some doctor is doing research about a disease that kills Mexican children."

"Esteban was not a child," Terry said.

"I know, but this doctor, he needs grown-up people who have the immunities for the disease. I pick them up when they arrive in the US."

"Where do you pick them up? LAX?"

"Near the border," Castaneda said, "but I don't know how they get there. Could be legal, could be not so legal. I don't ask for who was the travel agent. I just pick them up, three, four guys at a time, and I drive them to a medical lab."

"Where?"

"It's a van, so it's never in the same place."

"And what happens when you take them to this rolling medical research lab?" Terry said.

"I wait outside. They go in and some nurse takes blood and tells them piss in a cup. Then they each get assigned an ID number, and the nurse gives them a hundred bucks apiece. Then I drive them to a safe place."

"A nice, cozy place with beds in the living room, like here?" Terry said.

"Yeah. Here. Then maybe a week or two later, I get a call from this guy. Sometimes he tells me to release them all. Just tell them to go. But sometimes he gives me the ID number of one of them. I take that guy down to the Roadium in my van, and somebody comes and picks him up."

"But first he pays you for your trouble."

"It's no trouble, bro. It's all for medical science. Help the childrens."

"The guy who pays you," I said. "What's his name?"

"Don't know. This time I really swear. I call him the Professor's Assistant, because he's not the doctor, he's just, you know . . . like the assistant."

Terry had a screenshot of Tony handing Raoul the envelope. "Is this the Professor's Assistant?" he said.

Castaneda was amazed. "*Mierda.* Where you get these pictures?"

"They came with the wallet when I bought it," Terry said. "Answer the question, asshole."

"That's him. That's the Professor's Assistant."

Terry held up the picture of Esteban again. "And with so many border jumpers to choose from, why was the Professor's Assistant willing to pay for this particular one?"

"I told you, man. Esteban is one of the lucky ones who's got the immunities for this children's disease."

"And why is that lucky?

"Oh man," Castaneda said, "it's like winning the lottery. If you got the immunity, they give you an operation, and they pay you bigtime."

"How bigtime?"

"Twenty-five thousand dollars, US. You know what a guy can do with that kind of money back in Mexico? You live like King Tuck, man."

Normally Terry would have backed off and let me step in. Then I would go a little easier on the guy. But Castaneda was a scumbag who didn't deserve a Good Cop.

"You're lying through your rotten yellow teeth," Terry yelled. "Who pays twenty-five thousand dollars to let them cut you open? What kind of bullshit operation are you talking about?"

Castaneda was both scared and pissed. "I'm trying to explain, man. *Es verdad*. If I'm lying, God should strike my father dead."

"And your mother," Terry said.

Castaneda hesitated. "Okay, and my mother. The operation is on your back. I don't know what they do, but I think they cut out some cells that have the immunities, and they make medicine for these sick little kids. I'm not making this shit up. I know guys who did it. They say it's very painful, but for twenty-five thousand, it's worth it, man."

"Prove it," Terry said. "We need to talk to someone who had this bogus operation."

"Oh shit, señor, but with all that money, they go home to Mexico. My job is to make sure they get back safe. They call me, and I pick them up somewhere, like maybe the bus station. Then I drive them down to the bridge at San Ysidro. My brother, he's waiting. He has a nice little hotel in Tijuana. These guys have a pocket full of *dinero*. They need some pussy and tequila before they go home and give it all to the wife."

"And they pay you for the ride home?" Terry said.

"I don't charge so much," he lied. "It's for medical research."

"Right," Terry said. "For the little childrens. So I guess we can't talk to Esteban, because you drove him back to the border."

"Not me," Castaneda said. "This guy Esteban you looking for, he never called me. Maybe he likes it here in LA. *Quién sabe?*"

"Is he the only one that stayed here?" I asked.

"Yes. No."

"Pick one and stick with it," Terry said.

"Paco went back to Mexico, but then he came back to LA." Castaneda held up his hand, heading off the next question. "His name is Paco Saldamondo. He hadn't been home for a year, then he gets called for the operation. He wanted to surprise his wife with the money, so he went back to his village, but he got a big surprise himself. The bitch was pregnant. So he kept the money and came back to LA."

"Where do we find him?"

"He bought a taco stand. Eighth Street near Broadway. He's there every day except Sunday."

"And that's it?" Terry said. "He won the lottery, and he's running a taco stand in downtown LA six days a week? If that's not living like King Tuck, I don't know what is."

CHAPTER FIFTY-FIVE

"So if your name was Paco, and you sold tacos," I asked Terry as we drove downtown, "what would you call your place?"

"Shirley's Diner."

The real Paco, of course, wasn't nearly as droll as Terry. He went with Paco's Tacos. It was lunchtime when we got there, and the joint was jammed. The line outside was ten deep, and the picnic tables that surrounded the little building were filled with a multi-ethnic crowd munching and chattering away.

"Good vibe," Terry said. "We might as well get some lunch."

We walked to the front of the line, and were immediately bombarded with a chorus of 'where do you assholes think you're going' in two languages.

We didn't owe any of them an explanation, but it was smarter to flash a badge than start a riot. Even so, one woman yelled out, "You think that entitles you to buck the line?" Then she gave us the finger.

We stepped up to the window, ID'd ourselves to the counter-man, and asked for Paco. There was a barrage of Spanish, and a short, roly-poly man who looked like the Mexican version of the smiley-face icon came running to the window. He held up a framed copy of his California health permit.

"Excellent," I said. "Can we come in?"

He nodded vigorously, waved us around the back, and let us in.

Paco Saldamondo was all heart and no brains. Unlike the traditional immigrant-comes-face-to-face-with-authority-figure initial encounter, Paco seemed genuinely happy to see us, and immediately offered to feed us.

"We have a few questions first," I said. "We've been talking to your friend, Raoul Castaneda."

His face went grim. "He's no my *amigo*," Paco said.

"Good," Terry said. "Because he's a dirtbag."

That brought the smile back to Paco's face. Nothing wins trust like agreeing on a common enemy.

"I'm US citizen now," Paco said. "Pay *mucho* taxes."

"God bless America," Terry said.

We explained that Raoul told us all about the medical research, and we asked about his surgery.

"I'm so lucky," he said. "I have immunities. The doctor takes them out. They pay me twenty-five thousand dollars."

"Do you remember the doctor's name?" I said.

"No."

"*Gringo?*" I asked.

He laughed. "No. Doctor was Mexican. He had on mask, but we speak only Spanish. Real *Español*, no *gringo* Spanish."

"Do you remember where they did the surgery?" I said.

"Of course."

He turned around and lifted his shirt. There was a long scar that started near the center of his lower back and wrapped around the front.

"Right here they give me operation."

Terry and I exchanged a look. We had been to enough autopsies to recognize kidney surgery when we saw it. Paco was either too naïve or too mesmerized by the twenty-five grand to know it, but nobody had taken his immunities. They'd cut out a kidney.

"Thanks," I said, "but I meant do you remember where they did the surgery? What place?"

"Oh, sí. Los Angeles."

"What hospital?"

"No hospital. Some building. Maybe East LA. But is two years ago. Long time. Sorry. You hungry? I get you a nice lunch." He yelled out to one of the countermen in Spanish, and the guy hustled for two clean plates.

"You're right," I said. "Two years ago is a long time. Maybe we could talk to Esteban Benitez. He had the surgery recently. Do you know him?"

He beamed. "Nice boy. Good boy."

"Where can we find him?"

"*Quién sabe?* I'm thinking he maybe would come back for his grandfather's watch."

"You have his watch?"

"His grandfather's," Paco said. "These boys, they come to America, no money. They give it all to the coyote who helps him across the border. So they come here to my place to eat, maybe borrow a few hundred dollars, while they wait to find out if they have the immunities."

"So he owed you money," I said.

He grinned. "They all owe me money. *El Banco de Paco.* So he give me his grandfather's watch for how you call it, collateral. Is much more expensive than what he owes me. But he never come back after he have the operation. Not to thank me, not to pay me, not even to get the watch. He just disappear."

"How long ago?"

"Three weeks, a month, something like that."

The counterman gave a yell, and Paco escorted us to a little table in the back of the kitchen. There were two taco platters with rice and beans waiting for us, along with *dos cervezas*. We passed on the beer and opted for a couple of Cokes. He refused to let us pay. It wasn't a bribe; it was just who the man was.

He nodded gratefully as he watched us each take the first messy bite. We both gave him a thumbs up. I could see why the line was so deep, and so pissed to be cut into.

"Enjoy," he said. "If you find Esteban, tell him Paco still has his *abuelo*'s watch. Even if he has twenty-five thousand dollars, is still family heirloom."

He went back to his lunchtime customers, while Terry and I ate.

"It never ceases to mystify me just how dumb people can be," Terry said. "Here, let me cut a hole in you and remove your immunities. Oh, look what I found. A kidney. I wonder what I could get for that on eBay?"

"I'm willing to bet you that Esteban never went to a doctor's office in his entire life," I said. "He's a poor Mexican, and someone offers him a fortune for his immunities, which he thinks will save kids from dying. Do you think he's going to ask a lot of questions? He's not dumb, just clueless."

"So Esteban Benitez got a kidney harvested and then suddenly disappeared," Terry said. "To a cop, that means one of three things. He had complications from the surgery and is holed up somewhere, he got busted by immigration, or he's dead."

"If he's holed up, we'll never find him," I said. "If immigration has him, we'll be choking on red tape. There's only one morgue in LA. Let's start with dead."

CHAPTER FIFTY-SIX

The morgue was not only the smartest place to start, it was on Mission, only ten minutes away from Paco's. Twenty-five minutes with traffic. We parked in the rear and entered through the loading dock.

Anne Jordan, the senior tech, was sitting at the admissions desk. She looked surprised to see us.

"Do we have one of yours on ice?" she said. "I didn't see your names on my dance card."

"We're not here to commune with the dead," I said. "We're hoping to talk to a short, wiry, Jewish pathologist, who thinks he's funnier than my partner."

"Eli is up to his elbows in body parts." She looked at her watch. "He should be done by two thirty. About twenty minutes."

"We'll wait. In the meantime, can you check your database over the past two months to see if you admitted a male Hispanic, Esteban Benitez?"

It took her less than a minute to come up empty-handed. "Nobody by that name. Are we talking homicide?"

I shrugged. "We're not even sure the guy is dead."

She peered at me over the rim of her half glasses. "Honey, dead is one of our main criteria. We don't let them check in unless they've checked out. Let me go tell Eli you're waiting for him."

A half hour later Eli Hand emerged from an autopsy room. His scrubs were bloodied. He tossed his gloves and mask in a bio-waste bin. "Sorry to keep you waiting, boys. I have one more vital organ to deal with. Can you give me a few more minutes."

"Cut to your heart's content," Terry said.

"This particular organ was cut when I was eight days old," Eli said. "Sit tight. I've just gotta take a leak."

Anne Jordan laughed out loud. "He is funnier than your partner."

Five minutes later we were in Eli's office. "Is this about Marisol Dominguez?" he asked.

"No."

"I released the body yesterday. They're flying her down to Mexico to be buried with her parents and a brother."

"Any surprises?" I asked.

"Just the one," he said.

"Which one?" I asked.

"The one I wrote up in my report. Correct me if I'm wrong, but weren't you the guys who left the autopsy early on Monday and said you'd read about the gory details in my report?"

"Sorry. We didn't get to it yet. These dead people keep piling up and cramp our reading time. What did you find?"

"The murder was cut and dried," Eli said. "Bullet to the head. But what fascinated me about Dominguez were her lungs. Black as a coal mine at midnight. The woman would have smoked herself to death in less than ten years."

"What does that have to do with the case?" I said.

"Why does everything have to be about the case?" Hand said. "I'm trying to tell a story here."

"Once a rabbi, always a rabbi, eh, Eli?" Terry said. "Let's hear it."

"You know that Scared Straight program the morgue has for teenage drunk drivers? Last night I had a group I was lecturing to, so I figured, as long as I'm at it, I'll show them that it's not only alcohol that kills. I took a picture of Marisol's black lungs, and I put it side by side with a shot of a nice pair of healthy pink lungs. I wanted to show these kids the damage cigarettes can do."

"Sounds convincing," I said.

"You would think," he said. "But no. One kid looks at the pictures and he says, 'What did the poor bastard with the healthy lungs die from?' Damn punk kids. They've got all the answers. So what can I do for you?"

"We're looking for a John Doe."

"We get half a dozen a week," he said.

"This one would be easy to remember. He had a snake tattoo on his right arm, and he was probably the victim of a botched kidney surgery."

Hand smiled. "I don't have a John Doe," he said. "But I definitely remember a Juan Doe. A Mexican kid. And I think it's more than botched surgery when the deceased has two fresh scars and zero kidneys."

"Both kidneys were removed?" Terry said. "Are you sure?"

"I'm pretty sure," Hand said. "I looked around in all the usual places where people keep their kidneys, then I backtracked to the loading dock to make sure none of the technicians dropped any organs along the way. Of course I'm sure, you putz. But don't take my word for it. Sit tight, while I get the file."

He left the room and was back in a few minutes with a folder. "This is the autopsy on the guy you're looking for," he said. He opened it and flipped to a Polaroid of the dead man.

"That's Esteban Benitez," Terry said.

Eli pounced. "Are you sure?" He gave Terry a gotcha grin.

"So the cause of death is kidney failure," I asked.

"It's not that simple," Hand said. "The decedent was a young guy, in his twenties, but the autopsy showed that he had an obvious heart problem. A leaky valve. He wouldn't have survived another six months without a heart transplant, and I seriously doubt he was a candidate. He was probably always short of breath, got tired easily, but he might not even have known how sick he was. But even with all that, it wasn't his heart that killed him. Somebody removed both kidneys. The poor kid had a bad heart, and they never even cracked open his chest."

"Why bother?" I said. "Without his kidneys, wouldn't he die of renal failure?"

"No," Hand said. "He still could have survived on dialysis, but once they harvested his organs, I doubt if he ever woke up from the surgery. Whoever administered the anesthesia probably just dialed down the oxygen."

"Oh, I'm familiar with that medical technique," Terry said. "You take an unsuspecting guy with a bad heart and two healthy kidneys, you help yourself to the good parts, and you throw away the rest. It's called murder."

"According to the file," Hand said, "his body turned up in downtown LA. Two detectives from Central were handling the case. But there were no leads, so I doubt if they invested a hell of a lot of man hours in it. You ID'd the body, which is more than they could do. Do you know who cut him up?"

"No," I said. "But we have a pretty good idea of who brought him to the table."

CHAPTER FIFTY-SEVEN

There was a lot more that Terry and I needed to talk about. But not at the morgue. Not in front of Eli. We waited till we were back in the car.

"I guess Marisol was wrong," I said. "Tony wasn't cheating on her."

"Not in the slightest," Terry said. "Unless one of their marriage vows was 'I promise never to harvest the vital organs of another human being,' he was being completely faithful."

"Tony wasn't in this alone," I said. "He was in charge of recruiting illegals and bringing them in for blood tests so the doc could find a match. But once you find a donor, what else do you need?"

"Donees," Terry said. "People who are in desperate need of a working kidney and don't want to wait a couple of years to get one through legal channels. People who have the money to go to the front of the line."

"Or create their own line," I said. "And those kind of people don't travel in Tony Dominguez's circles. If you're looking for someone who can afford a couple of hundred thousand dollars to buy a kidney, where do you go?"

"Craigslist?"

"Dr. Ford Jameson, psychiatrist to the Rich and Famous."

Terry shook his head. "Darn, that was my second guess."

"The connection is right there on the video," I said. "Tony picked up Esteban from Raoul, a well-documented coyote. Then he delivers him to Jameson's car. And then Jameson takes him where?"

"A back-alley operating room," Terry said.

"I'm betting just the opposite," I said. "If Jameson's car is picking up a donor, then odds are the recipients are Jameson's wealthy patients, or their friends or relatives. And since I doubt that any of them are back-alley types, most likely he takes them to a state-of-the-art, totally sterile operating room."

"Who does the surgery?"

"Some Mexican doctor that Tony recruited to round out the team. Remember what Paco said—the doc spoke 'real *Español*, not *gringo* Spanish.'"

My cell phone rang. It was Anna DeRoy.

"Hey, Mike, remember when you told me I'm one of the few people in the DA's office who has balls?"

"I remember it as if it were yesterday."

"Thanks. It *was* yesterday, wiseass. Here's the problem," she said. "I may have them, but they are currently being squeezed. My boss wants these murders wrapped up, and I'll be honest with you—the case against Martin Sorensen is tight. The fact that one of the victims' husbands is inheriting money and another one was being tailed by his wife can't keep it open. Did any of those loose ends you were following lead you anywhere?"

"Yeah, but not where we expected," I said. "Our hero cop

looks like he's dirty, but it's got nothing to do with what you're working on."

"Then take it to Internal Affairs. Unless you can tell me you're going to substantially rewrite your report, I'm ready to close the case."

"Close it," I said. "We're on to the next one. We've got a victim and two principals connected to the murder. There's only one small problem."

"Let me guess," Anna said. "You don't have that damn proof thing that our system of justice is so finicky about."

"Proof is highly overrated," I said. "Did you ever think about looking the jury in the eye and saying, 'Trust Detective Lomax. Would a cop lie to you?'"

"First you'd have to convince me that cops don't lie," she said.

"Some of us don't, but I can't vouch for Tony Dominguez."

"Mike, if he really is connected to something dirty, you not only have to call IA, you need to warn the mayor's office before they embarrass themselves with a public display of affection for the guy."

"Thanks, Anna," I said. "I'll add that to my things-to-do list. *Prevent mayor's office from embarrassing themselves.* I'll put it right next to *end global warming.*"

I hung up and turned to Terry. "Anna's closing the case. She said if we have anything on Tony we should go to IA."

"It's a little late for that," Terry said. "If we tell them we investigated another cop without involving them or our boss, they'd just slap us with a Complaint 1.28. Even if IA was willing to listen, what can we say? We've got this really suspicious home movie of Tony

paying for an CD with an envelope, then escorting a border jumper
to a friend's car? They'd sit down and question Tony, he'd get all
unglued, raise holy hell, and we'd be crucified. *You're going after a
hero cop who was shot in the line of duty? What the hell are you thinking?*
Tony would get the Medal of Valor, and we'd get a Conduct Unbe-
coming or a Neglect of Duty."

"So what do we do?" I asked.

"Find a way to connect him to the surgery that killed Esteban," Terry said. "Anything less than that, and our asses are in
more trouble than his."

We got home to Sherman Oaks by four thirty.

"I love taking these personal days," Terry said. "It's good to
get some time off from being a cop."

I called Wendy Burns at the office to see if we were missed.

"Not as much as you'd like to think," she said.

I reminded her that we'd be out tomorrow to go to the funerals
for Nora and Julia, and she reminded me that most of the squad
room would be there too.

Marilyn was in the living room, looking happier than I'd seen
her in two weeks.

"I've been getting calls from real estate agents all day," she
said. "People are making offers on the flip house. The latest is
ninety thousand over our original asking price."

"I'll bet your partners would all be thrilled if any of them
were still alive to hear it," Terry said. "But I'm sure their estates will
be grateful."

"It's sick, isn't it?" Marilyn said. "Last week, when Stephen
Driscoll was lying dead on his bedroom floor, we got a few nibbles.

Now that we have real murders happening in and around the house, we've got a feeding frenzy."

"Proving once again that real murders are not only stranger than fiction," Terry said, "they're a hell of a lot more profitable."

CHAPTER FIFTY-EIGHT

The double funeral for Nora and Julia was painful. Painfully long, painfully tedious, and painfully boring.

Essentially, Nora controlled it all from the great beyond. Despite the fact that she had a normal life expectancy of at least another two decades, Nora apparently had begun preplanning her funeral years ago. Her casket was bronze and copper, solid as a Volvo, and probably just as expensive. Eight people gave personal eulogies, and a half dozen Hollywood celebrities read pieces assigned to them by their dear, dear friend Nora. One was a sonnet by Keats, the rest were all excerpts from Nora's bestsellers.

It took more than two hours to give Nora the send-off she always dreamed of.

Julia's ceremony felt like an afterthought. Charlie spoke for a few minutes, then read one of his wife's poems. His rhythm was off, and he pronounced a few of the words wrong, but thanks to Nora, at least Julia's poetry got exposed to a full house.

Finally, Helen Ryan, the blind woman we had met at Jo's funeral, spoke briefly, thanking Nora for giving her the audio versions of every one of her novels. Then she sang "Amazing Grace," and once again, her powerful, soulful voice gripped the crowd.

Six bagpipers led the procession as the coffins were carried from the church to the cortege of hearses and flower cars. Nora Bannister, the ultimate control freak, was still very much in charge.

After the burial, friends and family gathered at Charlie's house. It was the first time we got to talk to Tony. Aside from having his arm in a sling, he seemed in good shape and good spirits.

"I'll be back in the office tomorrow," he said.

"Isn't that a little soon?" I said.

"It's very light duty. In fact, it's no duty. I got a call that Mel Berger from the mayor's office wants to come over tomorrow morning and make some kind of a little fuss about me, so what the heck? You know politicians," he said. "They'll turn you into a hero, and then take credit for everything you did."

Terry and I told him we were happy to see him back and promised to be there tomorrow when Berger made that little fuss. I'd known Tony for five years, and his slick, suave mannerisms always seemed like part of his Latin charm. Now, knowing what I knew, every polished gesture was just further proof that he was a lying sleazebag, and I couldn't shake the mental picture I had of him leading Esteban Benitez to Jameson's Lexus. I was trying to think of how to politely get away from him when I was rescued.

"Detective Lomax? Detective Biggs?"

It was Helen Ryan.

"I hope that's you," she said. "You're kind of a visual blob, but I recognized your voices."

"It's *your* voice that should be recognized," I said. "Last week, when I heard some neighbor lady was going to sing at Jo Drabyak's service, I thought, oh, great. But today, I knew what to expect, and you didn't disappoint me."

"Thank you," she said. "I heard Marisol Dominguez was being buried in Mexico. In a way I'm glad. I sing in church, and karaoke clubs, you know . . . fun places. I wasn't looking forward to singing at yet another funeral."

"I guess you knew her pretty well," I said. "Your house is next door to the one they were renovating, and Marisol was on-site every day."

"Yes, and for me, her death was the most personal. I mean, I was a witness." She laughed. "Not an *eye*witness, but I did hear the shooting."

"We call that an earwitness," Terry said.

"You do not, Detective," she said.

"Were you in the house at the time of the shooting?" I asked. "Or outside?"

"I'm not embarrassed to tell you that I was cowering under the kitchen table with Dalton."

"And who's Dalton?" I said.

"My cat. It all happened so fast," she said. "It was a beautiful Saturday morning, and I was fixing Dalton's breakfast, when I heard the first gunshot. It wasn't very loud. Just kind of like 'pop.' At the time I just thought it was a kid shooting off a firecracker. But then bam, bam, bam! Well, there's no mistaking that, so I crawled under the table, and I had the open can of cat food in my hand, so Dalton crawled under there with me. I held onto her, and I said, 'Pussycat, we are not standing up until it gets real quiet out there.' *really* And sure enough, two more pops. Of course, by now I figured out they weren't firecrackers. It was two different guns. One much louder than the other."

"Did you dial 911?" I asked. *then*

"Oh heavens, no. When you're blind, and you don't know which way the bullets are flying, you don't stand up to make phone calls. I stayed under that table another ten minutes till I heard the police sirens. Dalton stayed with me and just ate her breakfast straight from the can."

"Helen, are you sure of that?" Terry said.

"Now, Detective Biggs, I made a mistake when I thought you and Detective Lomax were life partners, but I know when my kitty eats her turkey and giblets. Of course I'm sure."

"No, I meant the gunshots."

"Absolutely. There were six shots all together."

"Right," he said. Pop, pop, pop. Then bam, bam, bam."

"No, no, no," she said. "The first one sounded like a fire-cracker, then came the three loud gunshots, then two more fire-crackers. So it was more like pop, bam, bam, bam, pop, pop." She laughed. "Listen to me. I sound like a Rice Krispies commercial."

Terry and I thanked her, then moved outside where we could be alone.

"I think we just got some damning testimony from a blind eyewitness," Terry said. "According to Tony, there were six shots fired, and all of them were accounted for, so we didn't question him. But in Tony's version the sequence was pop, pop, pop fired by Martin, then Tony draws his gun and fires bam, bam, bam."

"But in Helen's version, there was only one pop," I said, "followed by a very deadly bam, bam, bam, any one of which would have killed Sorensen. And yet, with three .45 slugs in his chest, by some miracle his little pistol managed to go pop, pop, and shoot off two more rounds."

"I think the words Helen sang this morning have just come true," Terry said.

"How's that?"

"I was blind, but now I see."

It was time to reopen the case, and we knew exactly where to start.

CHAPTER FIFTY-NINE

Even before we met Ford Jameson we had heard of him. When you're shrink to the stars your name gets around. We knew from Tony that despite the fact that Jameson was supporting three ex-wives, he loved, and lived for, the finer things in life. Art, wine, travel, and a variety of candidates for Wife Number 4.

His home was smack in the middle of 90210. It was a substantial Tudor on Rexford, off Carmelita, that Tony had told us was magnificent.

Terry and I didn't get the tour. We rang the front doorbell, and Jameson, delighted to see us, quickly escorted us through a marbled foyer into his inner sanctum, a wood-paneled room that was more airplane hangar than doctor's office.

The furniture, the size of his desk, the degrees on the wall said it all. *I am highly educated and very expensive. You're sick. If you've got the money, I can fix you.*

"Detectives, what a pleasant surprise," he said, after we had all eased our butts into soft leather armchairs. "I'm so glad you took me up on my offer to help."

"Rumor has it you're a miracle worker," I said.

"My colleagues chide me constantly," he said, "but my goal is to get my patients out of analysis."

I smiled. "And dialysis."

It was swift and hit the target like a kick in the balls. There was no way he could hide his reaction. His face, his eyes, his body language all went into panic mode. I only wished I could watch from the inside, as his heart, brain, adrenaline, blood pressure, and other protective organs scrambled, kicking into high gear, opening up airways and shutting down sphincters, as the internal Klaxon screamed out DEFCON 1.

The best he could do was sputter, "I don't know what you mean."

"Let me phrase it another way," I said. "For a psychiatrist, you have an amazing track record of curing kidney failure."

"I don't know what kind of license you're taking with your authority here, Detective," he said, struggling to regain his composure, "but my medical practice is none of your business. The last I heard, you were being paid by the taxpayers of the county to solve homicides."

"You're right," I said. "I apologize."

His lips twitched into a half smile.

"Here's the murder victim," I said, handing him the morgue photo of Esteban. "I believe you knew him."

He grabbed it quickly so I wouldn't have a chance to see his hand shake. He studied it carefully. He knew who it was, but he needed time to think. "I don't recognize this man," he said. "I never treated him. Obviously he's dead."

"All but his kidneys," I said. "Are you still treating them?

Which one of your patients is walking around LA with one of Esteban Benitez's kidneys?"

"And before you decide to continue to play dumb, let me tell you something," Terry said. "We've been to all the major dialysis centers in LA. Once a patient starts going for treatment, they don't drop out because they've finished reading all the magazines. And yet, there have been a number of people who suddenly just stopped showing up for dialysis. But the records show that they didn't die, or get a transplant. At least, not one that's been recorded by the government agencies who like to keep track of body parts whenever they relocate. And here's the kicker. All those miraculously cured people are either your patients or close blood relatives of your patients. You, Dr. Jameson, have been trafficking in black market human organs."

It was total bullshit. Sure, it was information we could track down eventually, but there was no way we could have done it in such a short time without a fistful of warrants and the blessings of our department.

But Jameson believed it.

"My clients are all wealthy people," he said. "They can afford to have dialysis units installed in their homes. Or for that matter, they could have flown to some Third World country and paid a willing donor. Just because I may know someone who's been cured, doesn't mean I had anything to do with it."

"Let me show you another photo of the late Señor Benitez," I said. "Here's a shot of Tony Dominguez helping him into your car. And yes, it's definitely yours. We have footage of the license plate as it pulls away."

"My car, perhaps. But I don't see any photos of me. It sounds like you have something on Tony. Why don't you arrest him?"

"On what charge?" I said. "Tony is one smart cop. He's kept his distance from the real ugly stuff, but you . . . you're the doctor."

"I'm a psychiatrist, not a surgeon."

"I think when the jury hears the connection between you and all those people walking around with illegal kidneys, they're not going to say, 'What about that cop over there?' You're the one they'll convict, not Tony," I said. "As much as we'd like to nail him for chaperoning all these unsuspecting people into your organ factory, we have nothing on him. Tony will walk."

"Actually," Terry said. "You'll walk too. But after a few weeks in prison, a good-looking dude like yourself will walk real funny."

Jameson's lips quivered.

"Of course, if you help us convict Tony, he can watch over you in prison. Even better, the DA is willing to cut a deal," I said, hoping Anna DeRoy would back me up. "If you confess your involvement in Esteban's death, she'll give you a break."

"And I'm no shrink," Terry said, "but I hear confession is good for the soul."

Jameson didn't say a word.

"Dr. Jameson," I said, "I look at all these degrees on your wall, and I say to myself, 'This is a smart man.' But Tony Dominguez, that little Mexican kid you helped raise, may have outsmarted you."

I dropped my business card on his desk. "We can't put him away without your help."

"I don't know what you think I can tell you about Tony, but whatever it is, I have to stand behind doctor-patient confidentiality."

"In that case you'll also be standing behind bars in San Q," Terry said.

I nodded to Terry, and we both stood up. "Think about it, doc," I said. "If you don't talk, Tony walks."

"Y'know, there's a bright side to all this," Terry said. "I mean, you being a psychiatrist and all. These maximum security prisons, they just never seem to run out of crazy people. I'm sure you'll make more than your share of new friends."

We started for the door.

"Wait," he said.

We turned around and waited.

"I'm not an impetuous person," Jameson said. "I don't like being intimidated into doing things I haven't yet thought through. I need a little time to weigh my options."

"A little time is all we'll give you," Terry said.

"You'll know my decision sometime tomorrow morning," he said. "How early do you get to work?"

"We'll be at the office by seven," I said. "Plus my cell number is on the card. You won't have any trouble finding us."

We left the house, got into the car, and drove off. Then we doubled back and parked a block away. "If he calls Tony," I said, "Tony won't talk on the phone. He'll insist on talking face to face, someplace safe."

We watched the house for the next three hours, but Jameson never left, and Tony never showed up.

"Well," Terry said, when we finally headed home. "If Jameson is planning on doing something stupid, I can tell you this. He's gonna do it on his own."

CHAPTER SIXTY

I barely slept. It was 12:07 when I took my last look at the digital clock, and 3:14 when I woke up again. Not enough sleep for a middle-aged cop putting in eighteen-hour days.

Tony Dominguez had fooled us all, but I couldn't prove it. Jameson could help, but I didn't know if he'd hide behind doctor-patient confidentiality, hire an expensive lawyer, or call Tony and warn him.

Helen Ryan's testimony might help. Or she could be chewed up and spit out by a carnivorous defense attorney. For the first time in my life I wished I were a lawyer. I might have some idea of what would actually stick in court.

Your honor, the prosecution calls our star blind eyewitness to the stand.

And then the jury would have to believe that sweet Helen, cowering under a table, scared shitless and feeding her cat, was able to make an accurate mental recording of the gunshots coming from next door.

It's safe to say you were terrified, correct, Ms. Ryan?
Very.

So then was that pop, bam, bam, bam, or maybe it was pop, pop, pop, meow, meow, meow?

The jury would laugh, the prosecution would object, but Helen's credibility would suffer.

I felt Diana's hand on my shoulder.

"What are you doing up in the middle of the night?" she said.

"Worrying."

"About what?"

"What if I told you that maybe the guy who killed all of Marilyn's partners is still on the loose?"

"Then I'd tell you to get that cop car back in front of this house right now. Is that true?"

"Nothing I can prove," I said. "It's this damn system we've got about innocent until proven guilty."

"Can I help?"

"Not unless you went to law school."

"Do you think Big Jim can help?" she said.

"Why the hell would you say that?"

"Because you were mumbling *pop, pop, pop* before."

"It wasn't that kind of pop. It was gunshots, like pop, pop, pop, bam, bam, bam."

"Well, when you get to hug, hug, hug, kiss, kiss, kiss, roll over," she said. "I picked up a few interesting sleep aid techniques in nursing school."

I rolled over. The sex helped. I still couldn't sleep, but it was a lot more fun being awake.

Three hours later Terry and I were in the office waiting for the phone to ring.

Kilcullen was already there. Tony Dominguez's homecoming was scheduled for 9:00 A.M., and the boss left nothing to chance. He told one of the civilian clerks to order coffee, bagels, and Danish for breakfast.

"And make sure there's tomato juice," he said. "Deputy Mayor Berger will be here. He drinks tomato juice."

By eight forty-five, Kilcullen had gathered a small welcoming committee upstairs in the roll call room. Langer and Sutula, Eliot Ganek and Bob Kanarick from auto, Steve Venokur from burglary, and a handful of others who had better things to do, but who, in the great tradition of law enforcement officers everywhere, could be enticed by the sweet smell of fresh pastry.

Anna DeRoy, the lawyer I had wished for in the middle of the night, showed up early, and we filled her in on everything we had.

"So this Ryan woman heard the shooting," DeRoy said, "but she never actually saw it."

"She can't see anything," Terry said. "She's *blind*."

"A word I'm sure the defense will repeat constantly," DeRoy said. "Let's try not to use it too often ourselves."

"How about we refer to her as the crazy cat lady who was hiding under the table?" Terry said. "You think that'll affect her credibility as a witness?"

At eight fifty-five, the three of us went upstairs.

At nine on the dot, Deputy Mayor Berger entered. He looked fresh, neat, and trim in a blue suit, white shirt, yellow tie. "I hope you don't mind," he said to Kilcullen. "I brought a photographer along. This is not just a proud day for LAPD, this is a moment for everyone to share."

The photographer also had on a blue suit, but it looked like he bought it thirty pounds ago and never invested in dry cleaning. He was anything but fresh, neat, and trim.

"Where's the man of the hour?" Berger said, looking around the room.

"I just spoke to the watch commander," Kilcullen said. "Detective Dominguez is in the building. He's downstairs in ordnance signing for a new weapon. His gun was put into the evidence chain after the shooting."

"You mean after the heroic capture of the man who had been terrorizing the families of LA's Finest," Berger said. "You have to learn to spin, Brendan, spin."

"Good morning, Mel," Anna DeRoy said.

"Deputy DA DeRoy," Berger said. "This is a surprise. What are you doing here?"

"This is an important case. I want to make sure it's all buttoned up."

"Well, thank you for closing it," Berger said. "Good morning, Detective Lomax, Detective Biggs."

We said hello, but before we had a chance to say much else, Kilcullen quickly steered him to the refreshments.

"Tomato juice," Berger said. "Perfect."

Ass-kissing is learned, not acquired. Kilcullen poured him some juice, and then we waited.

At ten after nine Tony entered the room, and we all applauded.

His left arm was still in a sling, but other than that, he looked fit and healthy. "It's great to be home," he said. "Sorry I'm late. I was downstairs signing for a service revolver. I've been a cop a long time, so I've got to tell you, I was feeling a little naked without it."

"The important thing is that you know how and when to use it," Berger said. He tapped on his juice glass. "Let me just say a few words."

Mel Berger is the consummate politician. He needed no script. He hit all the high points. I'm sure it was a dry run of the speech the mayor would deliver at the Medal of Valor ceremony in the spring. He even charmed the room by saying a few things in Spanish, which pleased Tony no end.

"Picture time," Berger finally announced. "Let's get a couple of different shots. First me and Tony."

He set his glass down, and the photographer started lining them up against a wall.

Terry's cell phone rang.

"Take it outside," Kilcullen said.

"Yeah, yeah," Terry said. He left the room.

The photographer clicked off a few shots.

"Now let's get one with Lieutenant Kilcullen," Berger said, retrieving his juice glass from the table and taking another sip.

Suddenly the door crashed open. I saw several cops instinctively go for their guns. But they stopped when they saw it was only Terry.

"You motherfucking son of a bitch," Terry bellowed as he tore across the room and headed straight for the Deputy Mayor.

Berger backed up a few steps, but Terry charged him, grabbed him by the lapels and slammed him against the wall. I'd seen my partner angry before, but never like this.

"They shot her. They shot her," he screamed into Berger's face.

"You were in such a fucking hurry to wrap up the case. And now they shot her, you stupid, fucking political hack bastard."

By now Kilcullen and three other cops were doing their best to pry Terry away from Berger.

"Biggs, are you crazy?" Kilcullen said. "What's going on? What happened? Who got shot?"

"My wife. They killed my wife." And then the rage in his face turned to grief, and he ran from the room.

I looked around. Everyone was in shock. Anna was sobbing. The last thing I saw before I ran after Terry was Deputy Mayor Berger slouched in a chair, his blue suit, white shirt, and yellow tie covered with tomato juice.

The photographer was clicking away, preserving the moment for everyone to share.

CHAPTER SIXTY-ONE

Five minutes after Terry and I bolted from the station, Kilcullen gave everyone in the room the official report from the Sherman Oaks police. Marilyn had been shot in the back of the head. She was pronounced dead on the scene.

As soon as he heard the news, Tony Dominguez left. Thirty minutes later he raced down Rexford Drive and pulled his car to a screeching stop in front of Ford Jameson's house.

It was mid-morning, and the block was deserted, except for a cable repair truck and a crew of Mexican gardeners armed with leaf blowers, who were noisily cleaning up the fall foliage across the street on Carmelita.

Tony took the front steps two at a time, rang the bell with his good right hand, then grabbed the brass door knocker and banged it incessantly. Ford Jameson, dressed in a tan V-neck sweater and cream-colored slacks, opened the door halfway. Tony barreled in and stormed directly to the office with the doctor in tow. Jameson shut the door and calmly took a seat behind his mahogany island of a desk.

"Somebody just killed Marilyn Biggs," Tony blurted out, pacing the room. "It's a copycat of all the other murders."

"Oh dear," Jameson said. "I was afraid that might happen."

"What are you talking about? Afraid what might happen?"

Jameson interlaced his fingers, set his elbows on the desk and leaned toward Tony. "I was concerned that even after you got what you wanted you wouldn't be able to stop."

Tony's body jerked to a halt, and his head snapped toward Jameson. "You think I killed Terry Biggs's wife? Do you think I'm crazy?"

"No, Tony," Jameson said. "I have a patient who likes to shit in a bag and drop it off the side of a freeway overpass. He's crazy. You've murdered five, sorry—now six—people in cold blood. You, my friend, are a raving homicidal maniac."

Tony flopped down onto a chair directly across from Jameson. The doctor continued. "I had no idea how deeply this compulsion dictated your behavior."

Tony's jaw was clenched. He looked like he was about to explode, but instead the words came out in a slow, deliberate whisper that was far more menacing. "This is not a fucking compulsion. This was a plan. Carefully thought out and brilliantly executed. It was perfect."

"But apparently, it's not over for you," Jameson said. "Killing women has become the ultimate expression of your virility. You can't stop."

"What kind of psychobabble are you trying to mind-fuck me with, Jameson? Virility? This had nothing to do with my dick. This was about saving my ass. Mine and yours. I killed those women to keep us out of prison. But do you think I'm so crazy that I would do something that would reopen a closed case? I didn't kill Marilyn Biggs, because that would fuck up everything."

"I'm sure you've convinced yourself of that," Jameson said. "But you killed Marilyn for the same reason you killed Nora, Julia, Jo, and your wife. Because strong, smart women like them kept your mother chained to a mop until the morning she died."

"Don't even start with that mother bullshit, Freud Jameson," Tony said. "This wasn't about my mother. We had a dead fucking Mexican with two holes where his kidneys should be, and my bitch of a wife who wanted every nickel I had or she'd turn us in. Us. Me and you. I didn't kill Marisol because she was smart and strong. She was a selfish, greedy, blackmailing whore. She would have bled me dry and dragged you down with me. I killed her to save my ass and yours."

"My ass?" Jameson said. "I had nothing to do with the death of that Mexican boy. You made the call, Tony."

"And I'd do it again."

"There will be no *again*," Jameson said. "I am officially out of the kidney business. It's over."

"It *was* over," Tony said. "Martin took the rap for the four murders, but now, with Marilyn Biggs dead, the case will be reopened."

"Yes. And this time you won't get away with it. Especially when they find a lock of Mrs. Biggs's hair in your possession."

"My possession?"

"Oh, it won't be easy to find on your property," Jameson said, "but I'm sure the police dogs will sniff it out. Along with the gun that shot her."

"You son of a bitch," Tony said, pressing his hand to his forehead. "You stupid, arrogant son of a bitch. You shot Biggs's wife." He stood slowly. "Oh, Christ, you've fucked up everything."

"No, Tony, you fucked up everything," Jameson said, pointing a finger at Tony's chest. "I had a golden opportunity, a chance to save people's lives, and enrich my own in the process. Win-win. And when I needed a partner, who did I invite to be part of it all? You. I could have asked someone else, but I've always looked after you, always done my best to help you to live a better life. But then you got greedy. You figured if one of Esteban Benitez's kidneys is good, then two must be twice as good. For everyone but Benitez."

"He had heart disease," Tony said. "The surgeon said he had months to live. And we had two recipients that day. At a half a million a pop."

"Two recipients, one donor. Whose fault was that?"

"Shit happens, Ford. We've been through this. We had two young women stretched out on gurneys, waiting for us to snatch them from death's door. And we had one guy with two healthy kidneys who was not going to need them very long anyway. It was the smart thing to do."

"No it wasn't," Jameson said. "The smart thing would have been to call me. You never should have made that decision on your own."

Tony sat back in his chair and smiled. "Actually, Ford, I didn't make the decision on my own."

"What's that supposed to mean?"

"What were the odds of that one donor matching both those recipients?"

"A perfect match? Astronomical," Jameson said. "But the same blood type, and a partial tissue match? I don't know—a hundred to one? Two hundred?"

"Right," Tony said. "So I let God decide. If Benitez matched the second girl, then that's why God brought them together. So don't blame me for making the decision, blame God."

Jameson tapped two fingers on his chin, and stared at Tony, looking every bit the pensive psychiatrist. Finally, he spoke. "You're right, Tony. God made the call. But God didn't get caught by his scheming wife. You did. And if Marisol could figure it out, it's only a matter of time before the cops get there too. And then how long do you think it will take before it comes back to me? So effectively, Tony, you've forced me into early retirement, and I'll be needing a generous severance package."

Jameson stood up from his chair. "So be a good boy, sit down at the computer, and transfer eighty percent of your assets to my account."

"Eighty percent? You're crazier than the shit-bag bomber."

"I thought it was rather generous of me," Jameson said. "That still leaves you with plenty of money to get out of the country, before the cops find the lock of Marilyn Biggs's hair and the gun that killed her. You can start a new life. You're young, good-looking . . . newly single."

"And you're dead," Tony said, pulling the gun from under his jacket. "As you well know, Dr. Jameson, I'm not a very trusting guy, but I actually believed you were the one person who wouldn't fuck me over. I guess I was wrong."

He aimed the gun at the doctor's head.

"If you kill me, they'll know you did it," Jameson said.

Tony laughed. "You're damn right they'll know, because as soon as I pull the trigger I'll call 911. I just caught the ringleader of a multimillion-dollar human organ chop shop. And now that I know *you* killed Marilyn Biggs, I'll find some way of proving it. Do you know how many traffic surveillance cameras there are between here and Sherman Oaks? I'll nail you for her murder, and I'll find that lock of hair long before the dogs do."

"You don't have the balls to shoot me," Jameson said.

"You never did have any insight into who I really am," Tony said. He squeezed the trigger. The click was deafening.

He squeezed again. And again. And again.

Click. Click. Click.

Jameson smiled. "No insight, perhaps, but I did have the foresight to make sure Detective Lomax removed the firing pin from that gun. I'm sorry, Tony, but God helps those who help themselves, and to do that, I had to make a deal with the devil."

"Devils, actually," I said, as Terry and I walked through the door of Jameson's office. "There's two of us."

"Fucking Lomax and Biggs," Tony said.

"It's like poker," Terry said. "You got dealt the cards, you played your hand, you went all in, and you lost." He removed the useless gun from Tony's hand.

"Actually, we've got the whole deal on videotape," I said. "So it's more like *Celebrity Poker.*"

CHAPTER SIXTY-TWO

The plot to nail Tony had been hatched earlier that morning. After Diana and I had made love, I woke Terry and convinced him that it was time to get Kilcullen in the loop. We called him, then we called Deputy DA DeRoy at home. By six o'clock the four of us were in the office, and Terry and I came clean about investigating a fellow police officer behind the department's back.

Kilcullen bristled, but he kept his anger to himself. By the time we gave him the whole story, he no longer cared about crucifying us. He wanted Tony.

We strategized about next steps. "It all depends on whether or not Jameson calls," Anna said.

He never did. Instead, at six forty-five, he showed up in person. Accompanied, of course, by his lawyer, Robert Leitman.

"My client can help you put Tony Dominguez behind bars for the rest of his life," Leitman said.

Anna nodded. "In exchange for what?" she said.

"Total immunity."

"He walks," she said. "No time, no fine, not even community service mopping the floors at the local clinic."

"Yes."

"No," she said. "Let me phrase it another way for you, Counselor. Never. Not in a million years will your client go scot-free. We have a witness to Marisol Dominguez's murder. I'll take my chances on her, and then I'll put your client in jail for twenty to thirty for his complicity in the death of Esteban Benitez."

Leitman leaned over and whispered something to Jameson. It was legal theatrics. They had worked out their game plan before they walked in the room.

Leitman looked back at Anna. "If we're willing to deal, how low are you willing to go?"

"Ten years. He could be out in eight."

"We decline."

"Your client was involved in illegal organ transplants and the death of an unsuspecting donor," she said.

"He's an upstanding citizen, serves on several hospital boards, and donates his services to charities," Leitman said. "He'll do better than ten if he goes to trial. Two years, and you have a deal."

They haggled. They finally settled on five years in a medium security prison.

"All right, doctor," Anna said. "Start out by telling us how you got into the organ business, and Detective Dominguez's role in it."

"About three years ago, I was in session with one of my patients," Jameson said. "He was despondent over the fact that his twenty-year-old daughter needed a kidney. She was on the waiting list, but despite all his wealth, there was little he could do but keep waiting. He refused to accept the fact that he couldn't just go out and buy one. I explained that even if he found a donor, no American doctor or medical facility would do a transplant. Too many people are looking over their shoulder. He said, 'There are plenty of other countries in the world.' And then he said the magic words. 'Money is no object.' The next day I broached the subject with Tony. He jumped at it. He drove down to Mexico, and a week later we had a doctor and a donor. The surgery was done in Mexico City. The operation was a success, we were handsomely paid, and I thought that was that."

"But?" Anna said.

"The young woman who received the kidney had been in love with another patient at the dialysis center. He asked her to marry him, and as an engagement present, Daddy ordered another kidney."

"Volume," Terry said. "The key to success in retail."

"I was surprised," Jameson countered. "It never dawned on me that I might be asked a second time. What I didn't plan on was the word of mouth that would spread through the dialysis community. Oh, it was discreet, in a way. It was only leaked to those who could afford it, and at the prices we were asking, that was a select few. But the orders kept coming in, until finally we relocated our Mexican surgeon to Los Angeles. Then Tony came up with the idea of trucking in the potential donors in groups, blood and tissue-typing them, and calling them as soon as we had a match. We paid each donor twenty-five thousand dollars. Tony came up with the amount. He was confident that with that much money, they would go back to Mexico and we'd never see them again."

"And how much did you get paid?" Anna asked.

"Not relevant," Leitman said. "Move on."

"Did you ever inform these donors that you were removing their kidney?"

"No," Jameson said. "That was an unfortunate part of the deception. We told them we were looking for rare immunities to save children's lives. These young men were painfully unsophisticated, so they believed us. We couldn't tell them the truth, or we'd be known as that place in LA where you can get rich selling a kidney, and that wouldn't be smart, would it?"

"Removing two kidneys from the same patient isn't smart either," Anna said. "What was your thinking on that one?"

"It wasn't me. That was all Tony. We had two surgeries scheduled for the same day. The surgeon transplanted a kidney from Esteban Benitez, and the first operation was a success. But the second donor never showed up. We found out later that he was in jail. Meanwhile, the second recipient was in critical shape, and Tony was going ballistic. The surgeon went through his files on all the available donors, and there was only one possible match."

"Esteban Benitez," Anna said.

Jameson nodded. "Yes. He was the right blood type, and his tissue matched on three points, which is the acceptable minimum. The clincher came when the doc told Tony that Benitez would be dead soon enough from heart disease, so Tony made the call. They took the second kidney, and they saved the recipient's life."

"What about Benitez's life? Why did they let him die?" Anna said. "Why not just put him on dialysis until his heart gave out?"

"I asked Tony the same question. He said Benitez was a liability and had to be disposed of."

"Did you know that Tony killed Marisol and her real estate partners?"

Leitman held up his hand. "He learned it *after* the fact. Doctor-patient privileged conversation."

Anna ignored the lawyer and leaned in close enough to Jameson that he could feel her breath. "And when Tony told you that he was *disposing* of Benitez, was that doctor-patient, or just murderer to murderer?"

"Uncalled for, Ms. DeRoy," Leitman said.

"Don't tell me what's called for, Counselor." She snapped her head back at Jameson. "Let me ask another question, Doctor. What do you know about the deaths of Marisol Dominguez, Jo Drabyak, Julia Knoll, and Nora Bannister?"

Jameson turned to his lawyer for guidance.

"Don't look at him," Anna barked. "He made you a sweet deal. You're the one who has to deliver on it. Answer the question."

Jameson cleared his throat. "Tony was sneaking around so much for our little . . . for our little business venture . . . that Marisol thought he was cheating. She went to his computer and discovered he had an offshore bank account."

"Money from the kidney sales?"

"Yes."

"How much?"

"A lot more than most cops make in a lifetime."

"So she discovers his secret bank account," Anna said. "What did she do next?"

"She tried to hack into it," Jameson said. "She couldn't. But she smelled money, and she wanted her piece of the pie. So she hired somebody with a video camera to follow Tony around. He taped Tony paying off one of our coyotes. Marisol figured if Tony was paying someone off, somebody else must be paying Tony more. So she confronted him."

"How?"

"She showed him a copy of the videotape and threatened to

blow the whistle. Normally, Tony wouldn't have been worried. Slipping an envelope to a coyote wasn't that damning a transaction. Unfortunately, the guy on the video was Benitez, the one Tony . . ."—he groped for a word—"sacrificed."

"So Marisol is trying to bleed Tony for money, and he decides to kill her," Anna said. "Why did he kill all the others?"

"Who's the prime suspect when the wife is murdered?" Jameson asked. "The husband. Tony is smart. He knew he had to come up with a scenario that would allow him to kill Marisol without coming under suspicion. He decided he'd kill a couple of other cop wives first. By the time he killed Marisol, nobody would suspect the husband; they'd be looking for a serial killer."

"Was there a reason he chose those specific victims?"

"Absolutely," Jameson said. "I must say, his plan was ingenious. He needed to find someone to take the blame for the murders. Once he decided on Martin Sorensen, he couldn't just kill random cop wives. He chose women you'd believe Martin truly resented. Then he committed the murders to look calculated, angry, motivated by something personal. Cutting off the victim's hair did that, plus it gave Tony physical evidence he could plant on Martin. Of course, he knew he would kill Martin before you could ever question him."

"We know that Tony shot himself," I said. "What I can't figure out is why. Why not just shoot Martin and call 911?"

Jameson smiled. "You don't know Tony very well, do you? His ego is monumental. As long as I'm violating doctor-patient privilege, I can tell you that he often has dreams where he is standing on a balcony, and a throng of people below him are chanting his name. It's no surprise that he wants to run for public office some day. Killing Martin would have painted a picture of a loser cop who got to the scene too late to save his wife. Taking a bullet for her helps wipe away that image, and tells the world he was willing to die for her. People love a martyr, even if they don't actually die."

"Last question," Anna said. "When did you learn all this?"

"After it was all over. He confessed to me when I visited him in the hospital."

Anna turned to Leitman. "This is worthless," she said. "No deal."

"What the hell are you talking about?" Leitman yelled. "He gave you chapter and verse."

"He gave me hearsay," Anna said. "Do you think I'm going to put a corrupt doctor on the stand and have him testify against a patient? The defense will expose it for what it is. A plea to save his own ass. Nothing your client has said can help me put Tony Dominguez in jail."

"These detectives said you'd cut a deal."

"If you give me something I can convict with. Right now all you've got is 'and then Tony told me.' What I need is hard evidence that Tony shot any of those women." Anna looked at me, Terry, and Kilcullen. "I never thought I'd say this, but the blind cat lady is starting to look better and better."

"Then we'll just have to get Tony to confess," Terry said.

"And while you're at it, get him to paint my house," Anna said. "Detective Dominguez does not strike me as the confessor type."

"We need to do something he doesn't expect. Something that drives him crazy and throws his perfect little plan out of whack. Something that reopens the case."

"Like what?"

"Like another murder," Terry said. "Another .22 to the back of the head. A murder Martin Sorensen can't take the rap for."

Jameson stood up. "Wait a minute. Are you talking about staging a murder to look like all the others Tony committed?"

"Exactly like the other murders," Terry said. "Tony will realize we have to reopen the case, and he'll go batshit."

"He'll come running to me is what he'll do," Jameson said. "Eventually he'll decide that I did it, and if he thinks I put him at risk of getting caught, he'll kill me."

"Well, then, you may just have to be . . . *sacrificed*," Terry said. "But it's a small price to pay if we get to put a murderer away for life."

This time the lawyer stood up. "Ford, relax, they won't let him kill you. Ms. DeRoy, if you want my client to participate in a sting," Leitman said, "you'll have to do better than five years."

More haggling. Anna finally gave in to thirty months in a white-collar facility that is known in some circles as The Spa.

We hammered out the details of the sting.

"How soon can we set this up?" Kilcullen asked.

"We have to do it now," Terry said. "Tony is coming in at nine o'clock. It's now or never."

"We need a video unit to record this," Kilcullen said. "Do you know how long it takes to requisition a surveillance team? FEMA made faster time getting to New Orleans."

"Don't worry about surveillance," Terry said. "Mike and I know a guy."

"And who's the hypothetical victim?" Anna asked.

"That's easy," Terry said. "If this is supposed to be connected to all the other murders, there's only one logical choice. To quote one of my comedy idols: take my wife . . . please."

CHAPTER SIXTY-THREE

By late afternoon Jameson and Tony were behind bars, and Terry and I were behind on a whole new round of paperwork.

"It can wait," Kilcullen said, and the three of us drove out to the marina.

Reggie and Charlie were on the boat. They cracked open four beers and a bottle of Yoo-Hoo for Kilcullen, and we sat out on the deck, watching the rush hour air traffic approach LAX, as the sun dipped into the Pacific.

Reggie and Charlie had felt sucker-punched when they thought Martin Sorensen had killed their wives. He had been someone they knew and liked. But when we broke the news to them about Tony, they were both devastated.

We told them how it all unfolded, and when we described the sting we pulled at the end, Charlie smiled. "Nora would be proud of you guys. In fact, if she were still around, she'd figure out a way to steal that idea for her next book."

"I can't believe the bastard shot five people," Reggie said.

"Six," Charlie said. "Don't forget he shot himself."

"Technically he did," I said. "But he used Martin's finger to pull the trigger. That's why Martin tested positive for gunshot residue."

"Poor Martin," Charlie said. "Tony set him up, and I fell for it."

"Tony set everyone up," I said. "A witness put Marisol's car at Nora's house at the time of the murders. It turns out that Tony took it from the flip house, killed Nora and Julia, and returned the car before Marisol knew it was missing."

"Dr. Jameson gave up that little tidbit," Terry said. "It's amazing how that doctor-patient confidentiality shit crumbles when the doc is trying to save his own ass."

"It sounds like Jameson will only be doing Martha Stewart jail time," Reggie said when we told him how Anna let him plead down. "We'll never prove it, but don't you think he knew what Tony was doing *before* the fact?"

"Even if he did," I said, "the DDA was willing to let the doc off easy if he could help her nail Tony as the shooter."

"And she got him good," Terry said. "He's looking at six counts of murder 1, an attempted murder, transporting illegal immigrants, tampering with a crime scene, obstruction of justice, and drawing to an inside straight."

"And by the way, if we needed any more evidence, CSU tossed his house," Kilcullen said. "They found the scissors that were used to cut the three women's hair. I'll bet another bottle of Yoo-Hoo that the DNA they find matches one or more of the victims."

"Are you guys still planning on sailing to the other end of the world?" Terry asked.

"Not on this bucket," Reggie said, "but yeah. How about you and Mike? Are you two honeymooners still shacking up together?"

"Just for another two weeks," I said. "I hired my father to

work with my new contractor. I'm hoping that if he has one thing to do to help me out, he won't meddle in the rest of my life."

"Whatever happened to that first contractor?" Reggie said. "The one you were constantly bitching about? Did you ever work that out?"

"You mean Hal Hooper?" I said. "It worked out okay."

"It worked out better than okay," Terry said. "Hooper was really cocking it up in the beginning, but you gotta give him credit for finally nailing it down. There won't be any boners on his next job."

"I just want you two guys to know something," I said. "Terry and I never believed you were behind any of the killings. Neither did the lieutenant."

"You might not have *believed* I killed Nora and Julia," Charlie said, "but you damn well treated me like a suspect."

"Well shit, man, you didn't make it easy on us," I said. "You never did tell us who you were with the night Julia was killed."

"I know it looked bad, but I couldn't tell you."

"No problem. Now that it's official that you guys are going off into the sunset together, I finally figured out who your mystery friend was that night. You were in that hotel room with Reggie."

Charlie laughed. "He wishes."

"Well, then I guess we'll never know," I said.

"Lomax, you're about as subtle as a fart in an elevator," Charlie said. "If I tell you who I was with that night, is it going to wind up in the case report?"

"No way in hell," I said. "Right, Lieutenant?"

Kilcullen nodded.

"Alright, as long as I'm leaving the country, and it's off the record, I guess I can tell you what I was holding back. Remember a couple of months ago I caught a B and E up in Hollywood Hills? The guy was a chiropractor. His house was burglarized one night when he and his wife were out at the movies."

"Yeah, I think I remember you mentioning it a couple of times."

"Anyway, the wife was all upset and crying because some of the jewelry had been in her family for years. But the doctor, he was like, 'No big deal; we're insured, I'll buy you new stuff.' I never solved the case, but I kept in touch. In fact, a couple of times the doc adjusted my back. I know I'm not supposed to take freebies, but he's damn good."

"And that's what you were holding back?" I said. "You were getting free medical care from some chiropractor who was one of your victims?"

"No, asshole. I was in a hotel room with the chiropractor's wife. It's not exactly something I wanted to cough up the night Julia was killed."

"What about the next day when we came to see you in the hospital?"

"I told you I was with a friend," Charlie said. "You either believed me, or you didn't, but I wasn't gonna drag her into this mess as my alibi."

"Wow," I said. "Are you going to ask this chick to go to Australia with you?"

"Nah, she's happily married. It was just a fling. She's a nice woman, and she was just looking for . . . I don't know . . . she was looking for . . ."

"Someone who could bend her spine in a different direction?" Terry said.

Timing is everything, and Terry is a master. He not only cracked us all up, he waited till Kilcullen was taking a big slug of his Yoo-Hoo.

It's not every day you arrest a multiple killer and get to see your boss spray chocolate milk through his nose.

CHAPTER SIXTY-FOUR

Marilyn cooked us a victory dinner. A grilled butterflied leg of lamb, a broccoli and cheese soufflé, and just in case our cholesterol level was dipping, a tub of buttered orzo with asparagus and parmesan. And since she has a lemon tree in her backyard, for dessert she whipped up a fresh lemon tart.

"This dinner is fantastic," Diana said. "How do you do it?"

"First of all, rumors of my death are highly exaggerated," Marilyn said. "Second of all, it's a joy. For me, cooking is therapy."

"For me," Big Jim said, maneuvering a hefty chunk of lamb into his mouth, "eating is therapy."

He and Angel had been invited to join us for dinner. All he had to do was promise not to tell inappropriate stories, ask embarrassing questions, or cross personal boundaries. I knew it was a hopeless goal, but I didn't really care. After seeing the families of some of my good friends ripped apart over the past two weeks, I needed to be with people I love. Of course, I wouldn't tell Jim that. Some fathers and sons enjoy connecting over a couple of beers. Some go on fishing trips together. Jim and I seem to bond best when we're ragging on one another.

"So what was the biggest break that led to your solving the case?" he asked, still chewing.

"Not getting caught for illegally investigating Tony Dominguez," Terry said. "If they had found out about it, Mike and I would probably be working the parking lot at Dodger Stadium tonight and shoveling down a couple of red hots for dinner."

"Actually, our two biggest breaks came from a dead guy and a blind woman," I said. "In both cases, we weren't even digging. Helen Ryan came to us at Nora's funeral, and kind of blurted out the story about the gunshots. Same thing with Martin Sorensen's phone message. We didn't expect it, but it led us to the video of Tony paying off the coyote."

"It took us a while to figure it out," Terry said, "but that phone message really tripped Tony up. He made Martin look like a very smart killer, but no killer that smart would be dumb enough to drunk-dial the homicide detectives who are looking for him."

"How did you ever come up with that crazy plan?" Angel said. "I'm sorry. I don't mean crazy. I mean, how did you think to pretend to kill your wife?"

"I always think about killing my wife," Terry said, blowing Marilyn a kiss. "Pass the cheese soufflé, will you, honey?"

The doorbell rang.

"It's probably someone looking for one of the girls," Marilyn said. "I'll get it."

She came back a minute later with a padded envelope. "It was a messenger. Here," she said handing the envelope to Terry, "it's addressed to you."

"Uh, oh," Terry said. "The return address is from Mel Berger at City Hall. I may be working the parking lot at Dodger Stadium after all."

He opened the package slowly and I could see from the back that he had pulled out an eight-by-ten picture frame. He looked at it carefully and grinned.

"Do you remember I mentioned that little scuffle I had with the Deputy Mayor this morning?" he said.

A chorus of yeses.

"The way I remember," I said, "it was much more of a major throwdown than a little scuffle. But why not let the group decide? It looks like you might have photos to share with us."

"Just one."

He flipped the picture around. The sullen photographer in the rumpled suit had captured the moment perfectly. He caught Terry with his eyes filled with rage, his mouth contorted in a scream, and his hands ripping at Berger's lapels. The Deputy Mayor, a good eight inches shorter than Terry, had his head and back pressed to the wall, his face frozen in fear, and his shirt and tie splattered with tomato juice.

"Oh, my God," Angel said. "You told us you were playacting, but the poor man is covered with blood."

"I guess I really got into it," Terry said. "It was kind of a juicy role."

"You're in deep shit," Big Jim said.

"I don't think so," Terry said. "What do you think, partner?"

He handed me the picture frame. I read the inscription.

To Detective Biggs: You are the only person who has ever kicked my ass and saved it at the same time. With great respect, Deputy Mayor Mel Berger.

Thank You

There's a paragraph in the front of the book reminding you that this is a work of fiction, the product of the author's imagination. Here at the end of the book I want to remind you that there's one part that I can't leave to my imagination—and that's how my fictional cops go about solving murders. For that, I turn to real homicide detectives.

I am indebted to Detective Wendy Berndt of the Los Angeles Police Department for generously sharing her expertise and her time. Wendy was there to help when this book was just an idea, and has kept me honest every step of the way.

Thanks also to my East Coast consultant, Undersheriff Frank P. Faluotico of the Ulster County Sheriff's office. Like Terry Biggs, Frank is smart, funny, and plays poker like it's a contact sport.

Special thanks to my good friend Dr. Paul Pagnozzi, who is my technical advisor-without-copayment on all things medical.

They say God is in the details, and I'd like to thank the following people who helped me get the details right: Mike Romo at The Roadium, Marty Delaney of the Bergen County New Jersey Prosecutor's Office, Matthew Diamond, location scout extraordinaire, retired Poughkeepsie police officer Rich Sauter, Hortencia Goodman, who taught me some Spanish I didn't learn in high school, Greg Pliska, my music coach, and my go-to attorneys, Gerri Gomperts and my brother Joe Karp.

Thanks to everyone at St. Martin's Minotaur who encouraged, copyedited, proofread, marketed, publicized, and plied me with Rocky Road ice cream—Andy Martin, Sally Richardson, Matthew Shear, George Witte, Matthew Baldacci, Kylah McNeill, Hector De-Jean, Tara Cibelli, Meryl Gross, Margit Longbrake, David Rotstein, and most especially, to my editor Nichole Argyres, who managed to deliver both her baby and mine on their respective due dates.

Thank you to the many booksellers, librarians, fan magazines, bloggers, and readers, who continue to go out of their way to support my life of crime.

As always, my love and appreciation to Emily, Adam, Lauren, and Sarah, who read my manuscripts and offer inspiring feedback, and to my grandson Zach, who inspires me just by leaving a voice mail that says "Hi, Papa."

And finally, my gratitude to my friend and agent, the incredibly wise, patient, and supportive Mel Berger, who, despite the fact that I gave the fictional bureaucrat in the book his name, still returns all my phone calls.